THE Garden PATH

a novel

ANITA STANSFIELD

Covenant Communications, Inc.

Cover image: *Flowered Path* Jon McNaughton © McNaughton Fine Art Co.

Cover design copyright © 2013 by Covenant Communications, Inc.

Published by Covenant Communications, Inc.
American Fork, Utah

Printed in the United States of America
First Printing: August 2013

19 18 17 16 15 14 13   10 9 8 7 6 5 4 3 2 1

ISBN 978-1-62108-436-5

Chapter One

WHIT EDEN FOUND IT DIFFICULT to breathe as a palpable darkness threatened to suffocate him. He could see nothing. His surroundings were as dark as if he were in the deepest recesses of a cave with no accessible light. He held his hands in front of his face but couldn't see even their shadow. He gasped for air as the surrounding walls threatened to close in around him. The tiny space in which he was confined became tinier, and his ability to breathe became proportionately more strained. He sat up abruptly and gulped in air as if he'd erupted through the surface of water in which he'd been drowning. He gulped large mouthfuls of air again and again before he realized that he was sitting in his own bed. He'd been dreaming. He could see the subtle glow from a distant streetlight through the window across the room. Outlines of familiar furnishings reassured him that he was really here—really home, really all right.

Whit forced air in and out of his lungs until he was breathing evenly, glad to know his nightmare hadn't awakened Mary. But just knowing that his wife was sleeping close by made it easier for him to put his head back down on the pillow and breathe deeply. More than an hour later Whit was still staring into the darkness, wishing he could sleep half as well as his wife, who was sleeping beside him. But Mary needed her rest far more than he did. Being forty-one and pregnant was taking its toll on her, and the drama he'd recently brought into her life certainly hadn't helped. Now the drama was over, and Mary was sleeping peacefully. It was one of many items he could put on a very long list of things for which to be grateful. He'd often heard the adage that counting blessings could help you fall asleep, but at the moment it was having the opposite effect. Especially after such a terrible dream had given him a heart-stopping reminder of how things might have been.

Whit felt so deeply overcome with gratitude that he could hardly hold it all inside. The trial had ended today. The verdict had been a unanimous *not guilty* from the jury. But Whit knew very well how close he'd come to paying for someone else's crime. The evidence against him had been presented very adeptly by the prosecutor, and the fact that Whit had once been actively involved in violent gang activity, for which he'd done some hard time, had worked aggressively against him. Now the verdict was in, justice had proven itself on his behalf, and Whit was home in his own bed with his wife sleeping next to him.

It would be impossible, however, not to be preoccupied with the fact that he could have—at this very moment—been locked in a cell, embarking on his first night of a life sentence. He believed in people facing consequences for their actions, and he'd worked hard to face the consequences of all the regrettable things he'd done in his youth. But to face life in prison for something he hadn't done would have broken him. He couldn't even imagine how he might have coped—at the age of thirty—knowing that if the verdict had gone against him, he would never again have a day of freedom with his family in this mortal life. He had the reassurance of knowing that he and Mary were sealed for eternity, but getting through the remainder of this earth life—living under such deplorable circumstances—would have been unbearable. As if prison wouldn't have been hard enough, he wondered how he could have come to terms with leaving his wife to take care of herself and the rest of the family. She had a daughter that had become his own, they had a baby on the way, and his mother was failing with Alzheimer's disease and needed continuous supervision. Knowing that he might well have been within prison walls and knowing that Mary could have been left alone with so much responsibility made him sick to his stomach.

Whit sat on the edge of the bed and hung his head, again finding it difficult to breathe. He knew well enough that he was suffering some mild symptoms of PTSD. His time in prison more than ten years earlier had given him a vivid picture of that kind of life, and he'd had no false illusions about facing the possibility of what it would have been like to go back. The jail time he'd served prior to the trial had done well at refreshing his memory. Now it was over, but the residue of fear tightened his chest nevertheless, making him nauseous. He immediately turned his mind to prayer, as he always did when any kind of fear or distress threatened to overtake him. But his emotions were especially persistent, or perhaps they just needed the opportunity to be released. Assaulted with a fresh rush of emotion in volcanic proportions, Whit hurried out of the room and rushed down the stairs so he wouldn't disturb Mary. He slumped onto the couch in the common room and hung his head in his hands, sobbing helplessly, as if someone he loved had died. He found it ironic that he'd not grieved a single moment over the death for which he'd been blamed. But he'd certainly been punished for it.

Mary's father had surely been one of the most mean-spirited, bigoted men on the planet. Walter Cranford had loathed anyone whose skin was not the same color as his own, and he'd never made any effort to suppress his feelings. Whit still cringed to think of things he had personally heard Mr. Cranford say, as well as things Mary had repeated to him. He had never been able to understand what could make a man so hateful; he couldn't judge because he simply didn't know. However, there was still no denying how Mary's father had made life utterly miserable for everyone around him—especially Mary.

Then someone had broken into the house and shot him through the heart—with Whit's gun, a weapon that had been stolen months earlier, complete with Whit's fingerprints. Whit strongly suspected that one of his cousins might have been responsible; they were deeply affiliated with a well-known Hispanic gang, and there was little they detested more than a mean, white bigot. They'd known through the grapevine that Whit and his new wife were having trouble with the old man, and that was the only explanation that made any sense to Whit as to why someone would break into the house and kill Mary's father.

If it hadn't been one of his cousins, it was someone with whom they associated. The act had likely been some kind of warped, backward way of protecting Whit and his family. He knew well enough that the mentality of these people made no sense in any normal realm. But these guys hadn't been raised in any normal realm. Their world was violence and hatred, and Whit had once lived in the middle of it. He wished that he could help them understand that murder was no solution to anything, but they would never get it, and whoever was responsible had probably gotten away with it. They all covered for each other way too much, and it was difficult to pin a crime on someone in that culture and make it stick. But he wondered if the perpetrator had intended for Whit to get blamed, or if that had just been an unexpected backfire. He knew there were people who would be glad to see him go to prison, and others who would never want such a thing to happen—and several people in both of those categories were capable of committing murder. Consequently, Whit didn't know whether to feel that his family was safe or vulnerable, given the fact that the real killer was still out there somewhere.

While he sat there and allowed himself to freely vent his grief, the entire drama from its beginning until that crucial moment in court today replayed through his mind in vivid detail. He thought of all the times he'd *wanted* to cry, but he'd not had that luxury; or perhaps he'd been afraid to allow his emotions anywhere near the surface. Now he just cried. He cried for all the fears he'd been facing. He cried for all that Mary and little Adrienne and his mother had endured through these months between his arrest and the conclusion of the trial. And he cried for the life he'd lived, surrounded by bigotry and senseless violence that accomplished nothing but the perpetuation of heartache and grief. He cried for the people he cared about who were victims of the senseless crime machine, and he cried for the personal losses in his life that were a direct result of that machination.

Gradually Whit's tears evolved from grief to gratitude. As he allowed all of the pain to be vented, praying all the while, he allowed God to soothe his heart. He could clearly see God's hand in many good things in his life, too numerous to count. The very fact that he had Mary and her daughter Adrienne in his life was a miracle he never could have imagined before he'd met them. Adrienne and her twin sister, Isabelle, who had been killed in a car accident along with Mary's first husband, had been adopted because Mary had been unable to have children. And now she was pregnant—a miracle in and of itself. And on top of all that, he had been spared a fate worse than death. He was home and safe and free. He had a beautiful family, and he would never take for granted the miracle he had been given this day.

Whit remained there silently in the dark, pondering how far he'd come and looking toward the future with great hope and joy. Life was far from perfect but it was a whole lot better than it might have been.

"Are you all right?" Whit turned to see Mary crossing the room from the bottom of the stairs.

"I'm fine," he said, reaching out a hand toward her. She took it and sat beside him. "What are you doing up?"

"I'm pregnant," she said. "I never get through the night without at least one trip to the bathroom." Whit wrapped his arms around her and pressed his lips into her hair. "What's wrong?" she asked and eased back, touching his face with her fingers. "Have you been crying?"

"I'm afraid I have," he admitted, knowing if there was more light than the glow of night lights on the stairs she would have seen that his eyes were probably red and swollen. "Are you disappointed by my lack of manliness?" He asked the question lightly, knowing she would never see it that way.

"On the contrary," she said, "given all that's happened, I might be concerned if you *didn't* cry."

"Well then, you have nothing to be concerned about," he said, "because I've been bawling like a baby."

She made a comforting noise, like she might have if Adrienne had skinned her knee. "Do you want to talk about it?"

"Nothing that you don't already know," he said. "Mostly I'm just . . . grateful. I'm so grateful, Mary. There is nothing God could ask me to do that I wouldn't do after the way He saved my life today."

Mary made that soothing noise again, then said, "I feel the same way, Whit. He saved *my* life too. I don't know how I could have ever lived without you. We all have much to be grateful for, except that . . . I've tried to keep Adrienne buffered from it, so I don't know whether she realizes how bad it could have been."

"I prefer it that way," he said, "even though I'm glad she knows it was her testimony that saved me."

"She'll be proud of that for the rest of her life, I think." Mary sighed. "And I don't think your mother has been aware of much of anything except what she's watching on television, even though I don't believe she remembers the beginning of a program by the time she gets to the end."

"I hate to see her memory worsening," Whit said, "but I'm glad she hasn't been fully aware of all of this. After the way she lost my father . . . and Joseph . . . this would have broken her, I'm afraid." He hated bringing up the violent deaths of his brother and father, but he loved the way Mary stroked his hair gently and kissed his brow as if doing so might completely erase the painful episodes of his past. There were moments when he almost believed that it could.

Mary stood up and held out her hand. "Come back to bed," she said. "I don't want to be there alone . . . ever again."

"Amen to that," he said and took her hand.

Before leaving the main floor they looked in on Whit's mother. Ida was sleeping peacefully, and they went up the stairs to peek into Adrienne's room, where they found her equally content in slumber.

"She's so beautiful," Whit whispered while they both admired her in the glow of her Cinderella night light.

"She looks like you," Mary said, and Whit gave her a startled glance.

Back in the hallway, where they wouldn't disturb Adrienne, he said, "That is biologically impossible."

"Yes, but it's still true," she said. "I thought I'd told you before . . . that I think she looks like you."

"No, you hadn't mentioned it," he said. Since Whit was half Hispanic, his mother having come from Mexico, he had similar coloring to Adrienne, who had been born in the same country—although Adrienne's hair and skin were darker than his, since his father was Caucasian.

Mary was blonde and looked nothing like Adrienne, so he assumed her remark was in reference to his common ethnicity with the child. But she said firmly, "She looks like you. Anyone who saw her with you and didn't know the situation would think you're her father." She started down the hall to their bedroom. "It can be that way with adopted children, you know. They usually end up where they're supposed to end up; at least that's what I believe."

"Except that I'm not the man who adopted Adrienne. Her father died along with her sister."

Mary turned to look at him as they entered their bedroom. Since she'd left the lamp on, he could clearly see her smile when she said, "You're the father she was meant to have. That's why she looks like you."

Whit said nothing as they climbed into bed and Mary turned off the lamp, but he couldn't stop thinking about what she'd said. His tears had exhausted him, however, and he drifted quickly to sleep. He woke up to daylight, with the vague memory of a dream hovering in his mind. But this one had been far more pleasant than the nightmare that had nearly suffocated him earlier in the night. He'd been chasing Adrienne through the garden behind the house while she'd giggled and pretended to avoid his tickling. Then he'd realized that there was more than one child, and the other was almost identical to Adrienne. Isabelle, her twin sister. He barely had time to absorb the tenderness of the dream before Adrienne jumped on the bed in a flurry of giggles, not unlike those he'd heard in his dream.

"I'm so glad you're back home, Daddy!" she declared and smooched him on the cheek.

"I'm so glad too," he said. "I think Mommy doesn't tickle you nearly enough when I'm gone."

She squealed with laughter as he grabbed one of her bare feet and tickled it mercilessly while he and Mary laughed too. When the tickling finally subsided, Mary kissed Whit and said, "Good morning, Mr. Eden. It's good to have you home."

"It's good to *be* home," he said, then Adrienne snuggled down into the bed between them while the three of them silently reveled in a blanket of gratitude. Even without words, Adrienne seemed to sense the deep spirit of thankfulness, but she was like that. She had a special gift for appreciating the good in everything and for making the world seem a little brighter. And today was certainly a bright day!

"It's time for you to get ready for school," Mary said to the child, breaking the silence.

Adrienne protested, which was extremely rare, since she loved kindergarten. She then declared very maturely, "I shouldn't have to go to school today. We should celebrate! We could go bowling, or shopping, or out to lunch, or to a movie."

"Or all of it," Whit said, and Mary gave him a mild glare that made him smile.

"Can we? Can we?" Adrienne begged.

"I don't think missing one day of school will hurt when we really could use a celebration," Whit said.

"But I missed yesterday too so that I could be in court," Adrienne pointed out.

"Okay, two days of school," Whit said, then he looked at Mary and stuck out his bottom lip like a pouty child. "What do you say? I'll help her catch up on her schoolwork."

"I think it's a grand idea," Mary said. "We could all stand to get out. But I don't know if I'm up to doing *all of it.*"

"We'll have to see how Mommy feels," Whit said to Adrienne.

"You'd better go get dressed so we can start celebrating," Mary added, and Adrienne shot off the bed and out of the room.

Whit laughed, then laid his head back on the pillow, knowing he wouldn't get to stay there long. "Mary," he said gently, taking her hand, "we need to have the girls sealed to us."

She turned more fully toward him, surprised. "The girls? Both of them?"

"Of course, both of them. They're sisters; they're both your daughters, and that makes them mine in a spiritual sense. We were married in the temple; we need to have our daughters sealed to us."

"What brought this on?" she asked.

"What you said last night . . . about Adrienne being my daughter. And then . . . I dreamt of them—both of them. I think Isabelle wants to be a part of our family; we need to be a *forever* family. All of us."

Whit noticed tears in Mary's eyes before she put her head on his shoulder and wrapped her arms around him. "What a lovely idea," she said. "What do we have to do?"

"I don't know," he said, "but we'll find out how I go about adopting the girls so that we can have them sealed to us. Right now I think we'd better get dressed and get some breakfast before Her Majesty has a chance to get too impatient."

"I'm sure you're right," she said, but not with a lot of enthusiasm.

"Are you okay?" Whit asked.

"I'm fine," she said. "Just . . . much slower and more tired than I'd like to be. But it's all for a good cause."

"I'm thinking we should nix the bowling," he said. "A movie might be better. I'm sure there's some matinee Adrienne would love that we can probably tolerate."

"Excellent plan," Mary said, and Whit kissed her before he helped her to her feet and they embarked on a perfectly normal family day, something they'd not enjoyed for a very long time.

Whit got dressed and left Mary to take her time and oversee any help Adrienne might need. He found his mother sitting on the edge of her bed, looking confused. Since they used a baby monitor to be aware of his mother's needs, he knew she'd not yet made a sound before he'd come down the stairs. But it was becoming more and more common for her to wake up and just sit on the edge of the bed until she got some guidance.

"Good morning, Mother," he said, sitting beside her and gently taking her hand. It took a few minutes of careful conversation for her to become oriented to her surroundings, but even then Whit wasn't entirely sure that she knew who he was. Given the fact that he hadn't been living in the house during the trial probably made his presence there a little more strange. Prior to that, he'd been fortune enough to be under house arrest rather than having to spend months in jail. He'd not been able to leave the premises, but at least he'd been with his family. Today he was free and looking forward to their outing; he just hoped that his mother would enjoy it too.

Whit guided his mother into the bathroom with some simple instructions, then he closed the door to give her privacy and set out the clothes she would need. He went to the kitchen and kept his end of the monitor with him so that he could hear her if she evidenced any distress or need for help. He'd only been there a minute when Janel arrived to begin her day's work. She'd been employed by Mary's father for many years to do the cooking and keep the house in order. Since Walter Cranford's corporation was still willing to pay her salary and allow Whit and Mary to live in the house for the time being, they were all quite happy to enjoy it for as long as it lasted. Janel was like family to all of them, and she squealed with excitement when she saw Whit. She'd heard the news of the verdict the previous evening but she'd gone home before they'd returned from court, and she'd not yet seen him since the trial had begun several days earlier.

"Oh, look at you!" she said and engulfed him in a tight hug. She let go, then took his face into her hands. "I dare say you're glowing," she said.

"I would say that's highly likely," he said. "There are no words to express my relief."

"Oh, we've prayed so hard," Janel said as tears filled her eyes.

"I've felt those prayers," he said. Janel did not share their religion, but she was devoted to God and had a keen respect for their beliefs.

Janel insisted that she was going to fix an extra-special breakfast, and she was glad to hear that the family would be going out to celebrate. He invited her to come along, but she insisted that she had some things that needed to be taken care of around the house and would take a rain check. Whit could tell from sounds on the monitor that his mother was talking to herself while she was getting dressed, which was preferable to silence, because this way he knew exactly what she was doing. He took the monitor with him while he went out through the patio doors off of the common room and stood at the edge of the garden, admiring its beauty and familiarity.

Whit had first come here when he'd been hired to restore and care for the immense garden that covered a wide expanse of the property surrounding the house. Mary's mother had loved and nurtured the garden but she had been dead for years, and it had been neglected long before that due to her illness. Mary had wanted the garden restored to its original beauty, and her father—for all his difficulties—had given permission for a gardener to be hired, mostly because he wanted people in the neighborhood to be impressed by his yard rather than offended by his weeds. Whit had found great joy in the work he'd done here. The work itself was fulfilling, but doing it for Mary had warmed his heart right from the start. In spite of their considerable difference in age, it had practically been love at first sight for him. She was an amazing woman and he adored her—and her daughter. He still had an enormous amount of work to do in the garden, but the view from here was lovely. He'd done it that way on purpose, so that while he continued to hack away at years of neglect, Mary could have a nice view from the house, and the patio could be used for relaxing and for entertaining guests.

Whit was surprised when the little three-tiered fountain nearby began to flow. He turned around to see that Adrienne had flipped the switch just outside the door and was running toward him.

"Here," she said, holding out a nickel. "Make a wish."

"Do you have a nickel for yourself?"

"Of course!" she said somewhat indignantly, which made him laugh.

Whit tossed in the coin, wishing that he might never be separated from his family again. He followed it with a silent prayer of gratitude for being here with them now. He watched Adrienne make her wish, then they went inside to help Janel fix breakfast.

They were all seated around the table, sharing breakfast while they talked and laughed, and Whit had a moment of such overwhelming gratitude that he couldn't have spoken if he'd needed to. His mother was somewhat lucid and was enjoying Adrienne's antics, while Janel teased the child by pretending not to know the alphabet. Mary was laughing, then she turned and caught his eye. Seeming to sense his thoughts and what he was feeling, she reached across the table and squeezed his hand, smiling in a way that made everything perfect.

A few minutes later, Adrienne said to Whit, "We can't forget to go to the party tonight."

"What party?" Whit asked, glancing toward Mary.

"I'm ashamed of you, Whit Eden," she said lightly.

"Well, I *have* been a little out of touch," he said in the same tone, glad they could joke about it now.

"What day is it?"

Whit glanced at his watch, where the date was displayed along with the time. "It's May fifth," he said, then added as enlightenment finally dawned on him, "Oh! It's the fifth of May!"

"Cinco de Mayo," Adrienne declared proudly. "There's a party at the church for Cinco de Mayo."

"Of course," Whit said. "There's always a party at the church for Cinco de Mayo." Since they attended church with a Spanish-speaking branch, the holiday was always celebrated, and it was done with a great deal of festivity. "I guess that's good timing since we're celebrating today."

"I'd say that's perfect timing," Mary said and found it difficult not to cry as she observed Whit behaving so naturally in such a familiar setting. She thought of how she'd dreaded this day with the fear that either the trial wouldn't be over or the verdict would send Whit to prison. She never could have been brave enough to attend the branch party under such circumstances. And she'd avoided mentioning it to Whit, hoping that if he hadn't been able to go he might forget all about it and not be saddened by what he'd be missing. Now everything was perfect. Mary took in a deep breath and felt happier than she ever had in her life.

When it came time to leave for the celebration adventure, Ida seemed confused and didn't want to go. Janel graciously offered to watch out for Ida, certain she would be no trouble at all if she remained at home in her familiar surroundings. She promised to call if there was even a hint of a problem, and Whit promised to keep his phone on vibrate in his pocket if they went to a movie so he would be readily available. Janel had looked out for Ida a great deal and was comfortable with it. They were all thankful for her help but Whit felt concerned as they left the house.

Once they were on the road, with the radio playing and Adrienne distracted in the back seat of the truck with a book she was reading for school, Whit said quietly to Mary, "My mother is getting worse. I wonder if we'll ever be able to take her out any more at all."

"I've wondered the same," Mary said, and Whit sighed.

"I know we talked about this when she was diagnosed, but . . . a day will come when we won't be able to manage her. I'm not sure she even knows who I am."

"I know," Mary admitted, and Whit felt sick as he imagined her having to deal with such things on her own if he were now in prison. He was flooded with gratitude all over again. "We'll watch her closely and be prayerful. We'll know what to do." She squeezed his hand. "It will be all right."

They went shopping in their favorite bookstore, then they wandered through a mall, since the doctor had encouraged Mary to walk, and Adrienne enjoyed looking in all the store windows. Whit bought her some new shoes that were sparkly red and would match hardly anything that Adrienne owned, but the sale price had been a steal, and the shoes brought an equivalent sparkle to Adrienne's eyes.

After eating a leisurely lunch, they made it to a matinee and returned home to find that Janel had been productive and Ida had been cooperative and no trouble at all. Once Janel had left for the day, Whit realized that he might not be able to go to the church party after all. If his mother felt uncomfortable leaving the house, he would need to stay and look out for her. Mary would have been fine to stay home with him, but Adrienne had her heart set on the party, so they would possibly have to divide and conquer the needs of the evening. Whit kept talking to his mother about the party, hoping she might be up for it. He prayed about it, then had the idea to pray *with* his mother. Prayer had been a big part of her life for *all* of her life. Whit was amazed, though he figured he shouldn't have been, when the very act of praying aloud on her behalf seemed to calm her and clear her thinking. She quickly became excited about going to the party and seeing all of the people with whom she went to church, people she had grown to love over the years.

As they drove to the church building, Adrienne's presence helped Ida remain in a lucid and natural mental state. They arrived to find a sense of excitement in the air along with colorful decorations, festive music, and the aromas of fine Mexican fare. Food was being set out in the cultural hall, and people were talking and laughing as they mingled. Whit held Mary's hand in his, finding it difficult to keep his emotion in check. When he'd been arrested for the mysterious murder of his father-in-law, his bail had been set at an exorbitant amount they never could have afforded. Due to his gang history and the fact that he'd once served time, the judge had shown no leniency on that issue. Then, thanks to Donald Vega—a member of the branch and a great attorney—bail had been lowered with the agreement that Whit would remain at home with a monitoring anklet. At that point, members of the branch had taken money out of their savings accounts, pooled it together, and posted bail so that Whit could be at home with his family. That money had all been returned now, but

Whit would never forget the spontaneous goodness and charity of these people and how their love and prayers and support had gotten him and his family through a terrible time. Apparently, not one of these people had even remotely believed that he had been guilty—in *spite* of his violent history—and he marveled that people could be so good.

Whit felt Mary squeeze his hand, and he turned to see her smile, as if she perfectly understood what he was feeling. He was able to control his emotions, and they immersed themselves in the small crowd of people that was like an amazing extended family. Ida did well, and Whit and Mary were both pleased to see her enjoying herself. Adrienne quickly found some girls from her Primary class, and they had great fun. After the meal was finished but before the entertainment began, the branch president took the microphone and said, "I'd like to say that the timing of Cinco de Mayo couldn't have been any better for us this year. We are all so grateful to have Brother Eden back with us."

Whit was startled to hear his name then was quite overcome when everyone applauded. He was just thinking he could keep his emotions under control when they all came to their feet, as if simple applause was not sufficient to express their "amens" to what President Martinez had just said. Some of Whit's friends then nudged him, encouraging him to go the microphone and give a little speech. He could hardly decline, and he couldn't deny there were some things he wanted to say, but he knew he wouldn't get through it without some tears. He figured that was okay since these people all shared testimony meeting once a month, and there were always tears then.

President Martinez actually embraced Whit before handing him the microphone. Whit took hold of it and looked out over the faces of his branch members; the knot in his throat increased. "I cannot even find the words to . . ." His firm beginning faltered with the onslaught of such deep emotion that he couldn't get even a sound out of his mouth. It felt as if the tears in his eyes had burned their way up from his heart. He prayed for some help to get through this moment, although the problem was amplified when he heard many sniffles in the room. His prayer was answered after at least a full minute of silence, and he was able to add his heartfelt appreciation for both the literal hands-on help these people had given him and his family and for their prayers and fasting. He expressed his gratitude to a merciful Father in Heaven, and for the infinite Atonement of the Savior, stating firmly that without God's hand in his life, the outcome would have surely been very different. Once he'd managed to say what he felt needed to be said, he handed the microphone back to President Martinez and returned to where his family was sitting, but he didn't get there without first receiving about fifty hugs and at least that many more handshakes. He felt as if he'd come back from war after being missing in action. Perhaps it was an appropriate metaphor.

Whit sat down next to his wife and put his arm around her. He noticed his mother beaming proudly and smiled at her. Adrienne climbed onto his lap and kissed his cheek. He had everything in life he could ever want or ask for.

They were just getting into the truck after the party when Whit's cell phone vibrated in his pocket. He answered it right after he closed the door and before he put the key into the ignition. It was his Aunt Sofia. She spoke in Spanish and was obviously in a very agitated state. Whit's mother had two sisters still living. Whit was closest to Claudia, who was in a care center. They all visited her every Sunday, and she shared a close relationship with his family. Whit wasn't as close to Sofia, and Mary and Adrienne had never even met her. She lived in the neighborhood where Whit had grown up. It was overrun with gang activity, and he would never dare take his white wife into that neighborhood at any time of the day or night. It would be a risk to her safety, and he would never take that kind of a chance.

Claudia and Sofia both had children who were actively part of the gang to which Whit had once belonged. Whit and his cousins held a grudging respect for each other, but mostly they just tried to avoid contact. Now that Whit had reason to wonder whether one of his cousins might have had something to do with the death of Mary's father—and Whit's subsequent arrest for the murder—he felt even more skeptical than usual. But he also knew that Sofia's children weren't known for seeing to her needs as well as they should, and if she needed help, he was eager to give it. He concluded from her phone call that she needed him but she wouldn't say why. He told her it would take about half an hour to get there, and she assured him she would be fine until then. She just needed to talk to him. The truth was that he could have been there in ten minutes, but he wouldn't go see her without first taking his family home.

"What was that about?" Mary asked after Whit hung up the phone.

"I have no idea," he said, "but I'm sure it's nothing serious. Sometimes she just needs to see the face of someone she can trust." He muttered more quietly, "Too bad she can't trust her children."

"Yeah, too bad," Mary said. They were speaking in English, which meant that Ida couldn't understand most of what they were saying, but she was engaged in conversation with Adrienne in the back seat anyway.

Back at the house, Whit made certain all was well with his family before he left to drive back to his old neighborhood. He hated going there! The memories were uncomfortable at best and horrific in some cases. This place where Whit had grown up was smack in the middle of the territory of a Chicano gang. They hated whites. They hated the rich. What they engaged in—racially motivated theft, rape, assault, vandalism, and sometimes murder—were officially called hate crimes. The more they could get away with, the more they had to brag about, giving them additional power over other gangs in the city. When Whit had lived here, he could never leave home without making absolutely certain that he wasn't being followed, because he knew there were people watching and waiting for any possible opportunity to engage in mischief of the worst kind. Over time and through much difficulty, he had earned a kind of grudging respect with the members of the gang he'd once belonged to, especially those who were his cousins. But he certainly didn't trust them, and he knew better than anyone what they were capable of. Now he hated the whole spirit of driving into an area of the city that was controlled by a code of fear and violence that he loathed. He'd worked hard to get beyond all of that, but he knew well enough that the consequences would always haunt him, and they were never far away when people who shared his blood still embraced that lifestyle.

He parked his truck in Sofia's driveway, praying it wouldn't be subjected to any vandalism while he visited with his aunt. If so, it wouldn't be the first time. Whit suddenly felt very uneasy just before he knocked on the door, and he wondered if something might be more wrong with Sofia than he'd suspected. She answered the door, looking a little sheepish, and he felt nervous as he stepped inside. She closed the door behind him and said in whispered Spanish, "I'm sorry, Whit. They promised there would be no trouble."

Whit turned to see five of his male cousins lounging casually in Sofia's tiny front room. Jose and Carlos were Claudia's sons. Carlos was his only cousin that he could credit with some amount of decency. Jose was a loose cannon who was usually either stoned or drunk. The other three were Sofia's sons, all older than Whit and men whom he thankfully saw very rarely. At first glance, one might have thought it was a casual family gathering. But the feeling in the air suggested more subtly that Sofia was being held hostage, with Whit as the ransom.

Whit's heart beat hard with a fear that he kept carefully masked. They could *smell* fear, and he would never allow them to pick up on the scent. The collective sum of piercings and tattoos in the room was impossible to count, and the extreme hairstyles and manner of dress among Whit's cousins were astonishing. But Whit hated it most because it all reminded him of the way he used to be. He reminded himself once again that he'd worked hard to leave this world behind. He'd served his time, and he'd certainly paid a high price—over and over. But he'd just been made well aware of the fact that there are some things from which you can never fully be free. These people were part of his family, and apparently they weren't very happy with him.

Chapter Two

"WELL, ISN'T THIS FUN?" Whit said with a light voice and a little chuckle. He'd become a very good actor when it came to behaving with perfect confidence around these people. They had a keenly tuned sixth sense about intimidation, and they thrived on it. He knew he had to be stronger than they were to withstand it. "Are we going to watch a movie? I hope someone brought popcorn."

"We just got a quick item of business, cuz," said Julio, the oldest of Sofia's sons. Whit noticed that his aunt had left the room. They'd told her there would be no trouble, but what could she do about it if there were?

"And you couldn't just give me a call?" Whit asked.

"Sit down, bro," Angel said. He was Julio's younger brother, and his name was a sick irony.

"I'm fine, thanks," Whit said, folding his arms over his chest but being careful not to portray a defensive demeanor. He was the only one aware of his pounding heart and sweating palms. He knew for a fact that any one of them could pull out a gun or a knife and his life would be over in a heartbeat if that was their intent. He'd seen it happen, and he knew it was possible. He tried to focus on visualizing himself surrounded by protective, armor-clad angel warriors with weapons drawn, ready to protect him. He did his part by giving intimidation right back to his cousins through a purposeful, intense gaze that he shot back and forth among the five men. He included Carlos in his surveillance, not wanting the others to think that there were things Carlos might know that the others didn't.

"Come on and sit down," Jose said. "Relax," he drawled, as if Whit might be hypnotized enough by the word to take the invitation.

"I'm fine," Whit repeated. "Why don't you just say what you've got to say and get it over with. You didn't have to put Sofia in the middle of this."

"Fine, we'll say it," Julio said, standing up. The guise of this being a friendly encounter fell away, but Whit resisted the urge to run and instead took a step closer to Julio, kicking the façade of his firm stance up a notch. "You spent a lot o' time with the cops lately and—"

"Yeah, that happens when you get arrested and go on trial," Whit countered. "As if that was *my* choice."

"Cops did a lot o' sniffing around here while you was in jail," Julio added. "We gotta deal that you keep your mouth shut. We just wanna be sure we *still* gotta deal."

Whit took *another* step toward Julio, who didn't step back, but nevertheless seemed to retract just a bit. "I've *always* kept my part of the bargain," Whit said firmly, referring to the terms they'd mutually agreed to after Whit had boldly burned off his only visible gang tattoo and had declared his resignation from the gang. He'd been badly beaten up and had ended up in the hospital with multiple bruises and some broken bones. But he'd stood his ground and made it clear to them that although he knew a great many of their secrets, he was willing to keep that information to himself as long as they didn't give him or his family any trouble. That was before he'd married a white woman and moved into a much nicer neighborhood, but he needed to make it clear that the agreement was still viable. He didn't even want to think about what these men were capable of doing if they felt slighted in the tiniest way. And these men were his family; however, the ones Whit truly feared were the people his cousins associated with who shared no blood ties with him. But he held power over them too with his knowledge of things that they would never want *anyone* to know. Whit added with all the intense conviction that he felt, "I'm well aware we disagree on many things, but we're still family. I never gave the police any of your names, or said a word about anything I know. That's the deal. I've never backed down on it. And as long as you and your *homies* mind your manners with me and my family, I never will."

Julio, who had apparently been designated as spokesman for this little meeting, took a step back and put up his hands in a conciliatory gesture. "Okay, man. Okay. That's all we wanted to know."

"Well, as long as we're having this little soiree," Whit said as he again made eye contact with each one of them, "I'd like to know if you've held up *your* part of the deal."

"What you talkin' about, man?" Angel growled from where he was still seated.

"I'm talking about someone breaking into my home and killing my wife's father, and getting it pinned on me! I can think of at least one or two of your friends who would love to see me rot in prison. Any of you been passing around rumors about me?" He made eye contact with them all once more, his gaze coming to rest on Julio.

Whit knew he had them when Julio said with firm defensiveness, "We didn't say nothin'; we don't even know where you live. Why would we do that?"

"That's all I wanted to know," Whit said, mimicking the way Julio had said it a minute ago. "You keep the deal and I will too. No problems. No worries. Are we good?"

"Yeah, we're good, bro," Julio said and held out his hand.

"Okay, we're good," Whit said, so relieved he could have collapsed, except that he was still firmly keeping his tough persona in place. He took Julio's hand firmly, then his cousin put his other hand on Whit's shoulder in some kind of brotherly hug. The others stood and repeated the gesture with Whit. He *did* sit down to visit with them for a few minutes, not wanting to seem unfriendly or like he was cutting himself off from the family, even if he'd cut himself off from their gang affiliations. He felt acutely uncomfortable, and his senses were as alert as a young animal knowing that a hungry lion was nearby, sniffing out his scent. But he remained calm and cool and even managed to smile and make a few jokes. Sofia rejoined them; she'd obviously been eavesdropping and was relieved to have the confrontation defused. Whit hated the thought of these dear little old ladies being in the middle of all of this. He was glad to have finally moved his mother out of this neighborhood, and was relieved that Claudia was in a care center that distanced her further from the problems. But Sofia was still in the heart of it, and he prayed for these sweet ladies every night and day.

Whit left the house, acting as though the entire encounter had all been for the sake of family bonding. *If only,* he thought with a heavy heart as he got into his truck, grateful that it hadn't met with any damage during his visit. He called Mary to tell her that he was on his way home, and he thanked God more than once during the drive that he could leave that neighborhood behind and have a *real* home to go to, with a family that made him feel secure and loved.

Mary met him when he walked into the house, obviously having heard the garage door.

"Is everything all right?" she asked, putting her arms around him.

Whit held her tightly and said, "In a manner of speaking."

"What do you mean?" she asked with suspicion, looking up at him.

"It was an ambush," he said, moving to the couch where he slumped down with a sigh. Mary sat beside him and took his hand. "My cousins were there. The big five!" he added with sarcasm.

"What on earth . . ."

"They wanted to make certain I hadn't told the police anything. I made it clear I had kept my part of the deal, and I made certain they were doing the same. They swear that they don't even know where I live. Obviously Carlos hasn't let on that *he* knows. Glad I can trust him; at least I think I can."

"So you think they're innocent . . . of the . . . murder?"

"I don't know, Mary. I have no idea. But if I were to even *sniff* in their direction with any attempt to get information and find out if any of them were involved, they would be on to me and it would only put us all in more danger. If any of them had anything to do with it, or even if they know who did, we are not likely to ever find out. And neither will the police. The whole thing makes me terribly uneasy, but we can only do what we've done all along. We'll do our best to stay safe and protect ourselves and put it in the Lord's hands." He sighed more contentedly and looked at her face. "He's gotten us this far. I don't think He'll let us down now."

"No, I don't think He will," Mary said and kissed him.

Whit didn't have trouble falling asleep that night, but he woke up around four and couldn't go *back* to sleep while his encounter with his cousins wouldn't leave his mind. The problem was that their brief interaction had triggered memories of so many events of the past that were difficult to think about. His father and brother had both died as a result of gang violence, and his sister had moved far away and had very little contact with Whit or their mother, as if just talking to them more than two or three times a year might taint her life. He couldn't really blame her but it was one more piece of evidence that the neighborhood he'd grown up in had torn their family apart in more ways than he could count. He wondered what it would be like to have a family where you could hold family reunions and get together just to have a good time and become better acquainted. Since Mary was an only child and had no contact with extended family, their marriage was practically the only real family that either of them had. They'd talked about how they could begin new traditions, and how their children would live a different life and it would be better for them. Whit believed that to be true, but sometimes his heart ached for all the grief connected to his family. However, stewing over the ridiculous injustice of such a lifestyle was a fruitless endeavor that he'd given up on years ago.

There was only one solution, and he knew it well. It usually took him an hour or two of stewing now and then before he would have to figure it out all over again, and it was just past six when he replaced his thoughts with prayer, earnestly asking his Father in Heaven to take away the burdens that he was not strong enough to bear. He asked for relief from all of the heartache and grief of the past, and protection from the challenges of the present situation. He committed to doing all that he had the ability to do with his human limitations, then he agreed to give the rest to the Lord. He knew from experience that a willingness to give such burdens to the Lord wasn't an easy exercise when combined with human pride and ego. For years he'd somehow figured he still needed to carry *some* of it, or perhaps he might be able to handle it better on his own. He now knew that giving it to the Lord meant letting go of the worrying, the stewing, the fretting, the fussing, the pain, the loss, the sorrow, the grief, the heartache—whatever the burden might entail.

While God allowed human beings to experience their human emotions, Whit knew that a time came in every trial when human will had to submit fully to the fact that a Savior had already paid the price. Only pride could keep any person from fully accepting that gift and the peace that comes with it. Sometimes he had to pray a hundred times a day for peace to replace his fears and for hope to vanquish his difficult memories. But eventually the peace and hope always came, and Whit knew it was the *only* solution to *any* challenge. Even in the recent trauma of facing the possibility of prison, Whit had known that for all of how unfathomably horrible it would have been, he personally had held no control over the outcome, and he'd known that God would carry him and his family through—no matter what had happened. God couldn't take away the agency of people who could make bad choices and do great harm, but he could give good people the strength to carry them through their challenges, and the eternal perspective regarding things that were truly important.

By the time the usual morning routine was underway, Whit was able to put his unsavory visit with his cousins out of his mind somewhat and focus instead on the plentiful blessings in his life. He spent the day working in the garden, finding his efforts there more gratifying than they had ever been. In the back of his mind, he knew that a day might come when they'd have to leave this house—and the garden—behind. But for now, he enjoyed doing what he loved best and having his family always nearby.

A few weeks later, Whit found his work more fulfilling than ever as certain portions of the garden really came to life. The family ate on the patio nearly every evening, enjoying the pleasant weather and the lovely view of the many-colored roses and a myriad of other flowers. Mary's pregnancy nausea was subsiding, seemingly in proportion to the way she was blossoming into a stage where she looked *very* pregnant. Adrienne was doing well in school and actually dreading the end of her year in kindergarten, but they talked about many plans for the summer, most especially the anticipated birth of the baby, something Adrienne was really looking forward to.

Ida was also looking forward to the arrival of her new grandchild—at least when she had her lucid moments. Much of the time she just seemed lost in a world somewhere inside her own mind. In most cases, if Whit looked directly into her eyes and reminded her of who he was and what was going on, she would think about it for several seconds, then remember enough to seem all right. But she rarely knew Mary or Adrienne or Janel anymore. The doctor had told them she likely knew Whit because he'd been her caregiver for years. He'd spent some time in prison in his late teens, and then he'd cleaned up his life and served a mission in Mexico for two years. But since then, he'd taken care of his mother, and the symptoms of her disease had not set in until later. They were warned, however, that Ida's symptoms could at any time become unmanageable and they would have no choice but to rely on an assisted-living center in order for her to have the care she needed. They'd already had a couple of incidents where Ida had been frightened and confused and had adamantly refused to allow anyone to help her with simple tasks that she'd forgotten how to do herself. It had been upsetting for the entire family but Whit was adjusting to the idea that he was going to have to turn the care of his mother over to competent professionals who knew how to deal with the ravaging effects of this debilitating disease.

Soon after his mother's diagnosis, Whit had sought out the best facility in the city, which was a fifteen-minute drive from the house. They could visit often, and he knew Ida would be in good hands. He hated not being able to take responsibility for her care, but he wasn't naive enough to believe that his mother would feel any differently about him for taking this step. She'd made the decision about her own care back when her mind had been clear enough to do it; this was what she'd wanted, and they'd known it was inevitable.

Whit had been careful with his income ever since returning from his mission, and he had made some sound investments, so he had a fair amount of his own money put away. He also had the money from selling the house where he and his mother had lived. They certainly weren't well off by any means, but there was money set aside to see to his mother's care. He just dreaded the day when it would actually happen, and in the meantime he enjoyed every moment when she was mentally present to any degree, even though those moments were becoming less and less frequent. But Ida was having a good week so far, and she enjoyed sitting on the patio near the little fountain with the angel on top of it. Ida enjoyed the view and commented frequently on the beauty of the flowers, often forgetting that she'd just made a similar comment a minute or two earlier.

Whit was sitting there near his mother when Mary came out to the patio and sat some distance away before she motioned for him to come closer. He stood up and sat in a different chair, facing Mary and wondering what might be so important.

"Mr. Lostin just phoned," she said. Judging by the somber tone of her voice and her tight expression, he knew it had to do with the house. Mr. Lostin had been a loyal employee of Mary's father for many years. He'd taken care of all of Walter Cranford's finances and had served as a liaison between Walter and his hugely successful corporation. He'd been very kind to Mary, and following Walter's death he'd told them that the board had agreed to let them stay in the house for the time being, even though Mary's father had left her nothing in his will. They didn't know *where* the money had gone; they just knew it hadn't been to Mary, Walter's only child.

Mr. Lostin was also the overseer of Whit's paychecks as gardener, and they all knew that once the board of directors decided that the house needed to be rented or sold, his job could very well end. He and Mary were both exceedingly grateful for the time they'd been allowed to remain here rent-free following Walter's death, and Mr. Lostin had been kind and generous in convincing the board that Walter's daughter ought to be allowed to stay in the house. Mary believed that they all felt a little sorry for her. None of them had liked Walter, and they were all well aware that he'd kept his daughter out of his will for no reason other than his bigotry regarding the fact that she'd spent many years in Mexico and had adopted Hispanic children. However, Whit and Mary both knew that they couldn't depend on the company's charity indefinitely, and Whit knew from Mary's countenance that the situation was about to change.

"When do we have to leave?" Whit asked, preferring to get to the point.

"We *don't* have to leave," she said, which made him wonder why she looked so somber. "Although we do have to make some adjustments. Mr. Lostin explained that while the board is sympathetic to my situation, they have to be practical and consider profits and losses and . . . well, you know the drill. You've heard him say all of that before."

"Yes, I know the drill."

"He told me," Mary went on, "that there was a rather lengthy discussion on how the company could equitably make up for my father's stinginess—his words, not mine. I assured him that they had been more than generous with us, and we would completely understand if we needed to leave, or at the very least start paying rent—although I don't think we could afford what it would cost to rent a place like this in this area."

"Not likely," he said. "Especially knowing my mother's care will be very expensive before too long."

"Exactly," Mary said and sighed. He was still waiting for the bomb to drop. "So, anyway," she sighed again, "he said that if we would like, we could stay in the house and they will cut your salary in half in exchange for the rent."

"Really?" he said, pleasantly surprised. That didn't feel like a bomb dropping at all. "We can certainly manage with that. In truth, that's a very good deal on rent—for a house like this in an affluent area."

"Yes, I agree," she said. "I don't want to leave, even though I know that eventually we will probably have to. We're comfortable here. I worry about your mother and want her to be in surroundings that are familiar. When she goes into a care center, there will be full-time specialists to help her adjust. I'm not sure we could handle that if we had to move right now. Mr. Lostin brought that up. Apparently that was part of the board's discussion."

"My, he *is* thorough," Whit said.

"And he also said that they'd prefer not to see us uprooted with a baby coming. Also, he pointed out that since the house and property belong to the company, and they're well aware of the terrible condition of that half acre of 'a mess that used to be a garden,' is how he said it, they consider your working on the garden a benefit because it will raise the value of the property when, or if, it is sold. Therefore, keeping you on as a gardener is reasonably equitable for them. So . . . the bottom line is that we can stay if we can agree to that deal."

"I'm good with it if you are," he said.

"I'm more than good with it," she said. "Except that . . . there's one other concession."

"What?" he asked warily, now certain that a bomb *would* drop.

Mary sighed more deeply, hung her head for a moment, then cleared her throat before she looked at him with misty eyes. "We have to let Janel go."

Whit leaned back and drew in his breath sharply, wondering why he hadn't seen that coming. Janel just seemed like a part of the house, part of what made it a home. But of course she'd been hired to clean house and cook meals for Walter Cranford. Expecting his corporation to continue paying her salary made no sense at all. In fact, it was rather remarkable that they had continued doing so for this long. He didn't need any explanation, but he felt a little sick over the implications, and now he fully understood Mary's heavy mood. Neither of them said a word, as if nothing needed to be said at all. They'd discussed this possibility long before now, but it had been brushed aside due to other complications in their lives. There wasn't anything to say that hadn't been said before, so Whit just scooted his chair closer and put his arms around Mary so she could cry against his shoulder.

When she'd had a chance to vent her tears he asked, "Do you want me to tell her?"

"No, I'll tell her. But I want you to hold my hand while I do."

"Fair enough," he said and sighed deeply. "I wish we could afford to pay her salary ourselves. I wish that she could go with us wherever we might go."

"I know, and she knows that too. We all knew this was coming, but . . . it almost makes me miss my father. At least when he was here, Janel was needed to . . ."

"I know," Whit said so she wouldn't have to finish the sentence, and he made no effort to clarify that she might *almost* miss her father. While they had both been shocked by Walter's violent demise, neither of them had missed him for a moment. He'd contributed nothing positive to their lives except for giving them a roof over their heads. They were both readily grateful for that, but it wasn't enough to make them miss having to contend with his cantankerous personality and his obnoxious behavior.

A while later, when Ida was content in front of the television and Adrienne was upstairs playing in her room, Mary asked Janel if they could sit down and talk before she left for the day. She took one look at Whit's and Mary's expressions and said, "I can guess what this is about."

Neither of them responded, and they all immediately sat down at the dining table. Whit took hold of Mary's hand where it rested on the table. Mary just hurried and said it. "Mr. Lostin phoned today. The board has agreed to let us stay in return for half of Whit's salary, but they can't justify keeping you on any longer."

Janel took that in for just a moment; she sighed and forced a smile toward Mary, then Whit, then Mary again. "Your father was very ill for a long time. I knew well enough that when he died I'd be out of a job. The extra months I've been able to stay here have been a bonus." She forced another smile and took hold of Mary's other hand. "Don't you worry about me. I've got some money put away, and I've got grandkids to visit." She chuckled softly. "Now I can travel more to see them; most of them live out of state, you know."

"Yes, I know."

"It's not the job I'll miss." She wiped away a tear before it barely had a chance to fall. "It'll be you and your family. I've grown to love you all."

"And we've grown to love you," Mary said. "We won't see each other every day, but you can use some of your spare time to just come and visit. Adrienne will still be expecting to have sleepovers at your house."

"Oh, I do hope so!" Janel said.

"You're like another grandmother to her," Mary said. "We're not going to stop seeing each other."

Janel nodded firmly and smiled, as if she were feeling a little better. "But how will you manage?" she asked.

"Your help has been wonderful and very much appreciated," Mary said, "but we *will* manage, as most families do. You know Whit is very helpful, and we'll adjust."

"I'm sure you will. But I might just have to come over and help out here and there just for the fun of it."

"That's entirely up to you," Mary said. "When you *do* come to visit, I think I'd prefer that you just visit."

"I would agree with that," Whit said. "Although . . . we will surely need some help with that new baby." He chuckled tensely. "I know absolutely nothing about babies. We're going to need your expertise."

"Oh, don't you worry," Janel said and wiped another tear. "I'll not be letting that little one go too many days without seeing my face."

Adrienne came down the stairs, startling them all out of their somber moods, or at least motivating them to put on brave faces for the child. After Janel left for the day, Whit and Mary sat with their daughter and explained the reasons that Janel wouldn't be working at the house for very much longer. Adrienne handled the news as maturely as a five-year-old possibly could but she still shed some tears. She was assuaged by the reassurance that Janel was a very dear friend and they would see her as often as possible; she was also told she could still go to Janel's home for visits, and sometimes for a sleepover, as she was already in the habit of doing.

Since Janel had an official two-weeks' notice, they all had a transition period in which to get used to the fact that she wouldn't be around every day. Janel talked with both Whit and Mary about the things she took care of around the house, and they made notes so that nothing would get overlooked. Janel seemed to want to leave everything in as good an order as possible, even though they had assured her it wasn't necessary.

Whit and Mary were distracted from the prospect of Janel's impending departure when Ida began having some terrible episodes with her memory loss that made her terrified of not knowing where she was or what was going on. She actually became difficult enough to control that she punched Whit in the face with enough force to leave a bruise. Once that had happened, he wouldn't let Mary or Adrienne or Janel even attempt to help soothe her when she became upset.

Ida also tried to start cooking something once in the middle of the night, and since she'd left her room where the monitor had been left on, Whit heard nothing until the smoke alarm went off, which terrified all of them—especially Ida. The worst part of the experience was the way the alarm going off in the night reminded them all of the night their home had been broken into and Mary's father had been killed. It took them all a couple of days to recover from the trauma and to fully express their varied feelings of post-traumatic stress. Even Adrienne seemed to need to talk about what had happened. But they all agreed that it was in the past and they were glad to have it behind them. Neither Whit nor Mary voiced their fears that they still didn't know who had murdered her father, and therefore they could never feel completely safe. But Whit didn't admit to Mary that he was having more difficulty sleeping, and he was often convinced that he was hearing strange noises in the house that made his heart pound. Logically he knew there was a reliable alarm system in place but he could come up with all kinds of reasons why it might have failed—or been disarmed by someone with the intent to do harm. He was often up more than once in the night, making certain everything was as it should be, and that his mother and his daughter were sleeping peacefully. He usually managed to slip in and out of bed without disturbing Mary. On the rare occasions when she caught him, he simply assured her that he felt a little restless and that everything was fine.

Whit found he had less time and energy to deal with his fears— whether or not they might be well-founded—when he had no choice but to face the sudden decline in Ida's condition and accept the fact that they could no longer handle her on their own. They had planned and prepared well for this moment, and there was a room available for Ida at a facility that specialized in the care of Alzheimer's patients. The facility had a reputation for high-quality care, so Whit and Mary weren't at all worried that she wouldn't be in good hands. It was the very act of moving her out of the home and no longer having her in his care that broke Whit's heart. He knew well enough that his mother didn't even know what was going on most of the time; therefore, she was likely not going to notice his absence in her life nearly as much as he was going to notice hers. Mary and Adrienne had both grown very attached to her, and the transition would be difficult for them as well.

Less than a week after Janel stopped coming to work, Ida was moved to the care center. Members of the staff actually came with a van to pick her up and collect most of her things, so that if there were problems en route they would know how to handle them. Whit rode with them to Ida's new home, trying not to shed the tears that were building up. Ida stared out the window as they drove. Whit tried to hold Ida's hand, but she pulled hers away as if she didn't know him and the touch of a stranger made her uncomfortable.

Once they arrived, Whit helped put Ida's things away and get her settled in, even though it mostly seemed like her mind was a million miles away and she had no interest in what was going on around her. The thought occurred to him more than once that it was better than having her freak out over the change. He was afraid that would come when she woke up in the night in a strange bed in a strange room. But he had carefully examined the facility's monitoring abilities, and he knew the staff was competent, kind, and well-trained. He couldn't be doing anything better for his mother than this. The level of care she would be getting would cost him a fortune but he had enough money put away to handle it for a couple of years. After that, he'd figure something else out if he had to. Given the rate of her deterioration, the doctor wasn't certain she'd live that long. Whit didn't want to think about that, but the woman she'd become bore very little resemblance to his mother. He hadn't watched her die; he'd watched her disappear right before his eyes, and he couldn't help believing that death might be preferable.

Whit sat in his mother's room until she drifted off to sleep in a comfortable recliner while watching television. He carefully kissed her brow without disturbing her, whispering that he would be back to see her often, even though he doubted his visits would make much of an impression.

Mary and Adrienne picked him up outside the front door, and once he was in the car he stopped trying to hold back the tears. He felt as if he had just left the scene of his mother's death. Since Mary was driving and Adrienne was preoccupied in the back seat with the toys she'd brought along, he let the tears flow silently down his face, grateful to feel Mary take his hand and squeeze it. At least he had Mary. He tried to imagine how this might have all been without her in his life. It wasn't the first time he'd imagined an alternative existence to the one he was living now, but under such circumstances his gratitude was deeper than usual. He was glad he didn't have to return to an empty house and have no sense of purpose now that his mother didn't need his care. He'd been watching out for her ever since he'd returned from his mission, and not having her around was going to be a tough adjustment—but as Mary had pointed out more than once, Ida hadn't really *been* there for a while now. Not most of the time, anyway.

The school year ended for Adrienne, and their schedule became more relaxed without having to get her up and ready for kindergarten every morning. Since Whit worked at home, the three of them were rarely far away from each other. They were each doing their best to adjust to the dramatic changes in the household with Janel and Ida both gone. Janel came every few days for a visit, and she couldn't seem to keep from cleaning or cooking something while she was there. They were enjoying her regular visits, and they all agreed that having her around was not only enjoyable but helped keep things from seeming too quiet. Then Janel announced that her son who lived in Texas had called her the previous night to tell her that his wife was struggling with some severe depression. She'd struggled with it off and on ever since she'd given birth to their last baby, but it had gotten worse since she'd lost her father to cancer.

"I have to admit," Janel said tearfully, "that I actually felt grateful to know I didn't have a job. I told him I would get on a plane as soon as I could and be there to help with the kids until she can get feeling better. They're taking her to a good counselor and she's on some medication, but it's going to take time, and they really need the help."

"The timing seems like a blessing," Mary said. "Perhaps God knew they would need you, and that's why it worked out the way it did."

"I can't help thinking the same," Janel said, "but I'm sure going to miss you all."

"We'll miss you too," Whit said, "but we have email and telephones. Just keep in touch."

"Oh, I will. I will," Janel said. "You too."

Adrienne had a hard time saying good-bye when Janel left. She clung to her and cried, knowing that Janel was leaving the next day to fly to Texas, and she didn't know how long she would be gone. Janel's daughter, who lived nearby, would be keeping track of Janel's home until she returned.

Whit held a crying Adrienne in his arms while Janel drove away, then they all went inside and decided that they should stay up late and play some games. They played games that Adrienne loved until she was so tired that she was practically asleep by the time Whit carried her up the stairs to her bed.

"Now will you put me to bed?" Mary asked in the hall outside Adrienne's room. "I'm pretty tired myself."

"You ought to be," he said, rubbing her well-rounded belly. "Just a little more than a month to go."

"Yeah, I've held up pretty well for being such an old pregnant lady."

"I refute *old,*" he insisted.

"I'm too old to be pregnant," she countered.

"Obviously not." He smirked and glanced down at her belly, then he picked her up in his arms and carried her into their room, where he set her gently on the bed.

"And you just had to do that to prove how young and strong you are."

"No," he laughed softly and kissed her, "I did that to prove that I love you and I'm going to take very good care of you *and* our children."

"I know you will," she said and touched his face. "You already do. You're the best thing that ever happened to me. I just don't know how I could be so blessed to have you in my life, when I'd honestly believed that I was better off alone after Simon was killed."

Whit stretched out beside her and brushed her hair back off her face. He was well aware that her first marriage had never been good, and there had been no love lost when Simon had died. Her grief was more for their daughter Isabelle who had also died in the car accident with Simon. But that was now long in the past, and Whit could only smile at his wife and say, "I think we're both very much better off together. At least I know *I* am."

"Oh, *I* certainly am!" she said firmly. "And I want our baby to look exactly like you."

"I was hoping for it to look like you," he said, even though they both knew the Hispanic genes were more likely to be dominant, at least in hair and eye color. "But mostly I just want you both to be healthy."

Mary reluctantly got back up so she could use the bathroom and brush her teeth. Once they were both settled in for the night, they held each other close, with their heads on the same pillow, and talked about possible names for their baby. They'd discussed it many times, but as the time was getting closer, they were narrowing it down a bit. It had been a mutual decision to wait until the birth to know the gender of the baby. Therefore, they were trying out names for both boys and girls, but they both felt they wouldn't know for certain until they actually *met* the baby and decided what name really seemed to fit.

They finally fell asleep with Whit's hand over Mary's belly while Whit considered the irony of his mother's life nearing its end at the same time a child's life was about to begin. It reminded him in a strange way of the work he did in the garden, of the seasons and cycles of all growing things. There was both joy and sadness in the thought but he chose to focus on the joy and he slept well, without even a thought of the possibility of intruders entering his home.

Chapter Three

THE FOLLOWING DAY, WHIT TOOK Mary to her now-weekly checkup with the doctor. They dropped Adrienne off to play with her friend Rachel, who was near the same age and attended the same Primary class at church. Rachel's mother, Cinda, was divorced and had been a good friend to Mary ever since she'd first started going to church with Whit. The two little girls played together well, and it was nice for Mary and Whit to be able to trade child-tending time with Cinda.

Their wait in the doctor's waiting room was longer than usual since the doctor had left to deliver a baby, but Mary had been told that the doctor was back in the office now and would attend to Mary as quickly as possible. Mary tried to read a couple of magazines but had trouble focusing. She stood up and paced, feeling uncomfortable, then she sat down, then she stood up and repeated the ritual.

"What's wrong?" Whit whispered to her after she'd sat down for the third time.

"Just . . . restless. I'm all right."

"You look . . . tired."

"I *am* tired," she said. "I'm way too old to be having a baby, and the baby's making me too fat to get a good night's sleep." Realizing it had come out sounding grumpier than she'd intended, she softened her voice and offered her husband a gentle smile. "Sorry," she said. "I really am all right. I'll just be glad when you and I can take *turns* carrying the baby around."

"I'll be glad for that too," he said.

Once in the examination room, the doctor noted that Mary was a lot more swollen in her face and ankles than she had been the week before.

"Is that a problem?" Whit asked.

"It can often accompany high blood pressure, which can signal a problem, but it's completely manageable if we monitor it."

"Okay," Whit drawled while he waited for the doctor to take Mary's blood pressure, even though the nurse had taken it ten minutes earlier.

"Your blood pressure is fine," the doctor said, and Whit heaved a sigh of relief. Mary didn't seem as concerned as Whit felt but she had a kind of dazed, foggy look on her face that reminded him a little of his mother. She was likely just too tired to feel concerned. He almost felt a little guilty sometimes for the fact that Mary was pregnant. Of course he was the father and therefore the pregnancy *was* his responsibility. But when they'd made the decision to marry in spite of the ten years' age difference between them, they'd both believed that Mary couldn't have children, and they hadn't even discussed the possibility of pregnancy.

They'd talked about possibly adopting another child—or even more than one. They'd even discussed that fact that they might feel complete as a family of three. Mary's pregnancy had been completely unexpected. And while it was undeniably a miracle, and women certainly *did* have babies in their forties, there was no disputing the fact that a woman's body was not as strong and resilient at that age as it might have been in her twenties or thirties.

Whit worried about Mary more than he had ever admitted out loud, but it had only been in the last few days that she had shown evidence of not feeling well. It was something that hadn't been noticeable since she'd overcome the debilitating nausea and fatigue of her first trimester.

Whit wondered if the nagging uneasiness he felt now was just his own paranoia or if he should speak up. Deciding to err on the side of caution, he said, "She hasn't been feeling very well the last few days." Mary looked surprised by the comment, and he wondered whether she had actually noticed this herself more than she had cared to think about or acknowledge. Or maybe she just didn't want any attention drawn to something that didn't seem significant. Significant or not, Whit wanted to be reassured that everything was all right.

"What's going on?" the doctor asked Mary.

"I . . . don't know," she said. "I hadn't really thought much about it. I just . . . feel more tired, I suppose; less motivated to do anything. I just figured it's because I'm not sleeping as well."

"Okay, well . . ." The doctor was silent while she apparently pondered the situation, "this is what I want you to do. Walking should actually help the swelling, so I want you to be up and moving, but in small increments so you don't tire yourself out. Does that make sense?"

"Yes," Mary said.

"And given the swelling, I want you to get your blood pressure checked every day. If you live very far from here, I can arrange for you to go into another clinic or hospital to get it checked so that—"

"We're only ten minutes away," Whit said. "We can come here."

"Okay, good." The doctor wrote this information on the chart. "I'll tell them to expect you, and since we are on call this weekend, someone will be here on Saturday and Sunday in the mornings. I want you to get it checked every day. And if anything else changes, call me right away."

"Okay," Mary said.

"Thank you," Whit said, feeling a little better. He liked the idea of bringing her in every day. He didn't understand why, but even if it was just to help ease his own fears, he liked it.

Before they picked up Adrienne, they went out for a late lunch and did a little shopping, mostly purchasing more diapers and a few additional odds and ends for the baby. They were working on getting stocked up.

That evening Whit fixed a simple supper with Adrienne's help, and he did a couple of loads of laundry. He made certain Mary was comfortable in front of a PBS miniseries she'd been watching on DVD, but he paused it every little while and made her go outside and walk around the patio at the edge of the garden for at least five minutes.

The next day her blood pressure was still fine but she was more willing to admit that she just didn't feel well. A nurse checked her temperature and a few other vital signs and repeated what the doctor had said the day before—to call if anything changed.

Mary went to bed early that night, pleading exhaustion. Whit checked on her twice before he actually went to bed himself, and he found her sleeping soundly. But he was roused in the middle of the night by Mary's voice saying, with some alarm, "Whit, wake up. I need you."

"What is it?" he asked, abruptly sitting up once his brain had registered her words.

"I woke up a while ago with a terrible headache; I mean *terrible.* I've been praying about what to do, and I think we need to go to the hospital."

"Okay," he said and was out of bed with the light on in a couple of seconds. He was pulling on his clothes while keeping an eye on Mary as she carefully sat up and turned to put her feet on the floor. He was stunned by the evidence of pain in the grimace on her face. He pulled a shirt over his head and asked, "Do you think I should call an ambulance?"

"Don't be silly," she said, but she didn't lift her head enough to look at him. "Just wrap a blanket around Adrienne and . . ." She hesitated dramatically, and his heart began to pound. And was that a mild slurring he'd heard in her words? He held his breath, trying to interpret his instincts. She finally added, "I'll meet you downstairs and . . ." Definite slurring, and her head wavered as if she were dizzy.

"Mary," Whit said, going to his knees in front of her. "Look at me. Talk to me." She was conscious but apparently incapable of doing either. "Oh, help," he muttered quietly as he carefully eased her back into bed just before he grabbed the phone and dialed 911. He didn't know what was happening, but he knew it wasn't good, and he could never get her to the hospital in half the time it would take EMTs to get to the house, especially when he had a sleeping child to contend with. He explained the emergency, told them the address, and they asked him to stay on the phone with the dispatcher until the ambulance arrived. The kind voice on the other end of the phone asked him specific questions. He told them Mary was conscious but apparently dizzy, with slurred speech and a severe headache. He asked Mary questions to see if she was able to respond. She managed to tell him that her vision was blurry; when she seemed to go blank, Whit's panic deepened.

It seemed an eternity before the ambulance arrived. Whit ran downstairs to open the gate to the driveway via a button in the kitchen and to deactivate the alarm system. He went out the front door to meet the EMTs and guide them into the house. Then he ran up the stairs with two men right behind him, and once they were by Mary's side he felt a tiny measure of relief. That blank, dazed look on her face was gone, but he realized by the way she answered questions that she had no memory of Whit calling 911.

The EMTs quickly determined that Mary's blood pressure was very high and that she might even have had a mini stroke. They got an IV into her arm and medication flowing into it in record time, then they moved her onto a gurney and carried her carefully out to the waiting ambulance. Whit stood in the driveway and watched the vehicle leave with lights blazing and sirens blaring, wishing he could have gone with her. But he had Adrienne to consider. Oh, how he wished Janel wasn't in Texas! He could have taken Adrienne to her house, or he could have called her and she would have come over. He hurried inside, thinking that he would just have to take her with him to the hospital. Then he thought of Cinda, Rachel's mother, who had been helpful and supportive many times. He hated to call and wake her up, but he needed help, and he knew that he and Mary would have done the same for her.

"Of course, bring her over," Cinda said. "I can keep her as long as you need me to. She'd be far too nervous and scared at the hospital, not knowing what's going on."

"Thank you . . . so much," Whit said and hung up so he could hurry and pack what Adrienne might need for a day or two, not certain what was going to happen. He didn't want to think too hard about that. He focused instead on prayer—sometimes silent and sometimes zealously verbal—that Mary and the baby would both be all right. They were in good hands; they had the best medical care. Surely everything would be all right. He wondered what could have possibly happened in the hours since she'd had her blood pressure checked just that morning with normal results.

Adrienne barely woke up enough to hear him say, "Mommy's gone to the hospital, but everything's going to be fine. I'm taking you to Rachel's house and you can stay there. You can go back to sleep in the truck."

She nodded and he lifted her up, wrapped in a blanket, her bag over his shoulder. With the house locked up tight he drove through the dark, quiet streets, not even aware of what time it was until he glanced at the clock on the dashboard to see that it wasn't yet three A.M. He wondered what was happening at the hospital; he wondered how Mary was but he fought to remain focused on his driving and not complicate the matter by breaking any traffic laws.

Cinda opened her front door the moment he drove up, and it only took him a minute to get Adrienne settled on the couch without waking her. He thanked Cinda again, promised to stay in touch, and hurried to the hospital. He was glad when he arrived that he wasn't told to sit in the waiting room where he would have had to wonder what was going on. He was taken straight back to a room in the emergency area where Mary was lying flat on her back, wearing a hospital gown, a blanket tucked up over her rounded belly. Two different bags were hanging on an IV pole and dripping into the tube that went into her arm. A blood pressure cuff was on her arm, and it was apparently meant to remain there. Numbers on the monitor above the bed indicated her last blood pressure reading, her oxygen level, and her heart rate. He glanced at the numbers and knew enough about what was normal to know it wasn't good, but when Mary opened her eyes to look at him as he approached the bed, he saw immediately that she was more like herself than she'd been earlier. He smiled at her and got a faint smile in return before her eyes closed in a way that made him wonder if the medication was making her drowsy. The nurse standing on the other side of the bed, making notes on a computer there, turned toward him and said, "You must be Mary's husband. She's been asking about you."

"I am," Whit said, "and I'm very glad to hear it."

"She's going to be just fine," the nurse said. "I'll tell the doctor you're here. He wanted to talk to you himself, but he's dealing with a more urgent matter so he might be a little while."

"No problem," Whit said, "as long as she's okay." He liked knowing that Mary's condition was not the most urgent matter in the ER.

"She's fine." The nurse smiled at him. "She needs to stay down flat until those blood pressure numbers improve, but she's getting what she needs to help that, and if any of those numbers become a concern, we'll know immediately and be right in."

"Okay, thank you," Whit said, and the woman turned to leave. "What about the baby?" he asked before she went out the door.

"The baby's heart rate is normal and everything appears to be fine."

Whit listened to that with added relief. "Thank you," he said again, and the nurse left the room.

Once he was alone with Mary, Whit took a deep breath but found it difficult to fill his lungs. He tried again without success, glad to note that Mary still had her eyes closed and hadn't noticed. He finally just had to settle for being slightly breathless as he leaned over the bed, putting his hands on either side of Mary so that he could put his face close to hers as he said, "Are you awake?"

"Yes," she said, "but I can't keep my eyes open. Whatever they're giving me makes them feel . . . heavy."

"It's okay," he said. "Whatever they're giving you is going to fix this problem. You don't have to look at me, as long as I know you're going to be all right."

Her eyes came slowly open. "But I want to look at you." Tears gathered in the corners of her eyes. "There was a minute or two in the ambulance when I wondered if I would ever see you again."

Whit could now admit, "I had more than a minute or two of wondering the same thing." With his confession he was able to draw a deeper breath. "I can't bear to lose you, Mary. I've survived a lot, but I could never survive *that.*"

"Everything's fine," she said. Her eyes closed again, but she smiled faintly. "Everything's fine now."

"Just keep it that way," he said and pressed a kiss to her brow.

"I'll do my best," she said and he kissed her lips. She made a pleasant noise, then said, "I love you, Whit Eden. You're the best thing that ever happened to me."

"What about the gospel?"

"I never would have found that without *you,*" she said, sounding more sleepy.

"I love you, Mary Jane Eden," he said. "You should rest. I'll be right here."

Her eyes came open. "Where is Adrienne?"

"At Cinda's, sound asleep on the couch. She's fine."

"Oh, that's nice," Mary said and relaxed immediately.

Whit moved a chair close to the bed and kept Mary's hand in his while he prayed fervently that everything was indeed all right now. He prayed that the doctors and other medical personnel would be guided and inspired to take very good care of his wife and baby, and that there wouldn't be any more surprises. He wondered what the doctor would tell them. Would the baby be all right? Would Mary have to stay down flat until the baby came? Would she need to stay in the hospital until the baby was born? He was glad they had adequate medical insurance. He'd invested in a good policy years earlier when he'd become the official caretaker for his elderly mother, and he'd added Mary and Adrienne to the policy as soon as they'd officially become a part of his family.

It seemed forever that Whit waited for the doctor to come in so that he could know more about what was going on, and what to expect now. The same nurse came back twice to check on Mary, and she assured him that everything was fine, but she didn't know when the doctor would be available. Whit concluded that if this doctor had been busy saving someone he loved while others were waiting, he couldn't begrudge being on the other side of that equation. When Mary was obviously asleep, he let go of her hand and paced the room while he continued praying and pondering and glancing at the clock. Nearly two hours after he'd arrived at the hospital, the doctor finally came into the room, immediately offering an apology for the wait. "Car accident," he said, and that was all Whit needed to know. He didn't really want to hear any details or the outcome.

"It's not a problem," Whit said. "I hope everyone's okay."

"They will be . . . eventually," the doctor said, then put his password into the computer to pull up Mary's records. He made some contemplative noises and glanced a couple of times at the numbers on the monitors above Mary's bed. He tapped on the keys to write some notes, then he sat on a stool and motioned for Whit to be seated.

The doctor rolled his stool close to Whit and bent forward, speaking in a soft voice. "She appears to be sleeping and we'll let her rest. That will help those BP numbers to keep going down. What's happening here is a condition called *preeclampsia*. To put it in the simplest terms, sometimes pregnancy can cause blood pressure to become severely elevated, which of course can be very dangerous, but now that she's here and getting the proper care, there's every reason to expect that she will be completely fine. The biggest issue is that we can only control the blood pressure very minimally until that baby is delivered. Our best window of time to do that will probably be the day after tomorrow."

Whit kept himself from gasping, and before he could ask his most pressing question, the doctor answered it. "She's almost at thirty-six weeks, which means the baby should be fine. At the very worst, the baby might need a little assistance for a week or two, but there's no reason to believe there should be any problems, given this stage of her pregnancy."

The doctor glanced toward Mary in a way that made Whit believe he personally cared about his patients, in spite of his rushed schedule. "We'll get her checked in and moved to a room upstairs where she can be more comfortable. In the morning they'll do an ultrasound to determine the position of the baby, which will help determine whether a normal delivery can be induced at this stage of the pregnancy or if a C-section will be necessary. However we get that baby out, everything should be just fine. I'm recommending that we turn her over to a really great specialist who has delivered thousands of babies under difficult circumstances. He's very good at what he does. I just spoke to him on the phone, so he's aware of the details, and he has already spoken with Mary's obstetrician, who is completely comfortable with these arrangements."

"Thank you," Whit said.

The doctor made firm eye contact with Whit, and he wondered if there was some other bad news that needed to be delivered, but he only said, "Do you have any questions for me?"

"Is this because of her age?"

He wondered if the doctor might comment on the age difference in their marriage; it wouldn't be the first time it had come up. Some people thought it was funny, others had made flippant remarks that had been offensive. He wouldn't have expected either from this man, but he didn't comment at all. He simply said, "Women in their forties have been giving birth since the beginning of time. Yes, this problem can be more prevalent in later child-bearing years, but it can also show up in younger women. It's just one of those things that happens."

Whit nodded. "Thank you . . . for everything."

Both men stood and Whit shook his hand. "Glad to help. They should be ready to move her soon, and the specialist should be in to talk with you during his early-morning rounds, probably before eight."

Whit was left alone again with his sleeping wife, and he slumped back down onto the chair to take in the news. According to the doctor's reassurance, there was no reason to believe that everything wouldn't be fine with both Mary and the baby but he could see that even in the way the doctor had worded it, there was an implication of unpredictability. He wasn't naive enough to believe that *any* medical procedure didn't hold some kind of risk. He forced his mind away from the potential path of worry and anxiety and shifted his thoughts more toward a conscious effort to trust in the Lord that his wife and child would be cared for and the outcome would be positive in every way. He knew that putting their lives in God's hands was the only right answer. There was no ability or knowledge of any doctor anywhere that could supersede God's will. Whit just prayed that God's will would see them all through this.

A few minutes later three nurses—two men and one woman—came to take Mary to a room upstairs. They were efficient in working as a team to see to every little detail. Mary was awakened, and one of the nurses explained briefly what was going on. Mary nodded at the nurse, then looked around until she saw Whit. Then she visibly relaxed. She wanted his hand in hers as her bed was wheeled down long halls, into a large elevator, and down more halls. The room they took her to was indeed much more quiet than the ER, and she was moved to a bed that was obviously much more comfortable. Two nurses who worked on that floor came in to do the official changing of the guard in regard to all of Mary's needs. After the ER nurses had left and everything seemed to be in order, a nurse named Lita introduced herself to Whit and explained that she would be leaving in about an hour when the shift change took place, but the nurses coming on would see that they had everything they needed. She pointed out that the small couch in the room actually folded out into a single bed, and he was welcome to use it. Whit didn't know if he could sleep but he was grateful to know it was there. She also showed him a place where there were some snacks and beverages that were available for the family members of patients—but specified that Mary should eat only what was brought to her from the kitchen.

Feeling neither sleepy nor hungry, Whit sat down in a fairly comfortable chair near the bed and took Mary's hand. She opened her eyes and said, "They're obviously keeping me in the hospital. I'm not surprised, but . . . did you talk to the doctor? I must have been asleep a long time."

"I talked to him," he said and realized that it was falling to him to explain the situation, although he knew that a doctor would be coming later who could fill in the gaps and he didn't have to divulge all the details. "He said that everything should be fine with you and the baby, but they have to deliver the baby soon in order to get your blood pressure to go down; something like that."

"Will the baby . . ."

The effect of medication prevented her from completing the thought; Whit said, "He said you're far enough along that everything should be fine. A specialist is coming in a few hours to talk to us. I was told he's very good. You just need to rest and not worry."

He could see her thinking about what she'd been told, then she said with some resignation, "Okay." She sighed. "This isn't how I expected this to go."

"Me neither . . . but it will be okay."

"Is it because I'm so old?" she asked.

"I hate it when you say you're old," he said. "You're not old."

"Too old to be having a baby, apparently."

"To quote the doctor," Whit said, glad that he *could* quote the doctor, "'women have been giving birth in their forties since the beginning of time.' He said this can be more common with women your age, but it can happen with younger women too." He leaned over and kissed her with all the tenderness he was feeling. "I love you, Mary, and we're going to get through this. This baby is a miracle in our lives, just like you're a miracle in *my* life. The only thing you need to think about for now is getting rest and getting this baby here so you can be healthy again. I'll take care of everything else."

"What about Adrienne?"

"She'll be fine. Cinda said she's glad to keep her for as long as we need her to. I'll call her after we've talked to the doctor. I'm certain there are other people in the branch who would be only too happy to help. I'm going to stay with you every possible minute until everything is settled. I'm certain Adrienne will survive a few days without us."

"Can she come . . . here?"

"I don't know, but . . . truthfully, I think it might be best if we wait to bring her here until after you have the baby, then it will be a happy occasion, not a frightening one."

Mary sighed. "Yes, you're right."

"Okay, enough," Whit said, certain that such conversation couldn't be good for her blood pressure. He encouraged Mary to relax and he promised to wake her when the doctor came. A nurse came in and confirmed Whit's suspicion that Mary's blood pressure had gone up slightly from the numbers that had previously shown improvement. Whit talked in the hallway with her about the reasons, and she cautioned him to tell Mary only what was absolutely necessary, and that if his presence there helped keep her calm and relaxed, then he was good for her health. He was glad to hear it because he *wanted* to be there. He didn't want to let her out of his sight until he knew that she was healthy and strong again.

Whit dozed off and woke up when a nurse came in to check on Mary and officially take over the day shift. She introduced herself as Gail, and said that a man named Phillip would be assisting her. She wrote their names on a whiteboard and assured him that he could call on either of them if he or Mary needed anything. Mary woke up while they were talking, and Gail spoke soothingly to her as she checked every little detail. Whit felt reassured by the competence and kindness of the hospital staff, and Gail seemed even a little more personable than Lita had been. She was still in the room when Dr. Rosenberg arrived and introduced himself as the specialist that had been assigned to take care of Mary. Gail finished up but remained in the room to hear what the doctor had to say. Whit found him to be very straightforward, and certainly not impolite in any way, but not quite as adept in his bedside manner as the doctor in the ER had been. He reminded himself that it was the man's medical skills that truly mattered, and he just listened, holding Mary's hand tightly in his, while the doctor explained what was happening and why. The plan was to take Mary down to radiology for a thorough ultrasound sometime in the afternoon. This would give him the information he needed to deliver the baby. They were tentatively planning to either induce labor or schedule her for a C-section delivery the following morning. He'd put her as the highest priority on his schedule for the next day. Whit liked the sound of that.

He told them that qualified people who cared for premature infants would be in the delivery room, ready to care for the baby and handle whatever challenges there might be, although he didn't anticipate anything significant. He asked if they had any questions, but neither of them did since he'd been very thorough.

"See you tomorrow, then," he said and hurried out of the room.

"I'll check back in a while," Gail said and left as well.

Whit made eye contact with Mary and asked, "Are you okay?"

"I think so," she said. "It's just . . . overwhelming."

"Yes," Whit drawled in agreement, "but it's going to be okay."

"You keep telling me."

"I will," he said, determined to keep up his own confidence for her sake.

"Now," he glanced at his watch, "I've got to leave for a while. I'm going to hurry home and shower and make sure everything's okay so I can stay with you. I'll go see Adrienne and make certain everything's arranged with her, and I'll call Janel and let her know what's happening. I'll be back as soon as I can. You just rest."

"Okay," she said, seeming relieved to know that he would take care of everything and she didn't have to worry about her home or her daughter.

Whit kissed Mary and reassured her once again of his love for her before he forced himself away to do what needed to be done. He spoke with Gail for a moment at the nurses' station, and she reassured him that they'd take very good care of Mary. He felt confident that they would.

While driving toward home, the emotional impact of the trauma assaulted Whit and he found it difficult to breathe. He gasped with shallow, quick breaths while he prayed that all would be well. After he pulled into the garage, it took him a few minutes to consciously slow his breathing and fully fill his lungs with the hope and faith that all would be well.

Once inside the house, he phoned Janel in Texas and explained the situation. She expressed regret that she wasn't there to help but he assured her they were managing fine and that he would keep her apprised of Mary's progress. He then phoned the care center where his mother was staying to let them know why he might not be in for a few days. The woman he spoke to was someone he'd gotten to know through his regular visits. She was kind and wished him and Mary all the best. She promised to call his cell phone if she needed to get hold of him but understood he might not be readily available. She assured him—as she always did—that his mother was in good hands, and he knew that she was. Given his mother's situation *and* Mary's, he felt a renewed gratitude for the medical advancements of the twenty-first century and for the fact that they lived in a place where such services were readily available. He also felt grateful to know that his loved ones were getting *quality* care, when he knew that wasn't always the case in other places.

Whit then called Cinda, who assured him that everything was fine with Adrienne. She'd asked a few questions about her mother, but then she'd become involved in playing with Rachel and she seemed fine. Cinda assured Whit before he even asked that she could care for Adrienne for the next few days if that's what he needed. She said that she had one appointment the following day where she couldn't take children but she'd already spoken to another sister in the branch who was happy to take the girls during that time. She offered to call the Relief Society president and let her know what was going on with Mary, and she felt confident that when Mary and the baby came home from the hospital, many sisters would be eager to help with meals and any other needs the family might have.

Whit heaved a huge sigh of relief when he hung up the phone. It was far from the first time that Church members had come through for him and his family, but just knowing they were there and willing, and that someone like Cinda was eager to step in and help communicate, lifted a heavy burden from his shoulders. He could focus now on simply being with Mary and helping her get through this. For the first time since his mother had gone to the care center, he felt completely grateful—without any reservations—that she was in someone else's care. He couldn't imagine what they would have done otherwise.

Whit took a shower and put a few things in a bag that he might need if he remained at the hospital for a couple of days. He added a few things that he thought Mary might like, even though the hospital provided all that she needed. He then packed a little suitcase for Adrienne with clothes for a few days along with some of her favorite toys and books that might help her feel more secure. After making certain all was well with the house, he set the security system and left for Cinda's house.

Whit laughed when Adrienne ran into his arms and hugged him tightly. He sat and talked quietly with her for a little while, explaining the situation and answering her questions. When she seemed comfortable and reassured about the situation, she kissed him good-bye and ran off to play with Rachel. He thanked Cinda profusely and went to the hospital, where he found Mary resting, and he hoped that she hadn't even missed him. He realized as soon as he got there that he was starving. Phillip told him how to find the cafeteria and gave him a heads-up about the items on the menu to avoid along with some suggestions of what to eat that was actually quite good. He also said he would tell Mary, if she woke up, that her husband had been there and would return as soon as he got something to eat.

Whit returned to Mary's room to find her sitting up, with the head of the bed elevated. She looked utterly miserable but a quick glance at the numbers on the monitor showed that her blood pressure was improving.

"Hello," he said and bent over to kiss her.

She turned her face to offer her cheek instead of her lips. "After they let me brush my teeth I'll get a better kiss."

"How are you?" he asked.

"I don't know," she said. "The medication is . . . weird. It makes me feel . . . strange, but . . . they tell me I'm doing all right." He saw her shifting her position to get more comfortable, and he helped her adjust the pillows. "You're just in time to watch me eat my lunch. They just told me it's coming."

"Did you get any breakfast?"

"Yes, but I don't know that I have much appetite. What about you?"

"I just ate. I'm fine." He told her about his conversation with Janel and his visit with Adrienne. They brought in her lunch tray, and Whit quickly realized that the medication was also making her limbs feel heavy, so she had trouble eating. He helped her, and she joked about him getting practice for taking care of her when she was an old lady. But he didn't think it was funny. Without sounding too offended, he said, "I'm not even acknowledging that. I love you just the way you are, just the age you are, and I always will. Get over it."

"You always get so huffy about it," she said lightly.

"Only when you get in one of your insecure moods and start thinking that you being ten years older makes you somehow inferior. I should think it would be the other way around. Maybe my immaturity will eventually become a great burden to you."

"You've never been immature."

"Maybe one day I'll hit a sudden burst of immaturity," he said with such drama that she laughed, which made him laugh too. "Maybe I'll have a mid-life crisis when I'm thirty-five."

"I'll always love you," she said with no sign of humor.

"I'll always love you too," he said with the same intensity. "And we'll be the same age in eternity, you know. In the eternal perspective, it doesn't matter."

"So you've said . . . many times."

"As long as you keep bringing it up, I'll keep saying it. Now eat your chicken. You need your strength. We're going to have a baby tomorrow."

Chapter Four

"WE ARE, AREN'T WE," MARY SAID after she'd chewed a bite of chicken and swallowed it. "I never thought I'd actually be able to have a baby. I mean . . . one with my own DNA."

"I never thought that I would either. I couldn't imagine any woman actually wanting to settle down with someone like me."

Mary swallowed another bite and said, "You just say things like that to make me feel better."

"I say things like that because they're true. Maybe the medication is making you forget about your husband's tattoos." He held up his forearm where he'd burned off a visible tattoo before he'd gone on his mission.

"It doesn't matter."

"I know," he said. "Eat your rice, Mrs. Eden. Do you think it's a boy or a girl?"

"It's a baby. That's all I care about. They *are* doing an ultrasound in a little while. We could find out."

"What's one more day after we've waited this long?" he asked. "I think I can hold out until tomorrow."

"Me too," she said. "I can't eat any more. I feel a little nauseous sometimes, and I don't want to overdo it."

"No, we wouldn't want that," he said and stood up to move the tray.

He asked if she needed help getting up, thinking she might need to use the bathroom. He'd gotten used to her needing to do that frequently throughout the pregnancy. She told him that they wouldn't allow her to get up *at all,* and he realized she had a catheter that solved that problem.

He sat next to her bed and held her hand, asking gently, "Are you okay? I mean, really?"

"If you're asking about how I feel about all of this . . ."

"I am."

"I wouldn't say I'm afraid, or rather . . . I'm trying not to let myself be afraid, because it won't do any good. I admit to feeling unsettled." She relaxed her head and closed her eyes, overcome with their heaviness. "When things don't go according to plan, it can throw you off."

"Amen to all of that."

"So, I guess that tells me how *you're* feeling about all of this."

"I guess it does," he said. "It's not so surprising that we're both having the same feelings. We always have, haven't we?"

"Most of the time," Mary said and opened her eyes, giving him a faint smile. "You're very good to me."

"It's easy." He kissed her hand. "It's not like it takes any effort, Mary."

"I guess that's what amazes me," she said. "It doesn't seem to take any effort at all for you to make me feel loved and cared for. You *want* to do it. I suppose after having a terrible father and a husband who was completely indifferent, you can't expect me not to be amazed. I just want you to know I'm grateful."

"There's nothing I give to you that you don't give back and then some, Mary. You're very good to me, and . . ." He felt a little choked up. "I pray you don't suffer too much through all of this . . . however it might play out. I wish I could do it for you."

"That's not how it works," she said facetiously, but with her eyes closed. "Do we need to review the story of Adam and Eve?"

"No, I think I've got it down." He chuckled. "I still wish I could do it for you."

Whit stopped talking so she could rest, but she'd just dozed off when they came to get her for the ultrasound. He was glad they let him go along, and glad to be there when Mary was too medicated to tell the technician that they didn't want to know the gender of the baby.

"Glad you told me," the technician said after Whit had asked him to keep that information to himself. The technician smiled and added, "Because it's *very* obvious from what I'm seeing now." He took notes and measurements on the baby without saying much, pointing out that it was up to the doctor to give them any pertinent information after he'd had a chance to review it, but he could say that the baby would probably be about six pounds, give or take a few ounces. "If it had gone full term, it probably would have been a big baby," he said, and Mary was taken back up to her room without ever having to get out of her bed where everything was hooked up and monitored.

They hadn't been back in the room long before the Relief Society president and one of her counselors came to visit, bringing some flowers and much reassurance that Adrienne would be well taken care of and that there were many sisters eager to help once Mary came home from the hospital. They also delivered some beautiful crayon pictures of flowers that Adrienne and Rachel had made and that would look very nice hanging on the bulletin board. One of the ladies also showed Mary some pictures of Adrienne she'd taken with her cell phone camera just before coming to the hospital. The pictures made Mary a little teary, but in a good way. Both Whit and Mary laughed over how adorable their daughter was, and Whit asked if the photos could be forwarded to his own phone. It was done while they were sitting right there, and they talked with amazement about the advances in technology that were such a blessing in so many ways.

The ladies didn't stay long, but Mary felt worn out after their visit. She was only able to rest a while before the doctor came in to tell them that he'd reviewed the ultrasound. Everything looked fine with the baby but it was not in a good position for a traditional delivery. He believed that doing a C-section would be much more controlled, with less potential strain on Mary. The procedure was scheduled for nine o'clock the following morning.

"Wow," Whit said after he left. "This is starting to feel more real by the minute."

"Yeah," was all Mary said, but she reached for his hand and their eyes met with a mutual expression of silent support and a perfect understanding that they were in this together.

They'd barely had a chance to take in the doctor's announcement when Mary's supper was brought in, but she had very little appetite and Whit couldn't get her to eat much. When he told her she needed to take care of herself, she demanded to know how much sleep *he* had gotten and what *he* had eaten that day. He couldn't deny that he'd had only one rushed meal and he'd not slept beyond a little dozing since this drama had begun. She insisted that he go to the cafeteria and get something to eat immediately, and he did. She insisted that he go home and get a good night's sleep but he refused. *He* insisted that he wasn't leaving her side until the baby was safely delivered and he knew that all was well. But he did fold out the extra bed in the room and settled in for the night once the nurses had attended to all of Mary's needs and she indicated that she was ready to go to sleep. Whit slept surprisingly well—at least as much as he could between the nurses coming in the room at regular intervals to check on Mary. But his exhaustion lured him back to sleep quickly after each interruption.

When morning came, Mary was not allowed to eat anything—on doctor's orders—but she insisted that Whit get some breakfast, which he did, knowing it would be a long day and he needed to be in good condition to offer support for Mary. He didn't want to be the proverbial fainting husband in the delivery room because he hadn't bothered to eat.

All the while that Mary was being prepped for surgery and given an epidural to make her completely numb from the waist down, it was readily evident that Whit was far more nervous than the mother-to-be. Mary was calm and collected, but he wondered if the ongoing medication coming through the IV was contributing to her relaxed frame of mind. Or perhaps she was just too tired to care.

"I'll certainly be glad when this is over," she admitted, holding tightly to Whit's hand.

"You and me both," he insisted. At that moment, it was impossible to comprehend what it might be like an hour from now when the surgery was completed and the baby would officially begin its new life. He kept praying in his mind that everything would go well and that angels would stand at every post, guiding each person involved, so that there would be no unforeseen complications.

Once settled into the room where the delivery would take place, Whit was made comfortable on a stool near Mary's head, where he could hold her hand and talk to her. But neither of them could see anything in the area where her abdomen would be surgically opened in order to gain access to the uterus and remove the baby. As soon as the doctor came into the room, exuding confidence in his matter-of-fact reassurances, Whit felt a little more relaxed, and he sensed that Mary did too. The doctor had done this thousands of times. While it was a huge event in the lives of the parents, it was an everyday occurrence for the medical personnel.

The doctor told them each step he was taking so they would know what was happening, even though they couldn't see what he was doing. Only a minute after they were told that it would soon be over, an alarm on one of the monitors began beeping loudly, which immediately spurred frenzied conversation between the doctor and those in the room assisting. Whit had no idea what was happening, and he knew that it was futile to try to get any answers. Everyone was too busy trying to solve the problem to do anything but ignore him. He was just an observer. He held Mary's hand more tightly and saw his own fears reflected in her eyes. About the same time the words registered in his brain that she was bleeding too much, he saw her eyes drooping, and then he heard someone say she'd lost consciousness.

"I'm sorry, Mr. Eden," a kind voice said close to his ear, and he was firmly escorted out of the room by a nurse who pointedly ignored his hesitance in letting go of Mary's hand. "Wait down there." The nurse pointed toward a waiting area once they were out in the hall. "We'll come for you as soon as she's stable."

Whit could only nod and then stand there looking at the closed door as if it might give him the answers for which he was desperately praying. He had to take a minute to assess his own pounding heart and labored breathing before he could make some effort to exert enough control over them to move his leaden feet down the hall. His greatest motivation in following the nurse's instructions was knowing he was headed toward an area where he could sit down. He could feel the weakness in his knees threatening to take over in proportion to the growing heaviness in his feet, and he didn't want to faint *now* and cause a scene. And he didn't want to miss the report of what was happening when it came.

Whit wanted to believe that it would be only a minute or two before someone appeared to assure him that Mary and the baby were both fine. He slumped into a chair and hung his head in silent prayer for several minutes, but no one came. He felt as if he were drowning in quicksand, as if the world were literally being sucked out from under him. As he fought to get a handle on his fears, the drowning sensation suddenly burst into nervous energy. He got up and started pacing, glad the waiting area was mostly empty. The few people there were sitting apart from one another and took no notice of Whit. Their relaxed demeanors indicated their lack of stress. Since this was a general surgery area, they were probably waiting while someone got their gall bladder removed or a broken leg repaired. Nothing life or death on *their* minds. Life or death! Was that the case for Mary? Could it really be? Life or death? He had to sit down again and drop his head abruptly between his knees, not caring if anyone noticed.

Whit prayed more fervently, wondering with heart-pounding shock what he would do if he lost Mary. She had become everything to him! He needed her! Adrienne needed her! *The world* needed her! And would he ever be able to get over this consuming belief that all of this was somehow his fault?

Whit caught movement from his peripheral vision and shot his head up, glad that light-headed feeling had passed. But his heart pounded harder when he recognized Dr. Rosenberg approaching, still dressed in surgical garb. The doctor looked solemn, but not distressed. Whit moved toward him to close the distance more quickly so that he could get the news.

"Mary and the baby are both fine," the doctor said, and Whit let out such a ragged breath that he would have dropped to his knees if not for exerting great willpower.

"Oh, thank you," Whit said.

"I'm not sure exactly what happened," the doctor admitted, "but her blood pressure wasn't very cooperative with the surgery. It's under control now, but she lost a lot of blood. She's getting a transfusion now, and she'll need to stay in the hospital for at least a few days. It's going to take some time for her to get back to normal, but she's going to be just fine."

"Oh, thank you," Whit said again, this time more zealously.

The doctor smiled, and it was the first time Whit had seen him do so. "Glad to help, especially when the outcome is good."

"And the baby?" Whit asked. Once he knew Mary was all right, his mind snapped back to the fact that this entire ordeal had been centered in the delivery of their baby.

Dr. Rosenberg's smile turned to a chuckle. "The baby is fine. Good, strong lungs . . . especially for being early. Mary is conscious now. You should go in."

"Thank you," Whit said again and shook the doctor's hand, feeling like a broken record.

He hurried back to the room he'd left a short while ago, his fears completely eradicated by joy and relief—both of which were amplified when he entered the room to see Mary turn her head to look at him. She appeared to be fine, albeit somewhat weak and pale. Given that his own heartbeat hadn't returned to normal after the drama he'd just witnessed, he wondered if she had any of the same feelings. Then he recalled that she'd lost consciousness; she probably didn't fully comprehend what had happened. And she was still on those medications to keep her blood pressure under control. Whit took a deep breath, and his heart eased a little closer to its normal rhythm. Mary smiled faintly, reached out a hand toward him and said, "It's a boy, Whit. We have a son."

A gleeful jolt hit his heart, but before he could utter a word, a nurse stepped between him and Mary, holding what he could see only as a little bundle swaddled tightly in a white blanket with a little white cap on its head.

"Here he is," the nurse said in a tone that indicated she loved this part of her job. She glanced back and forth between Whit and Mary as she said, "He's breathing just fine on his own. We'll examine him more closely after you've had a chance to meet him, but everything appears to be fine."

"Thank you," Whit said and watched in silent wonder as the baby was laid in Mary's arms. He barely had a chance to note the tears in her eyes before his own vision became blurred. As anxious as he was to see his son for the first time, he leaned over the bed and pressed his lips to Mary's brow, holding them there while he whispered, "I'm so grateful you're all right, Mary. I love you so much."

"I love you too," she said, then laughed softly. "Oh, he looks like you!"

Whit looked down at the baby. He gasped to see the perfect little face, and he became immediately mesmerized by the dark eyes looking up at him as if they could see his soul. This tiny, little human life was only minutes old, but Whit had an impression of a very ancient and wise spirit gazing at its new environment with wonder and amazement. At that very moment, the newest member of the Eden family seemed to be surveying his father with the same kind of intrigue that Whit felt in looking at his son. He couldn't see any physical resemblance to himself, but there was a strange, subtle family likeness that he could glimpse. He heard Mary laugh softly and watched as she used her other hand to remove the baby's little hat to reveal a head of dark, curly hair. She laughed again and whispered, "He's beautiful." Touching the baby's hair, she added, "One of the nurses said that premature babies usually don't have much hair. Imagine how much he would have had if he'd come on time."

"He *is* beautiful," Whit said, touching the hair himself, so overcome with the experience that he could hardly breathe. He was a father! Mary was going to be all right! They shared a son!

Some conversation among the medical staff in the room drew his attention to the fact that they were not alone. The doctor had returned and had apparently been doing something out of their view to make certain the surgical procedure was completed to his satisfaction. Now he was turning Mary fully over to the nurses to clean her up and watch her closely.

Mary could still feel nothing due to the epidural, but Whit dreaded the time when it would wear off, and she would be able to feel what had happened to her body. He felt sure she would be in a great deal of pain. He focused again on the baby and basked in the joy of the moment.

"What will his name be?" Mary asked, as if it were up to him to make the final decision.

"We narrowed it down to two boy's names," he reminded her. "Which do you think suits him best?"

"I want to know what *you* think," she said.

"No, you go first," he said. "You tell me which name you think suits him, and I promise to be honest and tell you whether or not I'm thinking the same thing." He didn't want to tell her yet that neither of the names they'd talked about felt right. For some reason, he was thinking of his father, and he wondered why his father's name had never come up as a possibility in choosing a name for their son. Now it was there in his head, and he would tell Mary his thoughts, but not until she shared her own. It wasn't as if they had to make a final decision in the next five minutes.

"Okay," she said and took a deep breath as if it were some kind of drum roll to precede the announcement. "I don't think either name fits him at all. I think we need to go back to the drawing board . . . so to speak . . . or the baby name book, or . . . What's wrong?" she asked, noting the tears in his eyes he couldn't disguise. He figured a man who had just become a father—especially under such dramatic circumstances—should be prone to tears.

Whit chuckled to force back the tears, then he shrugged to give himself another moment to gather his composure. "I just . . . had exactly the same thought."

Mary smiled widely. "I guess that means we're being inspired."

"I guess it does."

"Maybe we should go back to that original list we made and look at it again, or—"

"Actually," he said, "I wonder what you would think of my father's name."

Her eyes narrowed on him. "I asked you about that once, but you said it didn't feel right."

He'd actually forgotten that, but she was right. It *had* come up, and he'd dismissed it as a possibility. "It feels right now," Whit said.

"Tell me his name again," Mary said, looking directly at Whit, even though he could tell it took great effort for her to take her eyes off the baby.

"Christian Werner Eden, the *Werner* being his mother's maiden name."

Whit watched her closely, waiting for a reaction. He heard her inhale deeply, as if to take it in. She looked again at the baby, with a deep, penetrating gaze, as if she might hear him tell her his name by virtue of some kind of telepathy. More accurately, he knew she was searching for the confirmation of the Spirit—the power of the still, small voice to confirm that this was the right name for their son to carry throughout his mortal life.

"Christian," she said gently to the baby, as if to try it out. She looked at Whit. "What better name in the world could there be to call our son? To name him after your father *and* to give him a name that represents something so precious to us . . ." She looked again at the baby. "I think it's perfect." Whit breathed out a sigh of relief to know she felt the same way, then she concluded, "Christian Whitmer Eden."

They'd discussed giving his own name as the middle name for a son, but that hadn't been decided on for certain either. He felt pride in the name Whitmer for its significance in regard to the great men with that surname who had been among the original witnesses of the Book of Mormon, and had done a great deal to support Joseph and Emma Smith through the early stages of the Restoration of the gospel. It certainly warmed him to know that Mary wanted their son to have *his* name, but it was the deeper significance of the name that really meant something to him in passing it down.

"I think it's right," he said firmly. He and Mary exchanged a smile, then the baby began to fuss and wiggle.

A nurse intervened and took him carefully from Mary after she'd put his little hat back on. "We need to keep his head warm," she said, which helped Whit know *why* they had put the silly little hat on him to begin with. "And it's time for him to get his first checkup and a good bath." To Whit she said, "You're welcome to come along since you're the new daddy. While we're gone they'll get Mom all cleaned up and settled in a comfortable room."

"We'll see you in a while then," Whit said, kissing Mary's brow again.

Mary took his hand and looked firmly into his eyes. "I love you, Whit."

"I love you too," he said, aware that the nurse was waiting, but he sensed no impatience. "I never imagined being so happy."

Mary smiled and nodded and Whit slipped away, following the nurse down one long hall and then another until they came to what was obviously the hospital nursery. There were other babies there and other nurses, all of whom seemed very busy.

Whit watched as they weighed and measured the baby. Five pounds, seven ounces. "A good-sized baby for coming a bit early," the nurse declared. She bathed him thoroughly, which made the newly named Christian very unhappy, but Whit couldn't help laughing at his newborn squawking. The pediatrician that had been recommended to them to care for the baby came in soon after the bath was finished to give the baby a thorough examination. Whit watched from a reasonable distance, trying not to feel nervous, but the doctor declared him to be perfectly healthy. A nurse pricked the baby's heel to draw blood, which again made Christian unhappy, but he calmed down quickly and was put into a little see-through crib. The nurse wrote his new name on a little blue card and taped it at the end of the crib, then she wheeled the little bed to Mary's new hospital room so that Mary could see him again.

Whit noticed that Mary had three different bags hanging on the IV pole, one of them with blood in it. He felt incredibly grateful for modern medicine and for knowing that Mary was going to be all right. The nurse who had taken over Mary's care told Whit his wife was doing well and that she'd eaten a little.

Whit and Mary were left alone with their son, knowing they could push a button and get help if they needed it. Together they unwrapped the baby and examined all of his fingers and toes and marveled between themselves at the miracle. A nurse came in and encouraged Mary to try to nurse the baby, even though her milk wouldn't be coming in for a day or two. The process didn't go very well, and by the time they had decided they would try again later, Mary was starting to feel pain as the epidural began wearing off. She was given some pain medication, and the baby was taken back to the nursery with the assurance that he would be well taken care of while his mother got the rest she needed.

Whit sat with Mary until the medication began to take effect and she was able to relax. Once she was sleeping peacefully, he left the room to make some phone calls and let the important people know that it was over, everything was fine, and the baby was a boy. His happiness blossomed as he told Janel and his aunts how much his son weighed and what his name was. He wished that he could call his mother and tell her the news and have her understand, but he knew that she wouldn't have any idea who she was talking to on the phone or what was going on. After enough time had passed that Mary and the baby were both well enough to go out, he would take them to the care center so that his mother could meet her new grandson. He could only pray that she might find some joy in seeing the baby, even if she would likely not have any idea to whom he belonged.

Whit most enjoyed calling Cinda's home so he could talk to Adrienne and tell her the good news. After giving Cinda a brief report, she put Adrienne on the phone, and he laughed to hear her sweet little voice say with excitement, "Daddy!"

"Hello, precious," he said. "Guess what?"

"We have a baby?"

"We sure do!" he said. "It's a baby brother."

"Oh, I knew it! I knew it!" she said with excitement, then he could hear her telling her friend Rachel, "I have a baby brother!" Into the phone she said, "Is he cute, Daddy?"

"What do you think?" Whit asked her. "He's the cutest baby I've ever seen. I've seen pictures of you and your sister when *you* were a baby, and you were awfully cute. But since I wasn't actually there I have to say that your brother is the cutest baby I've ever *seen*. He has dark, curly hair—just like you." Whit felt a tug of sentiment at those words. The fact that he and Adrienne shared an Hispanic heritage, even if she didn't share any blood with either him or Mary, had always meant something to him. But it hadn't occurred to him that having this baby inherit some of his Hispanic genetic characteristics would make him and Adrienne appear to be brother and sister. It really didn't matter what *any* of them looked like, he thought. They were a family. And being a part of this family was the best thing that had ever happened to him.

Adrienne strongly approved of the baby's name, and she immediately started referring to him as Christian instead of *the baby*. Whit talked to his daughter for several minutes and told her an age-appropriate version of all that had happened. He wanted her to understand that her mother had been through a difficult ordeal and that she needed time to heal, but he didn't want her to feel alarmed. She took it in with her usual childlike faith and unusual maturity. She asked him some questions, and he answered them candidly.

He talked to Cinda again about arrangements, then she gave the phone back to Adrienne so he could tell her that he was going to stay at the hospital for the rest of the day and probably until after her bedtime, so she would be having another sleepover with Rachel, but he would come and get her in the morning and take her to the hospital to see her mother and the new baby.

After he'd completed his phone calls, Whit checked on Mary and found her sleeping. He went to the big nursery window and found that Christian was doing the same. He admired him for several minutes before he went to the cafeteria to get a decent meal. It was easier to eat now that the drama was over, and he realized how hungry he was. He then returned to the nursery where the baby was awake, and the nurse let him come in and hold his son once he'd washed up and put a clean gown over his clothes. He sat there in an old-fashioned wooden rocking chair that looked completely out of place in the sterile environment, rocking back and forth while he just admired little Christian and felt as if they were getting acquainted.

He began to wonder how Mary was doing and turned the baby back over to the nurse's care so that he could check on his wife. He found her groggy from the medication, uncomfortable from the surgical pain, but in good spirits. When the nurses brought Christian to Mary's room so that he could be with his mother, Whit observed them together and knew why the principle of eternal families was at the heart of God's plan of happiness. He knew it more than he ever had in his life.

* * *

At Mary's insistence, Whit went home to get a good night's sleep. And he did. He'd slept very little ever since Mary's medical emergency had begun. Now it was over and all was well. He had to force himself to not relive those horrible moments when the situation had been so dire and his fears had been suffocating him. He focused instead on the miracles that had occurred, and he felt perfect peace.

In the morning he called the hospital first thing to make sure that his wife and son were still doing all right. After hearing a good report, he showered, then washed and dried a load of laundry, ate a good breakfast and made certain the house was in order. He'd never been so grateful for the flexibility of his employment that made it possible to ignore the gardening and know that he could catch up the time in order to maintain integrity in regard to his work agreement with Mr. Lostin. Thinking of Mr. Lostin, he gave him a call to let him know about the baby. This man who had known Mary for many years was genuinely thrilled with the news and promised to come over and see the baby once they were home and settled.

Whit was thrilled to see Adrienne when he picked her up, and he was even more thrilled with how excited she was to see *him*. Two years earlier he hadn't even known Adrienne or her mother existed, and he never would have imagined himself living the life he had now. He felt tremendously blessed!

Whit took Adrienne on a brief shopping excursion so she could pick out a gift for her new brother before they went to the hospital to meet Christian. Adrienne held the cute little gift bag while they took the hospital elevator to the correct floor, and Whit reminded Adrienne about the surgery her mother had needed and that she had to be very careful when hugging her because she would be very sore and it would take many weeks to heal. Adrienne declared that she understood, and she proved it well when they got to Mary's room and Adrienne restrained her excitement enough to climb very carefully onto the bed and hug her mother around the neck. Whit enjoyed just watching the reunion between the two of them as Adrienne got comfortable on the bed with her mother and they talked and talked. Since Christian was in the nursery getting his daily bath, the timing of their arrival had been perfect for Mary to spend some time with her daughter first.

Adrienne proudly gave her mother the gift for the baby, and Mary exerted as much excitement as a woman could while on pain medication and recovering from such an ordeal. A nurse then wheeled the little crib into the room, and Adrienne was able to meet her new brother. She oohed and ahhed and fussed with excitement over every detail, asking a hundred questions. Since she'd washed up very carefully, she was allowed to hold the baby while she sat in a big chair and Whit helped support the baby's head.

"When you've had more practice," Mary said to Adrienne, "and he gets a little stronger, you can hold him all by yourself."

Adrienne beamed with pride and couldn't stop looking at the baby. But then, Whit and Mary couldn't stop looking at him, either.

Two days later, Mary and Christian came home from the hospital. The baby was thriving and doing great, but Mary was miserable physically, which made it difficult to enjoy her new son the way she would have wanted. Whit reminded her more than once that most new mothers probably felt the same way in one form or another. She agreed that he was probably right, but it was still difficult for her. She had trouble sitting down, standing up, walking, and generally moving at all. The surgical incisions were deep and painful. The prescribed medication helped with that, but the doctor had warned her that at this stage of healing, she was simply going to have some pain and she just had to be patient and allow herself to heal. Her milk had also come in and she was having difficulty nursing the baby. Sometimes he was cooperative and sometimes he wasn't. They'd purchased a good breast pump that helped alleviate the pressure when the baby *wasn't* cooperative. It also made it possible for Whit to help feed him. Breast milk could be put into bottles, and the nurses had advised them that it was good for the baby to get used to bottles as well as the breast so that others could help care for him. Adrienne was also able to help feed the baby as long as she sat right next to her daddy and he helped hold the baby.

Whit often wished that Janel was still in their household when he felt certain that having another woman under the roof would have made things a lot easier for Mary. He did his best to be on hand and do everything he could to help where it was possible, but he often felt useless. He couldn't ease her physical pain, and she was insistent on taking on the majority of the baby's care. She encouraged Whit to work in the garden, reminding him that most women didn't have the luxury of having their husband around to continually wait on them. She promised to call if she needed him, and his cell phone was always in his pocket.

He did find that it was good for him to be outside and doing the physical labor that he loved, and he had to reason that it was good for Mary to have her time as a mother. He was grateful that he *could* be nearby but a little disappointed that he never actually got a call. Adrienne was very good at helping her mother get things she couldn't reach or access quickly, and they managed fine for the periods of time while he worked. When he wasn't working, he enjoyed every minute with his family. Even the challenging moments gave him a level of fulfillment he never could have imagined possible in the life he'd once lived as a gang kid on the streets and in prison. He felt humbled each and every day by how richly God had blessed him for taking the steps to turn his life around.

Whit didn't have to spend much time in the kitchen, since the Relief Society started bringing in meals as soon as Mary got home. The visits from the sisters in the ward lifted Mary's spirits, and it was always fun to see how they fussed delightfully over the baby. He usually just observed from a distance while these kind ladies admired the baby, then he'd discreetly make himself useful elsewhere in order to give Mary time with other women.

* * *

As Mary concluded another visit with kind women who always came bearing food or gifts or both, she returned carefully to the couch where the baby was sleeping and told herself that this should be the happiest time of her life. Everyone around her had nothing but good to say about how beautiful and precious the baby was, how kind and caring a husband she had, how sweet and helpful Adrienne was proving to be, and how very blessed they had all been as a family. Mary agreed wholeheartedly with all of that and more. She had a long list of blessings to count, but her list didn't make her feel any less inclined to go curl up in bed and stay there for as long as she could get away with it. Whit was so eager to do anything he possibly could to help her that she felt certain he would allow her to do just that. But instinctively she knew that staying in bed would not make her feel any better—and, in fact, would likely make her feel worse. Her physical pain certainly didn't help the situation but it wasn't her physical healing that concerned her. That pain felt *normal;* it felt understandable, easy to talk about. Everyone around her knew she'd endured having a baby surgically removed from her abdomen, and that she was naturally in pain. It was everything else she felt that she couldn't bring herself to talk about—not even to Whit.

Mary was glad to know that Whit was nearby, but she could never quite put into words how she *needed* him to allow her to care for the children so that she could focus on something besides her own disconcerted and confusing emotions. She reminded herself regularly that she had also lost a great deal of blood and it would take time to recover, but then most of that amount of blood had been given back to her through a transfusion, so that certainly wasn't a justifiable reason for her to be so discouraged. She also reminded herself that great hormonal shifts were taking place in her; that made some sense, but it didn't feel comforting in the face of her wavering emotions. She wanted to hold her baby and feel joy; she wanted to be in the midst of her family and feel nothing but the perfect happiness that any woman in her position should feel. But she just *didn't!* And she didn't know what to do about it.

Not wanting Whit—or anyone else—to be concerned, since she was certain it would pass with time, she just kept trying to do all the right things, kept praying for guidance and strength, and hoped that the clouds would soon lift and the sun would come out again, not wanting to admit even to herself what was *really* haunting her.

* * *

When Whit had a few minutes to spare, he phoned his sister to tell her the good news.

"Hello, Crystal," he said when she answered.

"Hello, Whit," she said, sounding disappointed and very tentative as she usually did when she heard from him.

He had come to accept years ago that Crystal's way of coping with the terrible losses in their life was to leave that life and everything related to it behind. She was married and living on a farm in Idaho. She had three children that Whit had never met, and he knew practically nothing about her life except that she was active in the Church. She knew that *he* was also active in the Church, but that hadn't been enough for her to warm up to him. She saw him, and even their mother, as being a part of her old life with all of its associated pain. Whit *had* come to accept it. As long as Crystal was safe and happy, that was good. But sometimes he missed her. It was rare that he ventured to bridge the gap, and he only called for really important reasons or to report significant family news. And he was always relieved when the number wasn't disconnected, since he didn't even know her married name and he knew she would never tell him.

"I won't keep you long," he said. "I just wanted you to know that I'm a father. My wife had a baby boy."

"Oh," she said with a positive lilt, "that's nice. What's his name?"

"Christian."

"After Dad," she said. "That's nice." Her voice sounded more sad. After a long moment of awkward silence she asked, "Is everything okay?"

"Everything's fine. There were some challenges with the delivery, but Mary is healing, and everything is fine. Mom's going downhill, but that's not surprising."

"Well, thanks for calling," she said, halting any possibility of further conversation. "Call me if anything changes."

He knew that meant to call her when their mother finally left this world, but he doubted that even then she would have any involvement in funeral arrangements or anything else.

"I will," he said. "You do the same. It's good to hear your voice."

"You too," she said. "I've got to go."

After she hung up, Whit stared at the phone for a few minutes, as if that might help him feel closer to his sister. He wished that something could change in that regard, but he was grateful to have at least spoken to her.

Whit counteracted his discouragement by picking up the Book of Mormon to read, if only for a few minutes. It had become a longtime habit that had begun during his time in prison when it had literally become the strength and power that had helped put him on the right path in his life. He found himself reading the testimonies of the witnesses at the beginning of the book, and he always found something comforting in seeing his own name there at the bottom multiple times, Whitmer being the surname of five of the eleven witnesses. He knew this was the reason he'd been given the name, and he felt warm pride in having it for that reason. This too had made a difference to him when he'd been making changes in his life; he wanted to live up to the name.

It actually startled him to realize that in combining his father's name with his own as he and Mary had chosen a name for their son, they had actually given him the name of one of those witnesses. *Christian Whitmer.* He daydreamed for a few minutes about the day his son might be old enough to understand the meaning of his own name and they could look at this page in the Book of Mormon and see it printed there. Then he went to find Mary and share his discovery with her, feeling much more hope than discouragement. Mary was genuinely pleased and agreed with his sentiment, but he sensed—as he often had since she'd come home from the hospital—that something wasn't right. When he asked about it, she assured him that she was healing, that everything was normal, that she was fine. But he felt a tiny nagging doubt that left him uneasy. Not knowing how to acknowledge what he felt, he determined to keep an eye on her, concluding that she'd been through a great deal and this was a big adjustment.

When Christian was ten days old, Mr. Lostin called to say that he would drop by that evening but wouldn't be staying long. He arrived with a large gift basket that had obviously been ordered from an expensive baby specialty store. It had a couple of different mix-and-match outfits for a baby boy, along with many accessories. He said it was from the company, and he handed Mary a card that had been signed by many people, most of whom she had never met. "We all wish you the best," he added.

Mr. Lostin admired the baby, expressed his well wishes for mother and baby, and hurried away to get home to his family after a long day of work. As Mary examined the contents of the basket she told Whit, "I think they all feel bad about the way my father treated us."

"Or the fact that he completely left you out of his will," Whit pointed out.

"Maybe. The money doesn't bother me. Most people don't get inheritances from a rich parent. It's the message of disapproval that I don't like."

"I know," Whit said. "It's sad. Very sad . . . more for him than for us."

"Yes, it is," Mary agreed.

"Does the gift basket make up for it?" he asked with a smile.

"It doesn't hurt any," she said and held up a funny little jacket with monkeys on it, which made them both laugh to imagine Christian wearing when he got a little bigger.

Chapter Five

THE NEXT DAY A BOX arrived from Janel, and inside the cardboard box was a wrapped package. Adrienne was so excited that Whit and Mary let her tear away the wrapping paper that was covered with little blue teddy bears. Inside they found a hand-crocheted blanket that Janel had made along with a little outfit she had purchased. Mary admired the blanket and commented on how she could feel all of the love that she knew Janel had put into every stitch. Then Adrienne noticed that the box wasn't empty. Inside was an envelope that said *Whit and Mary* and a little package wrapped in pink paper with a tag that read, *For the big sister.* Adrienne squealed with excitement and opened her gift to find that Janel had sent her a new shirt in just the right size and an adorable storybook about a little girl and her new baby brother. Whit read the story with her right then and there. It was above Adrienne's reading level, but he did stop on words that he knew she could sound out and encouraged her to do so.

After they had put Adrienne to bed that evening, Whit and Mary finally had a quiet minute to sit down together and open the envelope from Janel. There was a lovely card congratulating them on the baby, with some folded paper tucked inside on which she'd written a long, tender letter, expressing how much she missed them and telling them details about what was going on with her family. She thanked Whit for sending pictures of the children via email, and made him promise to keep doing so. When they finished the letter, Mary put her head on Whit's shoulder and started to cry.

"What is it?" he asked, putting his arm around her. He hoped he might get some information to help ease that little nagging doubt he'd been feeling.

"Probably just hormones," she said. They'd both become accustomed to her crying a great deal more than usual since the baby had come.

Pregnancy had made her more emotional, but now it seemed to have increased several notches.

Whit just held her and let her cry for several minutes, having learned from experience it was the best way to get to the heart of the problem—or sometimes there simply *wasn't* a problem and he just needed to let her cry. Her tears settled into a peaceful quiet, but that tiny nagging voice in his head suddenly became very loud. He prayed silently for guidance and knew he had to acknowledge that something wasn't right.

"Mary," he said carefully, "I need you to be completely honest with me." She didn't move, but he felt her become tense. "I get the feeling something's wrong, that you're . . . down, or . . . worried . . . or something. I know you've been through a lot, but . . . is there something else? Please tell me."

Whit expected her to perhaps reassure him the way she had been doing, and he would have to become more insistent to get her to open up. But she was quick to answer his question, which he hoped was some indication of the trust between them—although it also made him realize that her thoughts were not peaceful *at all.*

"I don't know why, but I can't stop thinking about the fact that someone actually broke into this house and committed *murder.*"

Whit shifted in order to look at her face. "I agree that it's unnerving, but it's old news, Mary. Exactly how much have you been thinking about it?" Under the circumstances, he didn't want to admit to her how much he thought about it himself. Right now he needed to be the strong one; his own fears and concerns would have to be addressed at another time.

She looked hesitant to answer, then she bit her lip to stop its quivering. She looked down as if she were ashamed of the answer and said with a cracking voice, "A lot."

Whit considered what she'd already said before that. Was it literal? "You can't *stop* thinking about it?"

She shook her head and became more emotional. "No . . . I can't." She sniffled and wiped her face with her sleeves. "It's just so . . . unsettling," Mary admitted. "In spite of appearances—that the killer was actually trying to protect us—the fact remains that some mysterious *person* invaded our home and committed a terrible crime. Will we never have answers? Will we spend the rest of our lives wondering what really happened?"

"A great many crimes go unsolved, Mary. It's a sad fact, but it's the way things are. And we both know that I cannot personally do *anything* that might even look like I'm trying to figure it out by myself. If the police didn't arrest me, my cousins would probably . . . well . . . there simply isn't anything I can do. I know how you feel, Mary; I do. But I'm afraid that being preoccupied with it will only drive us mad." He took her shoulders into his hands. "We need to trust the Lord, Mary. There is no other way to find peace—with this or anything else in this life."

"I understand what you're saying Whit. But it's easier said than done. You're a pro at this kind of thing. I have very little experience with such things."

"Such things?"

"You have so much . . . faith. You're so strong."

"Oh, Mary," he said, touching her face. "You're a lot stronger than you think you are, and you have *amazing* faith. We just need to keep doing what we've been doing all along. We've survived a great deal together. We will get through this just fine."

Mary forced a smile and tried to be convinced, but she couldn't deny the instinctive vulnerability she felt. Being responsible for this new little life had sparked something inside her that had been somehow dormant at the time of her father's death. Or perhaps her trauma over his death had quickly been swallowed up in the fact that Whit had been arrested for the crime. She'd been so focused on seeing Whit's innocence proven and having him free that perhaps she'd never really allowed herself to come to terms with how the crime itself had affected her. She then realized that Whit was staring at her, as if doing so long enough might allow him to read her mind. She looked down again but couldn't hide the fact that her emotions were resurfacing with a boldness that she just couldn't fight back or hide any longer.

"Mary," he said gently, "what's going on? What's *really* going on? You look terrified."

"Do I?" she asked, trying to sound completely ignorant as to what he meant, but knowing she'd failed miserably.

"Mary," he said in a gentle tone, encouraging her to speak her mind. A part of her had been wanting to tell him the whole truth, and a bigger part of her had preferred keeping it to herself. But perhaps it was best he knew.

"I don't know what's wrong with me, Whit," she admitted. "I don't know if it's the pain from the surgery . . . or that I was so sick before I had the baby . . . or the very fact that I gave birth or . . . or what. I just . . . I . . ."

"What?" he said with a tender firmness that let her know he would remain compassionate but he would not let her get out of completing this conversation.

"All I can think about are the bad things that could happen to us."
She started to cry again in spite of all her best efforts to keep the full depth
of her emotions out of it. "Maybe it's because I feel so vulnerable when I
can't even get in and out of bed without feeling practically helpless from
the pain. Maybe it's being responsible for this new little baby that's so tiny
and defenseless. Or maybe it's because what happened that night was so
awful and I never really processed it. Now it's all coming back to me . . . the
intrusion . . . the alarm . . . the gunshot . . . and then . . . and then . . . the
next thing I know they're taking you away and I have to face the possibility
that I've lost you."

"Listen to me, Mary. It's over. Do you hear me? It's over. I'm not
leaving you in any way, shape, or form."

"I know that," she insisted. "But it's really not *over*, is it? We don't
know who did this or why, and sometimes I fear that until I *do* know I will
never be able to be at peace."

Whit considered that for a long moment before he asked, "And what
if it's a mystery that will never be solved? After this much time has passed,
the likelihood of solving the crime has dwindled down to . . . . well, it's
practically impossible. It would take a miracle."

"Then we need a miracle," she insisted. Then she insisted even more
fervently that she didn't want to talk about it anymore. And since the baby
started to cry and needed attention, Whit could hardly force her to stick
with the topic until they came to a more settled conclusion.

Whit slept very little that night as his conversation with Mary haunted
him. He felt all the same things she'd expressed, except that he wasn't
obsessed by them in a way that implied some kind of budding paranoia. A
part of him felt desperate to have the crime solved, the same way he knew
Mary felt, but logically he knew that what he'd told her was true. It wasn't
likely going to happen. If that was the case, then the only way to find
peace was through spiritual means. Mary had a great deal of faith and he
knew it, which led him to believe that the problem wasn't about faith—or
the lack of it. The problem was something entirely different.

Whit prayed very hard for understanding and the ability to help his
sweet wife. He drifted in and out of sleep, afflicted with crazy dreams that
reminded him he had his own level of paranoia. Or maybe it was just
PTSD after having been faced with the possibility of life in prison. In
reality he was still linked to gang affiliations simply by the fact that he had
blood relatives who were actively engaged in such activities—and he had

the tattoos to prove that he had once been boldly on their side. *Someone* knew where he lived. Carlos did, but he knew Carlos wasn't behind any of this. At least he *hoped* he knew it. But someone else had discovered where he lived. Hadn't they? What other explanation could there be for someone breaking into the house and committing murder?

Whit hated the way that Mary's paranoia was apparently contagious. After he had gotten out of bed—twice—to carefully inspect the entire house, he had to pray even harder to get his thoughts straight, put his faith in place, and strive to put the matter in God's hands. He knew that if he was truly giving this burden to the Lord, he couldn't hold onto worrying and stewing over it in a way that completely contradicted the principle of faith. He did face daylight, however, with the belief that he needed to do his part, and right now that meant searching for answers. He doubted there was anything more that could be learned about the crime, and he didn't want to start digging around in his cousins' lives; that could prove more fatal than any other course of action. He considered the fact that God knew what had happened, even if they didn't, and it seemed to him that trusting in the Lord also included the fact that if God knew the whole story, He would protect Whit and Mary and their children.

Whit's impression to search for answers pointed more toward Mary and what might be going on with her. Later that morning, Mary was napping with the baby and Adrienne was busy playing on the patio with a dolly tea party set up meticulously along the edge of the garden. Whit took advantage of the time to himself and phoned Janel in Texas, praying she would be available. He might not be able to speak to her so candidly later on unless he left the house and called her from his cell phone.

Janel answered the phone, having known from the caller ID that it would be either him or Mary. She was pleased to hear from him but became immediately concerned when he told her that he needed her help.

"You told us," he said, "that your reason for going to stay with your son and his wife was mostly due to her struggling with some depression."

"That's right," Janel said, sounding suspicious. He felt sure she couldn't imagine how that might connect with Whit needing her help.

"You said that it initially started after she had a baby," he added.

"That's right," Janel said. "Is Mary struggling?"

"She is," Whit said. "I didn't really put the pieces together until last night. I just thought her mood was mostly due to her not feeling well. Now I know it's more than that. Please tell me what you know."

Janel talked to him about how postpartum depression was actually quite common, and it was mostly due to the huge hormonal shift that took place after giving birth. That shift, combined with not feeling well from the birth—which was the case for most women in one way or another—and not getting enough sleep due to caring for an infant often created a difficult adjustment. Some women came through it simply with time and rest; for others it was more severe and difficult to get past. It was evident that Janel had been doing her research in regard to her daughter-in-law. In that case the depression had been compounded by her father dying of cancer. Mary's father had died too—but that was a complex and horrifying matter in and of itself, and Whit couldn't begin to understand how all of it might have impacted Mary emotionally. She didn't even seem to know herself.

Janel's recommendation was that Mary might need to get some professional assistance before her distorted thoughts and feelings became too deeply ingrained or out of control. "Keep an eye on her," Janel said, "and if she's still struggling with it after a little time passes—or it gets any worse—I think you should act on it. That's my two cents."

"Thank you, Janel. I'm very grateful for your two cents."

"Oh, I do wish I was there to help," she said in a way that made it clear that she meant it. "I know I'm needed here, but I do miss all of you. And maybe you need me too."

"We'll be all right," Whit assured her. He too wished she was there to help, certain a woman in the house could help Mary feel more secure, but the situation couldn't be helped. "We miss you too," he said, "but we'll keep in touch. I appreciate your help more than I can say."

"You call me any time," she said, "and if Mary just needs another woman to talk to, have *her* call me."

"That might be a good place to start," Whit said. "You'll be hearing from one or the other of us before too long. I promise."

Throughout the remainder of the day, Whit remained close to Mary, discreetly observing her mood. He was grateful when it started raining. It required helping Adrienne move her dolls and their tea party into the house, but it gave him a good excuse to not be working outside so that he could more easily observe Mary. He tried to reopen the previous evening's conversation but she didn't want to talk about it.

That evening after Adrienne had gone to bed, Whit finally confessed to having talked to Janel and shared what she'd taught him about postpartum depression. For a minute he feared Mary might be angry with him but she quickly admitted that she knew something wasn't right and she needed help.

The following morning, Whit was thrilled to be able to care for the children on his own while Mary had a very long—and emotional—phone conversation with Janel. When they were done on the phone, Mary talked to Whit about it while she nursed the baby. She agreed that she would not hold her thoughts and feelings inside; she would either talk to him or Janel every day about what was going on inside. She also agreed that if the situation became any worse, she would be willing to get some professional help. They both knew from the things Janel had said that her daughter-in-law had very much turned inward and had descended into a terrible and deep habit of not expressing her feelings or acknowledging them, and it had only gotten worse from there.

"I need to be the best possible mother I can be," Mary said. "I can't let this undo me and affect my ability to be there—emotionally as well as physically—for my children."

"We'll get through this together," he said. "As long as you don't stop talking to me, we can handle anything."

"I believe you," she said and actually gave him a smile. "You're really very good to me."

"That's easy," he said and kissed her.

Mary sighed and relaxed with his arm around her. "I didn't have this problem when we adopted the twins."

"Well, first of all, they were adopted. No hormones. And secondly, you hadn't just been through the horrible trauma that took place here. Think about what actually happened through the course of this pregnancy."

"Oh, I have. Believe me." She sighed. "But I must admit that I think I dealt with a lesser version of this when we *did* adopt the twins, so maybe it isn't *all* hormones and trauma."

Whit leaned forward so he could see her face. "Tell me."

"I actually spoke to a counselor at the time. Some counseling was available as part of that particular adoption program to make certain parents were adjusting well to bringing children into their home from another culture. When all was said and done, it was *me* that figured out what was really wrong, although I think the counselor said some things that got me on the right track. The biggest thing was that I had secretly been hoping that having children in our home would change the way Simon behaved toward me. And it didn't. As you know, he was never unkind. He was just . . . absent. Even when he was home, he was emotionally absent. I was completely invisible to him. He loved the girls and gave them some attention, but not nearly as much as I'd hoped. So . . . I was naturally faced with some disillusionment. But I quickly pulled myself together and decided I would be a great mother no matter how he behaved."

"And you always have been."

"I've certainly tried, but . . . I also think that feeling vulnerable over having a new little life that needs protection and care likely incites some natural feelings of insecurity in a mother. I felt this way when the twins were infants; a little scared, paranoid perhaps. I got over that eventually as well. But I hadn't been dealing with a violent crime having taken place in my home."

"No, things are different now; harder in some ways, I know."

She took his hand. "And much easier in others."

"What do you mean?"

"I have you. I've never been invisible to you. You're such a good husband and father that I sometimes can hardly believe it. Of course, I have nothing to compare it to other than my own father and Simon, but . . ."

"As long as comparing makes me look good," Whit said facetiously. Then he laughed softly and kissed her again.

She settled her head on his shoulder once more as it became evident that Christian had fallen asleep in her arms. They were silent for several minutes while Whit's mind wandered, and he wondered what Mary was thinking. She answered that question when she said, "I really do wish we knew who killed my father . . . and why."

Whit wanted to tell her once again that they would probably *never* know, and they needed to make peace with that. But the truth was that he wanted the same answers. He hated not knowing, and even more so, he hated the likelihood that it had something to do with his past gang affiliations. When he'd made the decision to pursue a relationship with Mary, his biggest concern had been that he didn't want to bring the consequences of his past life into *her* life. But for all his efforts, he obviously had—however unintentionally. Not knowing exactly how or why someone had entered their home, or who was responsible for this horrible crime just ate away at him sometimes, making him feel like a hypocrite for all of his noble speeches to Mary about the need to give the issue to the Lord and make peace with it. He'd certainly prayed a great deal to have the Lord take this burden, but he *hadn't* made peace with it. He wondered if that meant he wasn't fully doing his part, or if it was some indication that there *were* answers out there somewhere, and there was something more he should be doing.

Not certain of anything, he began to pray daily that if there was some answer to be found, or if there was something he could do, that the Spirit would guide him to know what that might be, and that he would be willing to act on whatever prompting he might be given. And he continued to pray for peace over the matter—for himself as well as for Mary. *Especially* for Mary.

Whit didn't get any answers in regard to the unsolved crime, but he did feel some inspiration that he knew was Heavenly Father's guidance in helping him help Mary. It occurred to him that for a few months she'd not done much of anything with some ongoing humanitarian projects that had always meant a great deal to her. Earlier in her life she had been actively engaged in hands-on work in Mexico, serving in orphanages and doing other projects that would help ease the suffering of people whose basic needs were rarely met. Later when she'd become a mother, she had found other ways to make a difference and still be at home.

The first time Whit met Mary, she'd told him how she wrote a blog that she used to create awareness for the cause she believed in and that she did fund-raising projects and similar things, all from a home computer where she could write letters and make arrangements, connecting with people in many different places. It had been very satisfying to Mary, and had certainly become a large part of her identity. She had managed to keep up her obligations during all of the court drama in their lives. Then when she'd known the baby was coming, she'd made arrangements to have others cover for her in her absence. She'd left a statement on her blog that she was on maternity leave.

Now Whit realized that she'd not done *anything* with any of that since before Christian's birth. He felt certain that her getting back to it would help ease her discouragement and put her focus somewhere else besides on wondering who had murdered her father.

Whit prayed to know exactly how and when to approach Mary about it, and when he did, their conversation went very well. Mary tearfully agreed that she'd missed that part of her life and that she needed to get back to it. Whit agreed to watch the children for an hour each day so she could focus on getting her projects up and running again, and he offered to watch them longer if she needed him to. She thought that would be sufficient for her to get started, and she seemed excited at the prospect. She got to it the very next day, and within just a few days she was reporting that she'd made some connections on behalf of some children in Mexico and that she was getting positive responses to her latest blog post. They both agreed that it was something she always needed to keep close to as an active part of her life.

"It was one of the things that made me fall in love with you," he said. "Your desire and efforts to make a difference in the suffering of the world mean a lot to me."

She got a little teary when he said it. He just hugged her and silently thanked God for seeing some light in her eyes again.

When Christian was about seven weeks old, he was blessed in church and officially given his name. Whit felt grateful to be worthy of the priesthood he'd been given so that he could be the one to bless his son, and he also felt grateful that Mary was doing much better—emotionally *and* physically. That evening many branch members came to the house to visit and to honor the newest member of the Eden family. Christian was healthy and strong and adorable, and he apparently enjoyed being passed around to everyone who wanted to hold him. Even at such a young age, he seemed to have a very social personality.

As summer eased into autumn, Mary continued to battle a myriad of negative thoughts and feelings but she continued talking to Janel regularly on the phone, and she was open with Whit about what was going on. He didn't see any need to get professional help at this point. She was functioning well as a wife and mother and was gradually taking over more of the household chores as she continued to heal physically. Most of the time she seemed in fairly good spirits, even though certain things nagged at her and she had become somewhat obsessive-compulsive about keeping the doors locked and the alarm system turned on, even during times of the day when they had never kept it activated before.

Whit just did his best to honor any request she had that might help her feel more safe, and he continued to encourage her to talk. He also took every opportunity when it felt appropriate to give her a priesthood blessing. Again he was grateful to be worthy to do so. As Mary's husband, he could put his hands on her head and call upon the priesthood power he'd been given to offer inspired words of comfort and direction that always seemed to help her press forward, if only in baby steps.

Adrienne started first grade at the end of the summer, and she quickly grew to love school even more than she had in kindergarten. Whit and Mary took turns driving her to school and picking her up while the other one stayed with the baby. Once a week they went together and took the baby with them so they could have an outing with Adrienne after school. And now that Mary was feeling more like herself, Whit arranged for Adrienne to spend some time with her friend Rachel one evening a week so that he could take Mary on a date. Cinda was always happy to take Adrienne, and Whit and Mary watched Rachel enough in return that they didn't feel like they were taking advantage of her.

For the first few dates, they took Christian along. He was tiny and needed his mother. Then Cinda insisted that they needed to get out by themselves and emphatically declared that she would love to watch Christian as well. Since the baby was regularly fed with a bottle along with his breast feeding, Mary reluctantly agreed to leave her baby and go out for a *quick* dinner. Since everything was fine when they returned, and Cinda was actually enjoying the opportunity to help care for the baby, they were able to stay out longer the following week. Whit knew it was good for Mary to get out—in fact, it was good for both of them. They both agreed they needed to nurture their marriage relationship as well as work together to care for their children.

Whit made frequent visits to the care center to visit his mother, even though it was rare for him to get even a glimmer of recognition. Most of the time Ida still seemed to enjoy the visit. He enjoyed it too, as long as he could accept that she was conversing with him no differently than she might with a member of the staff or a perfect stranger who might have been kind enough to spend some time visiting with an elderly woman.

Once a week Whit took the family with him, and it was the same with them. Ida enjoyed Adrienne's sweetness, and she loved to see the baby. But she had no memory of who any of them were, and they shed a few tears shed once they were back in the truck following their visits. Since Ida's physical deterioration was becoming more intense, along with her memory loss, they didn't know how much longer she might remain in this world. Whit and Mary often talked about the situation with his mother and expressed their tender feelings over it. And they both agreed that death would be a blessing but would inevitably bring a great deal of grief when it finally happened.

The family continued to visit Whit's aunt Claudia every Sunday. She often talked about her sadness over her sisters. Reports of Ida's condition were heartbreaking for her, and she knew from regular conversations with Sofia that her other sister was very unhappy and often afraid, living in "that terrible neighborhood with all those hooligans." But Sofia refused to move, holding firmly to the same attitude that Ida had clung to before the Alzheimer's had made her confused and forgetful enough that moving her away had been possible—and necessary. Claudia worried about her sisters, and her children, and her nieces and nephews. She worried so much that it was all she could talk about, and it was difficult to keep the conversation at a level of cheerfulness.

Since Ida was the only member of her family who had joined the Mormon Church—about the same time she'd married Whit's father—it was difficult to offer Claudia the perspective of counteracting her worries with trusting in the Lord and accepting the peace of His atoning sacrifice. Claudia believed in God, but without the big picture of gospel principles being an integral part of her life, it was difficult for her to grasp the things that Whit tried to explain in the hope of providing her some comfort. He'd tried many, many times to share his testimony of the gospel with his aunts, always hoping they might embrace the truth and have *something* good in their lives. But they'd always been resistant.

Whit could only find comfort now in knowing that Claudia's health was also very poor, and he doubted it would be much longer before she passed away as well. He felt sure that once she got to the other side of the veil, she would have an opportunity to learn the gospel without the distorted perspective of this world getting in the way. He knew her heart and her spirit were strong, and he looked forward to the day when temple work could be done by proxy on behalf of his aunts.

Sofia was also getting along in years. Overall, her health seemed better than the health of either of her sisters. She was managing to take care of herself, at least. But she was so deeply unhappy that Whit felt a great deal of concern for her, as well. In fact, he felt *more* concerned for Sofia than he did her sisters. Just having her live in *that terrible neighborhood,* as Claudia always said, was always cause for concern.

Whit checked in on Claudia once or twice a week, knowing her children weren't very good at looking after her. But he never dared take his family along—simply because he refused to take them into *that terrible neighborhood.*

* * *

On a particularly beautiful Saturday, with the feel of a Los Angeles autumn in the air, the family shared breakfast as usual, with little Christian in his baby seat on the table. Whit then kissed his wife and children and went out to the garden where he intended to attack the weeds in a particularly stubborn area.

Mary found herself humming as she rinsed the breakfast dishes and put them in the dishwasher. She was still feeling some physical discomfort from her surgery and was certainly lacking the energy she'd once possessed, but she was healing and moving in the right direction, and she only had to take a glance at her new baby to know that it had all been worth it and then some. She considered—as she often had—what it might have felt like a few years earlier to look into the future and see the family she had now. She never could have imagined! Her blessings were tremendous, and too numerous to count. For that reason and many others, she found that she was even feeling better emotionally. She'd struggled a great deal with feelings of discouragement, some mild PTSD, and even some moderate paranoia. But she had a supportive husband, a good friend in Janel, and the foundation of the gospel to guide her to the correct answers that gave her peace. She felt certain it would continue to be a struggle, but in that respect she was also healing and moving in the right direction.

While Mary worked on putting the kitchen in order, Adrienne knelt on a chair and leaned over her baby brother who was still strapped into his infant seat. She talked to Christian in a funny voice and shared with him an adorable perspective about the world and all she intended to teach him as he got older. Just watching them made Mary feel deeply complete. She knew in her heart that their family *was* complete. She knew that being as old as she was, combined with the traumatic experience she'd endured bringing Christian into the world, it wouldn't be wise for her to try to have another baby.

She had discussed her feelings with Whit and he'd agreed, but they'd also agreed that they needed to take the matter to the Lord and both get a confirming answer before they made a firm decision. They had both done so, and they both felt at peace and complete as a family. Still, Mary intended to talk to her doctor about it at her next checkup—mostly based on curiosity as to what the medical perspective might be.

Her mind was wandering through the strange medical experience she'd endured when the phone rang and startled her. It wasn't very often that the house phone rang. Most people she conversed with knew her cell phone number and used that to reach her, since she took it with her almost everywhere she went.

Mary answered and immediately heard Claudia's voice speaking to her in frenzied tones, intermixing Spanish and English due to her stressed condition. Thankfully Mary understood both languages, but she still found it difficult to understand what Claudia was trying to tell her.

"Please slow down," Mary said calmly, even though her heart was pounding. She spoke in Spanish, knowing that it was Claudia's native language and it might be easier for her to get the message past the barriers of frenzy. "Tell me what's happened. Tell me what you need."

Claudia was still difficult to understand, even with her conscious effort to speak more slowly. Mary realized Claudia was crying—very hard. Her own frenzy rose immensely when she distinctly caught the phrase *there was a shooting*. Given the history of Whit's family and the things that some of them continued to be involved in, such news wasn't terribly surprising but it *was* shocking. And Mary had no idea *who* had been involved or *what* had happened.

Mary was finally able to conclude that the shooting had taken place at Sofia's home. Claudia had gotten a call from one of Sofia's neighbors, but this woman had known little except bits and pieces that all sounded horrible, and Mary didn't know what Claudia had accurately heard from this neighbor as opposed to what might be distorted by worry and fear. Claudia wanted Whit to find out what was really going on and let her know. Mary assured her that she would give Whit the message immediately and she knew he would do all he could. She made Claudia promise to try to stay calm and told her that she could call back in a while if she needed someone to talk to while they were waiting for Whit to get more information.

Mary ended the call and told Adrienne to stay right next to her brother and make certain he was all right while she went out to talk to Daddy for a few minutes. "If he cries, it's okay," Mary said. "I won't be long."

"Is something wrong?" Adrienne asked.

"Aunt Claudia is upset. Daddy will have to go and find out if everything is all right."

Mary hurried outside, wondering where to find Whit in the mass of the garden. If she didn't find him in a minute, she knew she could call his cell phone from her own. Then she heard the sound of the weed trimmer and followed it, wondering how bad the situation might be and wishing she didn't feel utterly terrified at the very thought of Whit going to investigate. She hated having him go anywhere near the violence related to his family—and his past. All of the unanswered questions that she'd been trying to suppress sparked into a new fire of concern, and she had to pray aloud as she moved quickly closer to where she knew Whit was working.

When Mary saw him, her heart pounded harder and her stomach tightened into knots. She told herself there was no reason to think that this moment had anything in common with the moment he'd been taken away by the police and had subsequently been arrested for a murder he hadn't committed. In her head, she knew there was no connection, but her emotions were in strong disagreement.

Whit saw her and turned off the trimmer before he put his safety glasses up on his head and smiled at her. His smile faded when he took note of her countenance. "What's wrong?" he demanded, setting the trimmer down.

"Claudia called," she said. "She was so upset I could hardly understand her, but . . . something's happened, and . . . she wants you to find out what . . . and let her know. A neighbor of Sofia's called her, but she didn't have much information, and . . . she's very upset."

Mary had purposely avoided the one thing Claudia had told her that she didn't want to say aloud, but Whit had a sixth sense about these things—or perhaps he just knew her well enough to know when she was holding back.

"What else?" he insisted, stepping toward her. Mary hesitated; he said it again, his voice lower. "What else did she tell you, Mary?"

Mary cleared her throat and looked up at him, gathering courage enough to allow the words through her lips. She was surprised that tears came to her eyes, but given her recent emotional state—and her knowledge of Whit's life—perhaps she shouldn't have been. "She said . . . there was a shooting."

Mary heard Whit exhale sharply as he dropped his head forward. He actually took a sidestep as if he might be dizzy. Mary took hold of his arms, and he lowered his head further as if to get the blood flowing back into it. "I knew something else would happen," he muttered. "I knew it was only a matter of time, but . . ."

"What do you mean?" she asked. He had told her some things about his cousins and the challenges between them, but she also knew he only told her the bare minimum in most cases because he didn't want to expose her to the ugliness.

"They're all just so . . . angry . . . and so . . . *stupid!*" He stood up straight, apparently having found his equilibrium, then he pushed his hands brutally through his hair. "They . . . deal drugs . . . and use drugs . . . and they wander around carrying guns . . . just itching for a chance to use them. But why does it have to be *my* family? Why?"

"I don't know, Whit," Mary said and wiped her ongoing flow of tears, "but . . ."

"Yes, I know. I need to go find out what happened, but . . ." He shook his head and squeezed his eyes closed. "I don't want to." He put a hand over his stomach. "My gut tells me it's bad." Mary wrapped him in her arms and he held to her tightly, as if he might be trying to draw strength from her that would carry him through whatever he might have to face. "I love you, Mary," he said and kissed her brow. He then took hold of her shoulders and looked at her firmly. "I want all of you to stay here. There is absolutely no reason to believe you have any cause for concern but I know this is all very hard for you, so just . . . stay put. Set the alarm if that will help you feel better. I will call you as soon as I possibly can."

"Okay," she said. "Don't worry about us; we'll be fine." She was glad to note that she meant it. She truly wasn't worried about herself or the children. "You be careful. Whatever *has* happened, don't get in the middle of it."

"I'm not worried about that. Whatever's happened it's over and done. They all lay low for a while after a big event. I'll be fine."

Mary felt a little better to hear that, but her stomach was still smoldering over the possibility of what *could* have happened, especially when it had apparently taken place at Sofia's home. Poor, dear Sofia. Ida and her sisters had been through so much, simply because of the neighborhood where they'd lived and the violence that their children had become involved in.

Whit and Mary went back into the house, where Christian had drifted to sleep with Adrienne playing quietly nearby. Both of the adults assumed an appropriate demeanor that would not alarm Adrienne. Since she had overheard Mary's phone call, she asked her parents if something was wrong.

"I don't know," Whit said, "but I'll go and find out. You have nothing to worry about. Just stay here and have a good day with Mommy and Christian, and I'll call Mommy as soon as I know anything. Okay?"

"Okay," Adrienne said, soothed by her father's comforting tone as well as his promise.

Whit kissed them all and left. Mary forced herself back to doing what housework could be accomplished while the baby slept, praying while she did so that Whit would be protected and strengthened, and that in spite of whatever he might discover, he would be comforted and have peace. She prayed for Whit's mother, grateful that her memory had failed her enough that she might be spared from knowing about any new tragedy in her family. And she prayed for Claudia and Sofia, that they too would be comforted and strengthened.

Mary reached a point where she was too worn out to do anything more, and since Christian was still asleep, she sat with Adrienne and read a story until the baby began to fuss. She changed the baby's diaper and nursed him—glancing often at the clock, wondering what had happened, and wanting to know for certain that Whit was okay.

Chapter Six

BEFORE WHIT PULLED OUT OF the driveway, he realized he should at least try to make some calls and find out what he could. He phoned Sofia's house and got no answer. He tried Carlos's cell phone and it went straight to voice mail. Carlos was the only cousin he trusted *at all,* and he had no desire to try to call any of the others. Not only did he have no desire to speak to any of them, he didn't want them to have his phone number.

Whit put the phone away and drove toward the neighborhood where Sofia lived. He always hated going back there, but today his stomach was tightly knotted and his mouth had gone dry. The combination of symptoms resulted in a mild nausea that he tried to suppress while he silently prayed that this would not be as serious as they had assumed based on the very minimal information they'd been given. His deepest concern was the fact that it had apparently taken place in Sofia's home—or on the premises—and he felt worried for how the trauma might affect her.

Maybe this would prompt Sofia to leave the neighborhood. He and Mary could take her in. He knew Mary would be willing; in fact, the subject had come up before. Perhaps this could be a blessing in the long run. He started thinking about how good it would feel to get Sofia away from all of this and have her in his care—then he came around the corner onto the street where Sofia lived, and his breath rushed out of him. Yellow crime-scene tape was draped across the front of Sofia's yard.

"Oh, heaven help me," Whit muttered and slowed the truck down, hoping to give himself a little more time to catch his breath before he pulled over and parked, as close to the house as he could get, given the barriers that had been set up in the street and the multiple emergency vehicles parked there—including an ambulance, three police cars, and . . . was it? No! *"No!"* he muttered. But it was true. A van was parked there, clearly marked as a vehicle belonging to the medical examiner. Just as it occurred to him that an ambulance was contradictory to the need for a coroner on the scene, the ambulance drove away in the other direction, no lights or sirens to indicate any emergency.

Whit got out of the truck and locked it with the remote on his key ring. He took a few slow, heavy steps. Then he ran. He was not surprised to be stopped at the yellow-taped barrier by an officer who asked, "Who are you?"

"My aunt lives here," he said. "Her sister called me, and . . ." Whit then recognized a man standing a short distance away, talking quietly with a couple of officers. The three men all turned his direction, and Whit met the eyes of Detective Wilson, the man who had investigated the death of Mary's father and who had fervidly believed that Whit had been guilty.

"Whit Eden," the detective said and stepped closer. "Why am I not surprised to find you here?"

"Because you know where my relatives live," Whit said. Not knowing how this man felt about him, Whit decided to just come right out and address the situation rather than trying to ignore it. "I don't know whether you still think I'm guilty or not, but I really need to know what's happening here."

The detective sighed. "A jury declared that you're not guilty. I do my best to uphold and respect the law. We'll leave it at that."

Whit nodded, grateful to know that much, but he still sensed that the detective hadn't fully let go of his belief that Whit had committed murder—one more reason to wish that they had any idea what had *really* happened that night.

He was surprised when the detective lifted the police tape for Whit to step beneath it. "Actually, I'm glad to see you, Mr. Eden. You're probably not surprised that we can't find any next of kin to help answer some questions. They likely scattered like scared rats as soon as the shots were fired."

"Tell me," Whit said, putting a hand on the detective's arm to stop him from walking toward the house. Whit didn't want to go in there until he knew *something*. The detective seemed hesitant, and Whit said, "Someone is dead in there, I'm assuming."

"That's right," Wilson said. "An elderly woman." Whit gasped and put a hand to his heart as the news gripped it in a painful vice. Wilson was quick to add, "But her death doesn't appear to have had anything to do with the shooting . . . not directly anyway. Coroner thinks she probably died of a heart attack—probably from the shock when the rest went down."

Whit knew he needed to ask what *the rest* entailed, but he had to lower his head and try to take in the numbing shock that his aunt was dead—and her final moments couldn't have been good, given what he already knew. He quickly reminded himself of what he knew about the gospel plan. She was in a better place. She was at peace. All of her fears and worries were over. She was free from this horribly challenging life she'd had to live.

"I'll give you a minute," Wilson said. "I know this must be shocking."

"Yeah," Whit managed. "Um . . . yeah."

"Let me know when you're ready, and I'd like to have you identify the body . . . to be certain . . . if you're up to it."

Whit took a deep breath and tried to separate the emotional shock from the need to do what had to be done. "Okay," Whit said. "Let's get it over with."

"Before we go in there," Wilson said, "I need to tell you that it's not pretty. Your cousin was shot. There's blood on the carpet, and—"

"Which cousin?" Whit demanded. "Is he dead?"

"One of them that testified for you," Wilson said. "Carlos, I believe."

Whit's head threatened to swim with dizziness, but he fought for composure.

"No, he's not dead," Wilson reported, and it became a little easier for Whit to remain upright. "Last I heard he's in surgery. Don't know any more than that."

Whit forced a deep breath in, then out. Then another. "Okay," Whit said. "Let's get this over with."

"Are you all right?" the detective asked.

"I'm in shock, Detective," Whit said, "but thank you for asking."

Detective Wilson put a hand briefly on Whit's shoulder, apparently as some kind of silent expression of compassion, then he led the way into the house. Whit's heart was pounding and he felt sick to his stomach, but he prayed fervently for the strength to remain composed and intact. Right now he just had to get through this. He could fall apart later. When he noticed the blood on the carpet, it took more effort for him to breathe deeply. He knew if he allowed his breathing to become too shallow he'd be in trouble. How well he recalled the night he'd come into this room to be confronted by his cousins. Thankfully, he'd had some pleasant visits with Sofia since that night, which helped offset the memory a bit.

Whit was led into the tiny hallway between the kitchen and bathroom, where a body was lying on the floor, covered. He heard the detective communicating with someone but a ringing in his ears prevented him from hearing what was being said. The man who was apparently the medical examiner squatted down beside the body and moved the sheet back just enough to reveal Sofia's face. Whit was relieved that her expression looked peaceful, which made it easier to imagine that her going had easy, even though it had been the violence taking place in her home that had initiated her heart attack. Or so they believed at this point.

"Yes, that's my aunt," he said with a shaky voice. "This is her home."

"Thank you, Mr. Eden," Wilson said, and the medical examiner covered Sofia's face again. "Let me get your current contact information, and I'll have them get in touch with you regarding further arrangements once they've done an autopsy."

Whit cleared his throat and rushed out of the house, relieved when the detective followed. He needed some fresh air in order to speak coherently. Once he was in the yard, Whit gave the detective his contact information, then answered some questions about his cousins—all of which had the same answer. He hadn't had any contact with any of them since the night after the trial had ended. He told the detective they had all been here that evening and had shared some chit-chat—nothing of any consequence. He left out the part of the conversation that he knew would make no difference to the detective and that might in fact just muddy the waters of the investigation of *this* crime, of which Whit knew nothing.

Whit prayed that this wasn't the beginning of a new nightmare for him. At least he knew that this time no one would find a gun with his fingerprints on it, because his gun had long since been confiscated and deposited in police evidence lockup.

Whit recalled that Carlos was in surgery, and he had no idea how bad off Carlos was. At the first possible moment, he said, "If you have all you need from me, Detective, I'd like to get to the hospital and see how my cousin is doing."

"Of course," Wilson said. "I know how to reach you if I need to."

"Yes."

"Are the two of you close?" Wilson asked, and Whit couldn't tell if the question was based on polite concern or on curiosity stemming from whether Whit might know more than he'd let on.

Whit just stated the truth. "We weren't *close,* but he's the only one who had any decency in him at all. I already told you the last time I saw him."

"I hope he'll be okay," Wilson said, and seemed to mean it.

"Thank you," Whit said and hurried to his truck. He hastened to start it and drove about a mile before he pulled into a mostly vacant parking lot and began gasping for breath. Now that he was alone, the shock that had kept him calm now reverberated through his entire body, erupting from his chest in heaving gasps. Sofia dead. Carlos in surgery. *He couldn't believe it!* Claudia would be devastated! How could he tell her? At least his mother would likely not even understand or remember who these people were. He never thought he'd consider Alzheimer's a blessing.

Once he could breathe almost normally, Whit remembered that Mary would be waiting to hear from him, as would Claudia. He reasoned that if Carlos was in surgery, he could do nothing at the hospital right now. It would be best to talk with Claudia first. But before he could do that, he needed to talk to his wife. He pushed the button that automatically dialed her cell phone.

"Are you okay?" she answered in lieu of any greeting.

"No, I'm not okay," he said, then just hurried to get the rest out. "Sofia is dead."

"What?" Mary gasped. "No! How? What happened? Did she—"

He knew her mind would immediately go to the possibility of some kind of violence, so he hurried to explain. "Apparently it was a heart attack, but *that* was apparently brought on by the shooting that took place in her home."

"No!" Mary said again. "So it's true?"

"It's Carlos," Whit said, his voice cracking.

"Is he—"

"He's in surgery. I have no idea how bad it is. And that's *all* I know. Our friend the detective was there."

"What a lovely coincidence," Mary said with sarcasm. He couldn't blame her. The man had not been kind to Mary when he'd believed Whit was guilty of murder. "How many detectives are there in this city?"

"I don't know, but . . . I'm glad it was him, actually. It prevented a great deal of explanation. He was rather kind, if you must know."

"Good," Mary said. "I'm glad to hear it." He heard her sigh, then knew she was crying. "I can't believe Sofia's gone, and . . . Carlos . . ."

"I know."

"What will you do now?"

"I know Claudia's waiting to hear from me. I'll call her and then go to the hospital. As soon as I know anything more, I'll call."

"Do you want me to meet you there, or—"

"No, I want you to stay put. I want you to keep your distance from this. Just take care of yourself . . . and our beautiful babies."

"I will," she said and sniffled. "I love you, Whit. I'm here for you."

"I know. I'm so grateful for that. I love you too. I'll call when I can."

When the call ended, Whit stared at his phone for at least a couple of minutes before he could bring himself to dial Claudia's number. He tried to think of the best way to tell her, but there were no words to buffer the truth. He wondered as the phone was ringing if he should tell her in person. Before he could rethink it, a voice answered, but it was the receptionist at the care center where Claudia lived. All calls went through the front desk, which made Whit feel like his prayers on Claudia's behalf were being answered. He knew the woman on the phone, and she knew him from his frequent visits and calls. He asked if he could speak to a woman named Nikki, who had cared for Claudia longer than any other nurse there. He knew she usually worked Saturdays, and was grateful that she was there now. He continued to pray while he was put on hold until Nikki could come to the phone.

Once Nikki said hello, Whit told her, "This is Whit Eden, Claudia's nephew. I have some very difficult news to tell her. I wonder if I could ask that you sit with her while I speak to her on the phone. I need to get to the hospital, or I would come and sit with her myself, and you know that having any of her children there would only make it more difficult."

"I *do* know that," she said. "I'll go to her room right now. Call back and have them connect you. I'll stay with her."

"Thank you so much!" Whit said. "You're a gem."

"Claudia's a sweet lady. I'm glad to help in any way I can."

"You know she can be forgetful. Just keep reminding her that I will call or come over as soon as I have anything more to tell her."

"I will," Nikki said, and Whit hung up then called again to speak to his aunt. He prayed while waiting to be connected, and he wasn't surprised to hear how upset she was, frantically asking him in Spanish if he knew what had happened and if everyone was all right. He told her what had happened in as straightforward a manner as he could manage between all of her tears and near hysteria. He could hear Nikki in the background trying to soothe her. When it seemed that Claudia wasn't hearing him at all, he was glad to hear Nikki say into the phone, "Obviously she's very upset, but we won't leave her alone."

"Thank you," Whit said, wishing the words could fully express his gratitude.

"Could you quickly tell *me* what's happened. I don't think I'll get it out of her."

Whit told Nikki the bottom line, and the nurse said, "Oh, my! I'm so sorry! You do what you need to do. We'll wait to hear from you."

"Thank you . . . so much," Whit said and hung up the phone. He had no choice but to do a repeat performance of his own gasping for breath in order to relieve the pressure that had been continually building in his chest and head. Once the bare minimum of pressure had been released, he gathered his composure and drove to the hospital. He was quickly connected with a nurse who had taken care of the formalities when Carlos had been brought in. She was glad to now have a relative there with whom she could consult. Whit explained the family situation to her, and she added names and contact information to her records for the patient.

When Whit asked about his cousin's condition, he was only told, "The bullet did a lot of damage. His condition is critical. We'll be able to better assess the situation once we see how the surgery goes." Whit understood the implication. *If* Carlos made it through the surgery, then his condition would be worth discussing.

The nurse guided Whit to a surgical waiting area where he met a different nurse who promised to notify him of any changes or complications throughout the course of the surgery. As of the last time she'd checked, Carlos had been stable, with his vital signs showing good numbers. She told him the surgery was very complicated, but she wasn't at liberty to explain any details. The surgeon would need to do that when he was finished. The nurse took Whit's cell phone number so she could reach him if he needed to eat or get some fresh air. He took that to mean that the surgery could be a long while yet.

As soon as Whit had nothing to do but wait, he wondered where his *other* cousins might be—especially Jose, Carlos's brother. Did his absence imply some guilt, or was he just oblivious? He could be stoned right now for all Whit knew. He didn't really believe that Jose would ever purposely allow his own brother to get hurt so badly, but these guys were all out of their minds, with the lines between good and evil so completely blurred that it was impossible to know what might have led up to this.

Whit didn't really care *who* was responsible. That was for the police to figure out—if it were even possible. Whit knew well enough that any energy put into trying to figure out who was responsible, and trying to hold them accountable, was simply energy wasted. He found it tremendously liberating to give such burdens to the Lord and to instead turn his attention toward prayer on Carlos's behalf and on behalf of the other family members who would grieve over Sofia's death. He felt an onslaught of grief on that count and even some anger. He knew such emotions were normal under the circumstances, but they prompted the need for more prayer. Whatever the outcome might be for Carlos, it was going to take time for healing—in many respects.

Whit phoned Mary to tell her what little he knew. He asked if she would call the care center and give Nikki an update. Mary offered to take the children and go sit with Claudia, but Whit insisted that they remain at home. His cousins had shown up at the care center before and had occasionally caused problems. He didn't know what had happened earlier today or what had led up to this trauma, but if anyone in the family went to see Claudia for *any* reason, he didn't want Mary and the kids there unless he was there with them. Mary promised to call the care center and to stay put at home. He promised to let her know as soon as he had any word on Carlos.

It took Whit a while to realize there was absolutely nothing he could do but wait. He paced for a while, trying to take in the reality that Sofia was dead and that he had no idea what the outcome would be with Carlos. He forced himself to sit down, and then he had to force himself to examine his feelings as opposed to trying not to even think about the horrid thoughts and images in his mind and how they affected him. Today's events tied into memories of other nightmarish days in his life, and he wondered if it would ever end. How could he ever forget the day that his brother had been shot and killed, and his father? Unable to even bear thinking about that, he thought instead of Sofia. Pondering the circumstances under which she'd left this world felt equally unbearable, so he thought instead of where she was now. He was grateful to feel some tangible peace on her behalf, and he found that his grief was more focused on the difficulties of the life she had lived as opposed to being focused on her death.

Whit's mind drifted far away to thoughts of the childhood years of his mother and her sisters and how they had grown up in poverty and with many difficulties in a small Mexican village. America had offered hope and promise, and one by one they had come here, each of them going about it legally and with great pride in becoming Americans. But he wondered what kind of life the next generations—his *own* generation—might have faced if they'd remained in Mexico.

Whit had more blessings than he could count in regard to growing up in the United States of America. He was grateful to be where he was and he would never deny it. Still, he couldn't help wondering if his family would have been exposed to—and been the victims of—so much violence if their circumstances had been different. His mother and aunts firmly believed they were better off here. And who was Whit to argue with them? He'd served his mission in Mexico, but he didn't know the area where his family had originated, and he knew very little of what life had been like for them there. He'd heard stories, but they had been cryptic in some ways, as if certain details had been omitted.

Whit knew his musings were futile. The reality was that he and his siblings and cousins had grown up in a violent neighborhood, and it had impacted all of their lives enormously. Now Sofia was dead, and Carlos might soon be following her. Again he thought of the deaths of his own father and brother. He'd also lost two cousins to gang-related violence, as well as a few of the friends of his youth.

While Whit had been trying to avoid looking at his watch, hoping the time would go more quickly, he glanced at it now, astonished at how many hours he'd been there waiting. He saw a surgeon coming up the hall and his heart quickened, but the doctor called out someone else's name then sat down across the room to visit quietly with an elderly man and a woman who appeared to be his daughter. From his discreet observations, Whit concluded that the news was good and the surgery—whatever it had been—had gone well.

The surgeon stood up and left, then Whit saw a different surgeon coming up the hall. He only had to wonder a moment before the man said, "Whit Eden?"

"That's me," Whit said and stood up.

"You're a cousin to Carlos?" the doctor asked. Apparently after having spent hours with Carlos in extensive surgery, he was on a first-name basis.

"That's right," Whit said, and the doctor sat down on a small sofa, motioning for Whit to sit next to him. Both men remained at the edge of their seats and faced each other.

Whit held his breath, wondering if he was about to hear the worst. But the doctor said, "He came through fairly well—better than I expected, to be truthful. And he's stable."

Whit exhaled a loud breath and dropped his head, but he lifted it again abruptly when the doctor added, "He's got a rough road ahead, but at this point his chances for survival are good."

Whit took in that information and asked, "How rough? What happened exactly?"

"What do you know?"

"Nothing," Whit said, and the doctor looked surprised. "What?" Whit demanded, although he tried to do so politely.

"The bullet severed his spinal cord. He will never walk again."

Whit sucked in a harsh breath and couldn't let it out.

The doctor continued, "There was also damage to his intestines, but that's all been repaired and should heal with time. The good news is that the damage is fairly low in his spinal column. He will have full use of his arms, and no problem with breathing on his own. I've certainly seen much worse, but I know that doesn't sound consoling when something like this needs to be faced."

Whit forced himself to breathe and comprehend all he was hearing. The doctor went on with some information on how Carlos would be well cared for here in the hospital until he healed sufficiently to be moved to a rehabilitation facility, where he would be taught everything he needed to know to adjust to his new way of living. Whit was reassured that the hospital staff would answer all their questions and help them get through this as smoothly as possible.

Whit thanked the surgeon profusely for saving Carlos's life. The doctor graciously accepted Whit's appreciation and his handshake, then he slipped away and Whit sank back into a hazy fog of shock and grief. It took him a few minutes to realize that he'd been told he could go sit in the room in ICU where Carlos would be coming out of the anesthetic in a while. And then there was the matter of Sofia's death and the need to make arrangements. He doubted her children would handle it well, if at all.

Whit couldn't even imagine where to begin to deal with all of this; then, without consciously thinking about what he was doing, he reached for his cell phone and pushed the button to call Mary. She was his lifeline! She would help him get through this! Without her and God, he would be utterly lost. And God had sent Mary into his life to be a strength and a support to him. She had done it over and over, and now they were heading into new and difficult challenges. He didn't want her directly involved with anyone in his family, but she could help him know what to do, and she could help give him the strength to do it.

"What's happening?" she asked, startling him back to the realization that the phone had been ringing. "How is Carlos? Is he going to make it?"

"Um . . . yeah," Whit said. "Um . . . he's stable. He's . . ."

"Whit? What is it? Tell me."

"He's never going to . . . walk again, Mary." He heard her gasp, and he added, "The bullet severed his spinal cord."

"I can't believe it."

"I can't either."

"Will he consider this worse than death?" she asked, and he was amazed at how she had perceived his exact feelings even though he hadn't had the presence of mind to formulate them into a precise thought. That was what he feared most—dealing with Carlos's emotional response to this.

"Absolutely," Whit said. "He will wish he had died, and no one beyond me and his mother will ever care."

"Then we will have to make certain he knows that we *do* care!" she said firmly, as if Carlos were every bit as much her own responsibility as his. And that's when he couldn't hold back the tears that had been brewing all day, tears that had been held back by shock and horror.

"How do you do it?" he asked, his voice breaking.

"Do what?"

"You just . . . love me so much that your love just . . . overflows toward these people that . . . you hardly even know."

"Whit, I *do* love you! And I understand why we have to stay away from most of your family; I understand the need to protect ourselves. But when it comes to something like this, Carlos will need us, and there's nothing more important than family."

Whit became more emotional but managed to say, "That's why I called you. I knew you could help me through this. I knew you could help me know how to handle it.'

"I should be there with you. I will call Cinda and see if she can watch—"

"No!" Whit said emphatically. "I need you and the children to stay at home! I'm not sure exactly how to deal with all of this, but with Sofia's death *and* this situation with Carlos, my cousins are sure to be involved eventually in one way or another, and I will *not* have you around them. At all! It's not up for discussion. You have no idea of the things they can do when they get some notion in their head that they are entitled to something that has nothing to do with them—especially when they get stoned, which happens far too often. Do you hear me?"

"I do," she said, sounding sufficiently convinced—perhaps even terrified—but it wasn't something he would toy with. "I understand."

"Okay," he said, his voice softening. "I love you. I just want you and the children to stay safe. Just talk to me. Help me know how to handle this. What do I say to Carlos when he comes out of the anesthetic? And how do I handle Sofia's burial if her kids get in the middle of it?"

"As for the burial, you can only do the best you can do. If they get in the middle of it, then you will have to put some distance between yourself and them. Maybe they won't want to be involved. You can do your best to make arrangements and see what happens. As for Carlos, I think you just have to be honest with him, and then he needs to know that you care and that you're not going to abandon him, because I'm betting his other cousins will. And his brother, no doubt."

"No doubt," Whit said. She had come to know his family well, even though she'd never met most of them.

They talked for a while longer, and he appreciated her insight and wisdom and compassion more than he could tell her. He promised to keep in touch, and he also promised to get something decent to eat as soon as possible. After they ended their call, he found Carlos's room and spoke to the nurse overseeing his care. She answered some questions with a great deal of kindness and patience. She left him alone with Carlos, which gave Whit a chance to get used to seeing his cousin hooked up to more tubes and wires than he could count. He prayed very hard on his cousin's behalf, then he left to go to the cafeteria once he'd been assured that Carlos would not be anywhere near consciousness for a while yet.

Whit didn't feel particularly hungry, but he forced himself to eat enough to sustain his strength. Then he found a place where he could make some calls and find out all he could about the arrangements that needed to be made for Sofia. He spoke to someone at the medical examiner's office, then he spoke to someone at the mortuary where the body would go. He realized that if he made arrangements for her burial, he would likely end up paying for it. His mother and Claudia had both asked for his help in financial matters long before their minds had begun to deteriorate, so he had control of how such things would be handled. But the same was not true for Sofia. If he'd even attempted to help her in any such way, he would have only been accused of trying to take possession of her property and bank account, and it would have gotten him into trouble.

He had no idea if Sofia had any money to her name or any life insurance. And even if she did, her sons would probably have their hands on it as quickly as possible, and he doubted a cent of it would ever go toward a decent burial. Whit knew he needed to do the right thing by his aunt, however, and after he'd spoken to the mortuary, he called Mary and she agreed that they would have to use some of their savings to pay for a decent burial if it came to that. Of course he knew she would agree to that. She was just that kind of person, and he wondered once again why a man with his own tattered past would be blessed to have such a good woman in his life.

Having done all he could do for the moment, Whit went back to Carlos's room and sat near his bedside, listening to the monitors and rehearsing the words he might use to tell him that their aunt was dead and that he was likely going to wish that he'd died too. The nurse he'd spoken to before came in every few minutes, and he quickly realized that patients in Intensive Care were monitored very closely. She told him that Carlos should soon be waking up, and they needed to bring him to full consciousness and make certain he was responsive before they increased the dosage of pain medication that would help him sleep and give him some relief.

Whit observed the signs of Carlos coming around, and his heart pounded with the thought of what the next little while was going to be like for his cousin. A horrible thought then occurred to him. Carlos had been the victim of a crime, and the police would inevitably show up to question him. Detective Wilson, no doubt. It could be worse. At least he seemed to care. But Whit knew that Carlos would never say that his cousins had been responsible for this—even if they were. Whit had no idea whether they had anything to do with it or not, and a part of him didn't want to know. But he hated to see Carlos having to face police interrogation and the possibility of needing to lie in order to protect himself from any further danger.

Whit couldn't imagine that one of his cousins had actually pulled the trigger. However, having seen their behavior in the past when they were stoned out of their minds, he could never be sure of anything. But he knew from experience that even if one of them hadn't personally pulled the trigger, they very likely could have picked the fight that ended in this disaster, and at the moment he was having trouble not feeling angry over the existence of that whole package of gang violence and the rotten luck that had planted his family in the middle of it.

Whit was brought out of his troubling thoughts when Carlos muttered something in an attempt to speak. Whit stood and took hold of his hand, leaning over him so that his face would be easily in his cousin's view.

"Carlos," he said earnestly. "I'm here. It's Whit. I'm here with you."

Carlos moaned and seemed to drift back into drug-induced sleep for a minute or two, then he once again attempted to speak, and his eyelids fluttered a bit. Whit was glad when the nurse came in and stood on the other side of the bed. She spoke very loudly to Carlos, saying his name and asking him if he could hear her. After a few minutes of groggy and undecipherable answers, Carlos finally focused on the nurse and managed to mutter, "What happened?"

"You were hurt and you're in the hospital," she said in a loud, clear voice that made it clear she'd had a lot of practice communicating with patients in this condition. "You had surgery and it was very complicated, but you're stable now. Do you understand what I'm saying, Carlos?"

"Yeah," Carlos said. Then he muttered, "Whit," and turned his head as if to search for his cousin, knowing he'd heard his voice and seen his face at some point during the last several minutes.

"I'm here," Whit said and leaned closer, at the same time squeezing his hand.

"What happened?" Carlos repeated, and Whit instinctively knew he wasn't seeking for a repeat of what the nurse had told him. He was wondering about what had happened *before* that.

"I wasn't there," Whit said. "What do you remember?"

Carlos became slightly agitated, closed his eyes, and shook his head very slightly. When he seemed cognizant of the physical pain he was suffering, he restrained himself from moving but still seemed agitated. Whit glanced at the nurse, hoping she might take the hint to leave them alone. When she didn't, Whit said kindly, "Would it be all right if we have a few minutes?"

She seemed hesitant, but he wondered whether she was concerned for Carlos's well-being or whether she was curious about the situation, knowing that Carlos was a victim of a shooting. Whit knew that all of Carlos's vitals were being monitored at the nurses' station, so he just gave the woman a firm stare, accompanied by a strained smile. She returned an equally strained smile and left the room, saying, "Just push the button if you need me."

"I will, thank you," Whit said, then turned his attention fully to Carlos as soon as the door closed. He squeezed his cousin's hand and felt a weak response. "What do you remember?" Whit repeated.

"Sof . . ." he sputtered. "Sof . . . Is she . . ." His agitation increased slightly.

"You need to stay calm, bro, or that nurse will be back in here breathing down our necks. But this is hard to say, so . . . bear with me."

Carlos's eyes showed fear that deepened into horror, as if he already knew. Whit wondered if he might have seen their aunt collapse before he'd lost consciousness or if he just feared that she'd been hurt.

"She had a heart attack," Whit said right off, figuring it was best to make it clear right up front that she'd not been a victim of the violence that had taken place. "Or at least that's what they think." Whit swallowed hard and cleared his throat. "She didn't make it, bro. She's gone."

Carlos groaned and turned his head on the pillow as if it were the only movement he could manage in response to the news. Whit knew that Carlos had a tenderness and concern for Sofia that the others didn't, and this would not be easy for him to face. But he had yet to hear the worst news. And Whit still didn't know how to tell him. He kept praying for the words to come to his mind, but they just wouldn't.

Whit saw tears leak out of the corners of Carlos's eyes, and he just squeezed his hand again to silently let him know that he was there. After a minute or two of silence Carlos said weakly, "It was my fault."

"How was it your fault?" Whit asked with more compassion than accusation. He knew Carlos well enough to know that it likely *wasn't* his fault, but Whit needed more information. He hoped he might even be able to help keep the police at bay and handle their questioning rather than having it fall on Carlos to endure under the circumstances.

"I shouldn't have . . . gone to her house," he insisted weakly, showing evidence that he was in pain. He muttered a few more fragmented phrases that made it clear he had been with his brother Jose, and it had been

Jose's idea to hang out at Sofia's house even though he'd been aware that members of a rival gang were out for payback over some typically ridiculous thing. When it became evident that Carlos was in pain and becoming more agitated, Whit insisted they not talk about it anymore for the time being. Carlos then asked, "What happened to me, man? I'm messed up pretty bad."

"Why do you say that?" Whit asked, holding his breath with the hope that Carlos might be able to figure out the problem to some degree on his own.

"My middle hurts bad," he said, "but . . ." He hesitated and looked at Whit as if it had just fully occurred to him.

"What, Carlos?" Whit asked.

"I can't feel my legs, man," he muttered weakly. Whit could only stare at him and knew that his gaze said what he couldn't find the words to say. Carlos groaned, then repeated the same statement with more anguish. Then he became so upset that his blood pressure went up, which set off a monitor, which brought the nurse returning in a hurry. She was kind and efficient and apparently had guessed that the patient had just gotten the bad news. She spoke gentle words to Carlos as she put medication into his IV, but he ignored her and for a minute seemed almost like a caged animal frantically trying to escape—except the cage was now the lower half of his body that had no feeling and would not respond.

Whit stood back and felt tears wet his cheeks. He'd seen his family members endure a great deal of suffering but this moment was high on the list of things he would rather not remember. The nurse motioned him to come back to the bedside and she whispered to him, "Try to help soothe him if you can. The pain medication will calm him down in a few minutes, but . . ."

Whit nodded and took hold of Carlos's shoulders and looked into his eyes firmly. "Listen to me," he said. "I know this feels like the end of the world, but we're going to—"

"You don't know nothin', man," Carlos snarled. "Get out o' my face!" He then uttered profanities that forced Whit to say quietly to the nurse, "Sorry."

"I've heard worse," she said. "When people are in pain they lose all inhibition."

Whit didn't bother commenting that this was common language among his cousins and that matters of pain and inhibition had nothing to do with it. He ignored Carlos's anger and got in his face anyway, saying over and over that they would get through it together, that he was never going to abandon him to this, and that his life was not over. Carlos insisted, along with more profanities, that it might as well be.

Whit was deeply relieved when the medication began to take effect quickly except for the way that Carlos went from cursing to sobbing to moaning in emotional anguish before he finally drifted into a drug-induced sleep. His most prominent thought when the quiet settled over the room was that people who didn't have any comprehension of a Savior in their lives had no hope of having anything to ease their pain. And this was a pain that could no longer be masked by Carlos's bad habits and criminal companions. Whit knew the most they could expect from anyone else was a possible visit to the hospital that was more likely to cause a problem than it was to give Carlos any comfort. Whit prayed that they would just stay away.

Chapter Seven

WHIT WAS STILL THERE WHEN Carlos woke again. He'd spent the hours pacing and praying and talking to Mary on the phone. He'd hoped that when he had a chance to speak with Carlos again, he might be just a little more rational, and that Whit could say something that might make him at least want to live beyond this day. But it quickly became evident that Carlos would hear nothing. He had ceased his ranting, but he wouldn't talk at all, and he insisted that Whit needed to leave and stay away—that he didn't want to see or talk to *anyone*. Whit finally had to give in to Carlos's plea when the nurses caring for him were adamant about honoring the patient's wishes for the sake of his well-being. A different nurse than the one who had been on shift earlier quietly reassured Whit that this kind of behavior was common for patients who had experienced disabling injuries and that with time, Carlos would come around. Whit wanted to think so, and he thanked the nurse for her kindness, but he knew that Carlos had a lot of ugliness in his heart, and he wasn't sure he had the strength to get beyond this in any kind of positive way.

Whit mourned silently all the way home, and it was only when Mary met him with open arms that he allowed himself to weep. The following week was one of the worst of Whit's life other than the experiences connected with prison or being on trial for murder. Dealing with Sofia's burial proved to be a nightmare. Her children became involved in the most dysfunctional ways that exceeded even his own worst fears.. He finally stepped away from the entire situation and just quietly attended the brief graveside service. Mary felt sad at not being able to attend, but Whit remained firm in his insistence on keeping her distanced from his cousins, and she couldn't argue his point. The one positive thing was that Sofia's children *did* pay for her burial in full from money that had been in Sofia's bank account. Whit knew that beyond that, her money—what little there was of it—and her home would become a source of contention among her children and create new opportunities for ugliness. Whit was simply glad to be out of that neighborhood, and now that Sofia was no longer alive, he had no reason whatsoever to interact with her children—ever!

Detective Wilson eventually caught up with Whit to question him about the shooting that had occurred at his aunt's home. He declared that Carlos had refused to tell him anything. Whit just said, "Well, he didn't tell me anything either, and he won't talk to me at all, so I can't help you. I guess you can chalk it up to one more unsolvable crime." As he said the words, he felt haunted by his father-in-law's murder that still remained unsolved but he pushed the thought away.

"You really can't tell me anything?" the detective asked, but his words were kind and genuine, which was a huge step above how he'd treated Whit when he'd believed he was a murderer.

"I tried to get Carlos to tell me what had happened. He honestly didn't tell me anything except some hints that it was gang-related. I wish I could help, Detective. I really do. I would give a lot to see the hate crimes in this city reduced even a little, and I would certainly like to see the man who shot Carlos punished for his crime, but I don't think Carlos will ever talk about it. If he does, I know where to find you."

The detective conceded, but Whit kept thinking about their conversation and how it had triggered the same old feelings about the unsolved murder that had taken place in their home. He and Mary rarely talked about it, but he knew it bothered her greatly. He only wished there was something he could do about it.

Whit went to the hospital every day to try to see Carlos, but his cousin absolutely refused to have him there. Whit resigned himself to just calling the hospital at least once a day to see how Carlos was progressing, and he became familiar with some of the nurses who worked regular shifts in the ICU. They reported that Carlos was doing as well as could be expected physically, but he exhibited many classic signs of depression. They also reported that no one except Whit had even attempted to visit him. Whit wrote Carlos some letters that he hoped might make a difference, but a nurse told him frankly that she knew for a fact that Carlos had torn the letters to pieces and thrown them into the garbage without a single glance. Whit then resigned himself to just praying very hard for Carlos, although he did continue his regular phone calls to the hospital to remain apprised of his progress. When he knew that a date had been set for Carlos to be moved to a secure rehabilitation facility in order for him to learn how to manage his altered way of life, he invested in a renewed hope that his cousin might then be ready to see a familiar face and accept some help from Whit.

Meanwhile, Whit's mother's condition became steadily worse, and Claudia's well-being went downhill significantly after the sudden death of her sister. She'd not taken the news of Sofia's death well, especially when she knew that violence had been to blame. Whit tried to reassure Claudia that if Sofia's heart was weak enough to stop beating under such circumstances, it likely wouldn't have lasted much longer under *any* circumstances. But Claudia wouldn't be convinced, and her health declined; it was as if she had lost her will to live. One of her sisters was dead, and the other one couldn't remember she even had a family. One of her sons was completely lost in the world of drugs and violence, and the other was crippled from that same violence and refused to even take a phone call from his mother.

In spite of all the drama, Whit was grateful for the sanctity of his own home, the love of his sweet wife, and his beautiful children. The baby was thriving, Mary's health was improving, Adrienne was enjoying school, and by all accounts was happy and well-adjusted. And Whit also enjoyed his work. Gardening was in his spirit, and the time he spent there five days a week was fulfilling and satisfying, even if he was mostly just trying to conquer weeds or nurture struggling shrubbery.

As they were heading into the holidays, Whit went with Mary to a final follow-up visit with the specialist who had delivered the baby. He reported that everything appeared to be in order, and Mary seemed to be in good health. As their brief visit was winding down, Mary said to him, "Do you mind my asking . . . from a medical perspective, after what happened, and considering my age, would you recommend that I not have any more children?"

"That's a difficult question for a man in my position to answer," the doctor said. "Logically . . . medically . . . the odds of your having problems with another pregnancy would probably be very high. Given your age and the likelihood that such problems tend to repeat themselves, it would probably be wise to not have any more children. *However,*" he raised a finger, "you're looking at a man who was born *after* a doctor told my mother not to have any more children. So how can I say for certain? My medical opinion is that you should do something to permanently prevent any future pregnancies. My personal opinion is that the two of you need to make that decision together and be sure about it before you move forward either way." He chuckled and added, "You can't quote me on that personal opinion. It's only my medical opinion that's on the record."

"We understand," Whit said. "Thank you." He considered for a long moment whether he should say what was on his mind, then decided that when in doubt about such a thing, you should just go for it. "Doctor? Are you . . . a religious man?"

"Not particularly," he said, not sounding at all offended by the question. "But I do believe in miracles. I've been in this business too long to not believe that someone or something a lot more powerful than I am is in control."

"Amen," Mary said.

Whit pulled a card out of his pocket, something that he always carried with him. "We believe in miracles too, Doctor. And we're very grateful for all you've done for us." He held the card out. "Sometime when you're on the computer and have a few minutes, just check out this website that shares some of our beliefs." The doctor took the card, looking mildly skeptical as he glanced at it. Whit added, "Just give it a try. You might be surprised." He felt he had said enough and changed the subject, holding out his hand, "Thank you again." The doctor shook Whit's hand firmly.

"Glad I could help," the doctor said with a chuckle, then added, much to Whit's surprise, "And I'll check this out." He held up the card. "Thank you."

That evening before they went to bed, Whit brought up the conversation with the doctor, wondering how Mary was feeling about the situation. She still firmly insisted that she felt that their family was complete, and she felt spiritually at peace with that decision. Whit agreed and knew that he had felt the same. He figured if they were both getting the same answer through spiritual channels, then it meant that they were making the right decision.

* * *

It was at Christmas time that a little miracle occurred with Carlos. He had been in the rehabilitation center for a couple of weeks, and Whit's home teaching partner, Brother Perez, had asked—as he often did—how Whit's cousin was doing. When Whit gave him the same report, telling him that visits and phone calls were being refused, this good brother told

Whit that a few families in the branch were looking for some service opportunities, and he wondered if they might take Christmas to the rehab center for Carlos. Whit thought it was a great idea, but he felt that he should not go with the little group of branch members who were going to take gifts and goodies and sing carols. As the date approached, however, he felt distinctly prompted that he *should* go; then Mary came to him and said she'd had the same feeling. Once again, he had to conclude that if they were getting the same answers, they had to be on the right path. So they went along as a family, but remained in the background, quietly observing how Carlos was obviously touched and overwhelmed by what was happening.

Whit's heart began to pound when he realized that Carlos had settled down from the initial surprise of this little Christmas party in his honor, and he was taking in more of what was going on around him. When Carlos's eyes settled on Whit, he feared an angry outburst of some kind. In fact, the other adults who had come along to be a part of this project had been warned about the situation and were prepared to handle it carefully. But when Carlos saw his cousin, his eyes got teary and a hesitant smile crept into his countenance.

Whit stepped with some trepidation toward Carlos, then stood in front of him. "Did you do this, man?" Carlos asked.

"It wasn't my idea; we just came along for fun." Carlos looked confused, and Whit said, "I go to church with these people. They've helped me through a lot of tough things. They're good people."

"Yeah," was all Carlos said, but he held out a hand, and Whit grasped it firmly before he bent over and he and Carlos shared some semblance of a quick hug and a strong pat on each other's backs.

"It's good to see you, man," Carlos said. "Thanks for coming . . . and for not giving up on me."

"It's good to see you, too," was all Whit said. He didn't want to make too big of a deal out of it, but he did let Carlos hold the baby, and Carlos became reacquainted with Mary and Adrienne. They had crossed paths a few times during his visits with Claudia. Carlos seemed to enjoy their company and they promised to come back.

Before they left, Carlos quietly asked Whit, "Do you think you could bring Mama to see me . . . for Christmas?"

In all honesty, Whit had to say, "She hasn't been doing very well, but . . . I know she really wants to see you. I will see if she's up to it."

"Thanks, man," Carlos said.

"No problem," Whit said. He wondered if it would be more practical for Carlos to go see his mother; he was certainly strong enough to help his cousin in and out of a vehicle. But as soon as the thought occurred to him, he knew it wasn't a good idea. Carlos would know that his brother and cousins sometimes went to visit Claudia, and he would not risk running into them. Carlos surely felt safer here, and Whit would certainly honor that. He had a distinct impression that he shouldn't even suggest such an idea.

In the truck on the way home, Whit and Mary marveled over the miracle, and they both agreed that perhaps now they could work on not only visiting Carlos regularly, but perhaps even work toward helping him find a better life.

Claudia was eager to see her son for Christmas, and she mustered up the strength to go to the rehab center. A couple of the nurses graciously assisted her in getting dressed up and fixing her hair, and Whit and Mary picked her up and drove her to the rehab facility. Whit had to practically lift her in and out of the truck, and they used a wheelchair on loan from the care center, since she was simply too weak to walk more than a few steps. The visit went well in spite of Claudia being overly emotional, but she was so thoroughly worn out by the visit that Whit couldn't imagine her ever having the strength to leave the care center again.

Of course they visited Ida for Christmas and took gifts, but she didn't recognize them any more then than she ever did. They had all learned to just give her unconditional love with no expectations, and they figured that if she felt any joy from their visits it was a good thing, even though she considered herself a stranger to them. Her health was rapidly deteriorating, and they knew that her time on earth was rapidly winding down.

Whit began visiting Carlos regularly, even though their conversations usually didn't go beyond discussing the weather and cracking jokes about wheelchairs and being crippled. Whit knew these attempts at humor were Carlos's way of trying to cope with his situation. He knew Carlos had received some counseling as part of the rehab program, and he believed it was making a difference. He was amazed during one visit to hear Carlos mention that "Perez" had been coming to see him a couple of times a week.

"Alejandro Perez?" Whit asked. "From my church?"

"Yeah, that's him," Carlos said casually, then changed the subject.

Whit called Alejandro later and asked him about it. He simply answered, "I thought he could use some company." And *he* changed the subject. Whit was truly amazed at such charity being so humbly exercised.

A few weeks into January, Whit knew he shouldn't have actually said aloud to Mary that things were going much better. They got a call less than an hour later from Mr. Lostin, asking if he could come over and talk to them. Mary knew the man well enough to know from his tone of voice on the phone that he had bad news.

"We both know what it will be," Mary said to Whit while she methodically rinsed dishes and put them into the dishwasher. "We've both known that living in this house was temporary. It's been good, but we knew it couldn't last forever."

Whit sighed and leaned against the counter, folding his arms over his chest. "Yes, I'm sure you're right." They both remained thoughtfully silent until he said, "But you know . . . it doesn't take much thought to consider that getting away from this house could be a good thing." He sighed again. "That doesn't mean it will be easy, but . . ." He realized Mary was crying and attempting to hide her tears from him by turning her back and trying hard not to sniffle. "Hey," he said, putting his hands on her shoulders. "I know this house means a lot to you. I would never make light of how difficult this could be, but . . . maybe that's not even what he wants to talk to us about."

"What else could it possibly be?" she asked, not making any effort to hide her emotion. She grabbed a paper towel to wipe her eyes and blow her nose. Whit eased her into his embrace and held her while she wept openly for a few minutes, then she blew her nose again with another paper towel and threw them both away before she looked out the kitchen window and sighed. "Don't get me wrong. I *do* believe that getting away from this house could be a good thing in many respects, but . . . I grew up here, and you and I have become a family here, and . . ."

"I know," he said, reminding himself that this was one of those moments when he had to overcome his male instinct to try to fix it or talk her out of feeling the way she did. Instead he just needed to listen and let her talk. And talk she did. She rambled for several minutes about memories of her mother and the good times they had shared in this house and in the garden. She talked about how Whit had come to this house seeking employment, and this was where they had met and gotten to know each other. This was where they'd shared celebrations with loved ones, where they'd begun their married life together, and where they had brought their son home from the hospital.

Then, in an obvious shift of mood, her memories drifted toward growing up in this home with an angry and neglectful father, of visiting here after her marriage when her first husband had been equally neglectful and had caused her a great deal of pain. She continued to stare out the window toward the garden while she talked of returning here after the deaths of her husband and daughter, and how cruel her father had been. She showed signs of anger as she spoke of her father's bigotry toward her Hispanic daughter and then her Hispanic husband. And then she finally got to the memories of her father being murdered in this house and the horrible trauma it had caused in their lives. Tears trickled down her face as she recalled in perfect detail how Whit had been taken away by the police after he'd been arrested for the crime and how he'd been under house arrest on these premises while waiting for a trial.

As her tears increased, Whit just handed her another paper towel and continued to listen. She talked and cried for a few more minutes, then turned to face him abruptly. "You're right, Whit. It would be *very* good for us to leave this house. We can hold onto the good memories and get away from any reminders of the bad ones. Maybe it's time we made a new start somewhere else."

"We don't even know yet that leaving will be necessary."

"Maybe we should leave anyway. Maybe it's time."

"Maybe it is," he said, actually feeling a deep relief that he decided to expound on at another time. He'd been feeling mildly unsettled over staying here for a while now, but he hadn't wanted to take Mary away from this place where she was comfortable and at home. He would certainly have regrets about leaving here, but the relief would far outweigh the regrets. Mostly he would be glad to live someplace where his relatives could never find them. He didn't know where that might be, but he had a strong feeling that it was time to relocate. In his heart he hoped that Mr. Lostin *was* coming to tell them it was time to move. He'd initially felt dread when the phone call had come, but while listening to Mary's oration of her memories, his feelings had shifted. He had begun to feel the calm and comforting sensation of the Holy Spirit, guiding him unquestionably to the knowledge that leaving this house was the right thing to do. Or at least it was right to begin preparing for that step—no matter *what* Mr. Lostin had to say to them.

When their visitor arrived, Whit felt calm, and he knew that Mary did too. Whatever Mr. Lostin had to say, they could accept it and deal with it together. They had certainly been through enough together to know that was true.

Once they had exchanged greetings and were seated, Mr. Lostin got right to the point. There had been changes on the board of directors, things were shifting greatly at the company, and the house needed to be sold. There was simply no getting around it any longer. He seemed surprised at how well Whit and Mary took the news, and Whit wished he could explain the principle of the Holy Ghost and how, in just the last hour, it had undoubtedly guided both of them to peace regarding this upcoming change.

Once the initial bad news had been well received, Mr. Lostin regretfully notified them on behalf of the company that they had until the end of February to be out of the house, which was a little more than a month. Of course, this not only meant that they would be without a home but it also meant that Whit would be officially unemployed. Mr. Lostin handed Whit an envelope, explaining that it contained a check for his salary for the remaining time plus a bonus that he had been able to negotiate into the company budget. He all but came out and said that he wished it could make up a bit for how Mary's father had treated her so unfairly, and for a moment it seemed as if he might cry. Whit and Mary both thanked him for his generosity and kindness over the years, and they parted on friendly terms.

After Mr. Lostin left, Whit opened the envelope with some trepidation as Mary hovered close by, holding her breath. They had some money in the bank, but his mother's care had been very expensive, and their portion of the medical bills for the baby's delivery had not been small. Starting over could be expensive, and they had no idea how long Ida would continue to need full-time care. Whit hesitated and looked at Mary, feeling the need to say, "You know, it doesn't matter how much it is. We have been very blessed to live here as long as we have. The Lord has taken very good care of us, and I'm certain He will continue to do so. I know how to work hard and I will do whatever I have to do to see that our needs are met. I mean it, Mary."

She looked into his eyes, and he saw a glisten of tears as a peaceful smile teased her lips. "I know, Whit. I'm not worried. Not only do you work very hard to take care of us—in so many ways—but you also have a great deal of faith. I know we'll be all right, as long as we are together."

Whit smiled in return and kissed her before he resumed his effort to open the envelope but she put her hand over his to stop him, and he looked at her again. "I don't say this very often, but I think of it frequently, and I am going to say it now." The glisten of tears increased, and her voice cracked. "This is one of so many moments when I have to stop and thank God that you are not in prison." She put both her hands on his face. "That very fact makes every day together a miracle, Whit. As long as we are together, we can face anything."

"Amen," his said, his own voice breaking slightly. He kissed her again, then he finally managed to get the envelope open. They both gasped, then laughed and hugged. The bonus was more than another two months' salary. It wasn't a huge amount, but it was certainly some good severance pay, so to speak, and it would help them start over.

That night after the children were both asleep and Whit and Mary had knelt together by the bed to share their usual nighttime prayer, Whit lay looking at the ceiling while cradling Mary's head on his shoulder. A thought occurred to him and he said, "I hate to say this, but if my mother and Claudia didn't need us, I think I would like to move far away from here and *really* make a fresh start, where no one in my family would *ever* find us."

Mary leaned up on her elbow to look down at him through the darkness. "I must admit I had the same thought. If that is how the Spirit is guiding us, then . . . well . . . we *do* know that they are both elderly and struggling. If their need for us being near is temporary, then perhaps we need to simply look for a temporary solution. We can rent an apartment. We can manage with minimal space—put some things in storage if we need to."

"And I could do what I can to find any work at all . . . anything temporary that will make some money without a long-term commitment."

"And we can just take it one step at a time. Then when the time is right, we'll know, and we'll know where to go. Perhaps we could do some searching online and be aware of job openings for a gardener. If we're willing to move anywhere but southern California, something's got to come up."

"And if we're trusting in the Lord to look out for us, then it will come up at the right time."

"Exactly," Mary said with a tone of triumph, as if they'd just concluded weeks of complicated meetings to come to a grand business decision. Perhaps they had, but the guidance of the Spirit had condensed it down immensely. Perhaps the Lord knew that with everything else that had happened in their lives, it was a great tender mercy to not have this life-altering decision be unduly stressful.

"We also have to consider that Carlos needs us, as well. I think until his new way of life is more settled I would not want to be too far away."

"We've already concluded we would be willing to take him in to live with us if necessary, and that decision stands. So, we might just take him with us. We'll just have to see."

"Okay then," Whit said and chuckled. "I will start apartment hunting right away, and I'll keep putting in my hours on the garden. I want to make sure that I've earned what I've been paid for, and we want to leave it in the best condition possible in order to facilitate the sale of the house."

"And I will start sorting and packing," Mary declared. "There is a lot in the house that belonged to my parents that can just be donated to Goodwill. There are only a few things that hold sentimental value for me. It all just needs to be thoroughly sorted, and I can work on that every day, especially if I spend less time in the kitchen."

"We can invest some of that money we were given into getting more takeout food for the next few weeks while we get ready to move."

Mary put her head back on Whit's shoulder and relaxed. "I'm glad that's all settled." She sighed and snuggled closer to him. "Truthfully, there's only one thing I truly regret leaving."

"What's that?" he asked, kissing her brow.

"The garden, of course. It's so beautiful. And it's like a tangible representation of . . ."

"Of what?" he asked when she hesitated to find the words.

"Of your love for us," she said. Now *he* leaned up on *his* elbow as she continued. "You came here to revive the garden. I fell in love with you while that transformation was taking place, and you have admitted to me that you felt like you were doing it for me. And the fountain! I love the fountain! I'll miss that, but . . ." Her words faded into some mild emotion.

"Mary, my love," he said firmly, "I *am* a gardener. That's not going to change. And wherever we go, wherever we end up, I will give you another garden—a place where we can always find respite and peace, where our children can play the way you played in *this* garden when you were a child. I can *always* create a garden, Mary. As long as God has provided soil and sun and water and the glorious variety of plants and flowers that we know He has, I can always put them to good use."

"Oh, of course," she said, touching his face. "What a lovely thought. You're right. And it will give us something to look forward to . . . something to work toward."

"Exactly," he said with a softer tone of triumph. "And," he said dramatically, "we will be taking the fountain with us."

"We can do that?"

"Of course," he insisted as if it were nothing. "Did I not buy it with my own money and bring it here in the back of my truck and install it? I can just as easily uninstall it and take it away. We will put it in storage until we have found a new home and we have a place to put it."

Mary sighed, and Whit relaxed again on the pillow. "Oh, that's a *lovely* thought. We can just imagine *that* when we have difficult moments."

"Imagine *what,* exactly?"

"Imagine throwing our coins into the angel fountain to make our wishes for the rest of our lives, with our children and grandchildren—somewhere far away from the violence and the difficulties of both our pasts."

Whit sighed and held her closer. "That *is* a lovely thought."

With that thought lingering in their minds, they both fell asleep until they were awakened by the baby's cries, signaling his need to be fed. But Whit was surprised to hear his cell phone ring while Mary was changing the baby's diaper. He always left it on, given that the people caring for Claudia and his mother might need to get hold of him in case of any unforeseen problems. Logic dictated that the call had to do with one of them, but as he reached for the phone it occurred to him that it could have something to do with Carlos. His caretakers also had this number.

The person calling introduced herself as a worker at the care center where Claudia had been living for years, although this person had just been hired recently and Whit had never spoken to her before. She then regretfully informed him that one of the nurses had just discovered minutes earlier that Claudia had passed away quietly in her sleep. Whit was struck with dumb silence for a good minute but the woman on the other end was silently patient until he could manage to thank her for letting him know. Then he asked what he needed to do. She informed him that they would follow standard procedure and call a mortuary that had been prearranged with Claudia a long time ago. He could come in the following morning to finalize a few things, and then meet with the mortuary for any details beyond that.

"You are the only contact number I could get hold of," the woman said. "I was told her children aren't generally available. Could you—"

"I can notify them," Whit said, even though he didn't want to talk to Jose at all. But they could hardly get through this without enduring some interaction. Telling Carlos was an entirely different matter. But he was the only one who had any contact with Carlos at all, so of course it was up to him to handle this.

Whit forced himself to his senses and hurried to clarify, "I will take care of it. Please don't worry about trying to get hold of them. Thank you for calling, and for all that you do. Please pass along my gratitude to the staff. They've been very kind."

"I'll do that," she said. "I only met Claudia a couple of times, but she was a very sweet woman."

"Yes," Whit said and heard the emotion seeping into his voice. "Yes, she was."

He hung up the phone and hung his head and wept for only a moment before he heard Mary say, "What's happened?"

He looked up to see her holding the baby, who was fussing for want of his feeding.

An eerie feeling assailed him as he thought of their conversation earlier about Claudia being one of their reasons for needing to remain in the area. It took him a long moment to gather his thoughts into words. "Um . . . it's Claudia. She's . . . gone."

"Oh, Whit." She said the words on a long exhale. "Are you all right?"

"Um . . . yeah," he said, his voice breaking. "I just . . ."

While he was gathering his thoughts, Mary sat down and leaned against the headboard of the bed to nurse the baby, which quieted him immediately.

"It's a blessing, of course. We've been praying for this for her . . . we know she's free of all her worry and turmoil now. It's just . . ."

"I know," she said, confronted with her own onslaught of tears. He was glad she *did* know, because he honestly couldn't come up with the words. Instead of trying to talk about it, he just got into the bed beside her and wrapped his arms around her waist, holding her close while she fed the baby. She pressed her free hand repeatedly through his hair while they both cried silent tears. Once baby Christian was fed and back to sleep, Mary put him back in his crib then returned and flipped off the lamp before she got back into bed and eased her arms around Whit.

"You know," he said, "I feel much the same as I did about Sofia. I feel more grief in thinking of the hardships of her life than I do about her dying. I have some wonderful memories of good times with her when I was younger. But most of the memories also have difficult associations mingled with them, and now I know the best of her will have the opportunity to be nurtured, and she can finally have true and lasting peace. I'm glad she's gone. I'll just . . . miss her. But I won't miss worrying about her, or trying to convince her that everything will be all right when I have no idea if it will be. Well, it *will* be all right where she is now. It's those of us left in mortality that have to deal with all the . . . garbage."

"That's well said," she muttered quietly. "I suppose it falls on you to tell the family."

"Yeah," Whit said with chagrin. "And I'll need to make whatever arrangements need to be made. No one else will do it. Carlos would if he could, but . . ." Whit groaned. "This is going to be really tough for him. I think I'm worried about him more than anything else."

"We will do everything we can to help him through this."

"I know," Whit said and kissed her brow. "You're amazing, you know. I love you for the way you have been so loving to my family . . . in all their dysfunctional glory."

"The few that I know have many sweet and redeeming qualities; they're not so hard to love."

"I know, but not everyone would see it that way. I'm just grateful that you do."

Whit didn't think he would be able to go back to sleep, but he actually did. All the lack of sleep created by having an infant had apparently caught up with him. When morning came, he managed to eat a little breakfast before he made a few phone calls, then he made certain everything was under control with his family before he left to go to the care center and to visit Carlos, and then he had an appointment with the mortuary.

Whit arrived at the care center and was informed that Jose had responded to a message that had been left for him, and he had been to the care center and had caused a bit of scene. In the words of the woman Whit talked to, he had "been drunk or maybe stoned and was demanding to know where his mother's money was hidden, because now that she was dead, he was entitled to it." Jose had been escorted out by security, then picked up by the police and was probably in lockup for disorderly conduct.

Whit was pleased with that last part. Life was the most peaceful when his cousins were in police custody. It could actually be a blessing if Jose was out of commission long enough for his mother's burial to take place. He was grateful—not for the first time—that Claudia had eagerly given him power of attorney years earlier. It would eliminate some of the complications he had dealt with in regard to Sofia's burial. In this case, Claudia had no remaining assets. They had all been used up for her care, and she had mostly been living on government aid. The costs for her burial had been paid for in advance, and she had chosen her own casket and simple headstone a long time ago. Nothing Jose did or didn't do would change any of that.

Whit boxed up Claudia's very few belongings that had any sentimental value, and he left the rest—some books and clothing and a couple of afghans—with the care center to be used by other residents there. He would have Carlos look through her things when he was ready and keep whatever he wanted. But he would save that for another time. He then went to visit Carlos at the rehab center and found him sitting in a wheelchair, staring out the window. It seemed to be all he did except when he was actually enduring the rehabilitation exercises.

"Hello," Whit said when it became obvious that Carlos hadn't heard him come into the room.

"What's up, bro?" Carlos asked, barely glancing at him in acknowledgment.

"I have some difficult news," Whit said soberly, not wanting to beat around the bush.

Carlos looked up at him with a furrowed brow. "Someone died?" he asked, completely serious. Whit felt a moment of sadness to think of how many times such news had been a part of their family experiences, and most of those deaths had been violent. He was glad at least that this one hadn't been.

"Your mother," he said, and Carlos's eyes widened before they filled with tears and he turned away abruptly as if he were ashamed of his emotion. "Go ahead and cry, cousin. I have been. We're both going to miss her."

"What happened?" Carlos asked.

"She died in her sleep."

Carlos nodded, and Whit could hear him sniffling. He discreetly handed his cousin a tissue and Carlos took it before he said, "At least she went peacefully, right?"

"Right," Whit said and sat down on a chair that he moved close to Carlos's side, positioning it so he could face him. But Carlos turned his wheelchair slightly so that he could look the other way.

They sat together in silence for several minutes, while Whit handed Carlos a few more tissues and just allowed him to vent his grief. He prayed silently for Carlos—that he could find some peace, some comfort, some hope. And he still couldn't help hoping that Carlos might have some inner strength that could help him reach beyond all of this and turn his life around.

Carlos suddenly took a deep breath and straightened his back. "I shoulda been there for her, man. She was a good lady, you know. She deserved better than she got."

"She *was* a good lady; she still is. Her spirit lives on, you know. And she *did* deserve better than the life she lived. But God will make up for that. She's at peace; she's in a better place. And as for what you did or didn't do, it's difficult to measure such things, given the way we were raised. In my own opinion you did a whole lot better than anyone else in this family. Remember how you would take her those cookie-dough shakes she liked so much, and you'd take her out to eat, and for rides. She loved it when you took her for rides."

"Those was good times," Carlos said, then added with sharp self-ridicule, "then I went and got myself shot and ended up crippled and couldn't do nothin' for her! Nothin'!"

"Now you listen, and you listen good," Whit said, and Carlos looked at him in response to his firm tone. "Getting shot was not your fault. Is that what you've been sitting here thinking? That this was your fault?"

"I was in the middle of it all when I knew I shouldn't o' been."

"I don't know what went down, Carlos. And I don't really want to know. But you were always the best of them. Whatever you did, you didn't deserve *this*. You *didn't!* Do you hear me?"

"I coulda been better, man. I *shoulda* been better."

"And how exactly do you think you would have gone about that?" Whit asked, knowing from vast personal experience that undoing such a life was like changing the Nile in its course. Possible, but not very probable.

"I don't know!" Carlos said and hit the arms of his wheelchair with clenched fists. "But I shoulda done it! I wondered a hundred times what I could do t' get out, but I shoulda asked. I shoulda tried harder! I shoulda been there for her!" His anger melted into an immediate visible sorrow as he looked at Whit with the bewildered eyes of a child. "I shoulda been more like you."

Tears welled up in Carlos's eyes again and he was silent for long moments without breaking eye contact. Whit could barely breathe, much less speak. Something deep and powerful and profound was happening inside of Carlos; he was tapping into a level of self-honesty that most gang-hardened kids could never achieve. Whit had been praying for it to happen, but a part of him had never believed it would. But even then, he'd never imagined any conversation taking *this* turn.

He had no doubt that whatever charity Alejandro had sincerely and humbly offered to Carlos surely had to have contributed to this moment. He couldn't even imagine what to say in response to something like that. He was relieved when Carlos added fervidly, "I wanted to ask you about a hundred times, man, what you did to get out, but I was scared, you know. I saw what they put you through. Sometimes I thought it would be worth it just to get away and have a real life, you know? But most of the time I just knew I couldn't do it. I'm not like you, bro; I'm not as strong as you."

Whit scooted his chair closer, leaned toward his cousin, and put a hand over his arm, saying with all the fervency that he felt, "You can do *anything*, Carlos. *Anything!* You want to know how I did it? I will tell you! I will teach you! I will be right by your side all the way! I won't mess around with back and forth, bro. It's got to be all or nothing. But if you are really willing to change . . . if you are ready to let that life go—completely and for good—I will be there with you, man. I will! Just say the word!"

Carlos gave him a hard look, filled with the skepticism and distrust that Whit understood well. He was examining those street-hardened instincts to try to determine if Whit really meant it, if he could really trust him. Whit saw his cousin's expression soften, and new tears glistened faintly in his dark eyes. "What have I got to lose, man?" He threw his hands up then dropped them in his lap. "I got nothin'. You're the only one who comes to see me, the only one who cares." He let out a sardonic chuckle. "I don't have t' do nothin' t' leave that life. It left me when I ended up crippled. What am I gonna do? Sit in some handicapped parking spot an' deal?"

"It happens," Whit said. "In spite of how your life has changed, you still have to make a choice. You still have to mean it. Because you never know when one of them will show up and get in your face and try to lure you back into that world. Do you hear what I'm saying?"

"I hear you," Carlos said, his voice cracking. "I been thinkin' about it a lot." He threw up his hands again. "What else have I got t' do? And now . . ." his voice cracked even more, "Mama's gone. You're all I got, man. And I wanna know how you did it. I really want t' know."

Whit looked deeply into his eyes, attempting to measure his sincerity. He not only undoubtedly found it there, but he felt a huge rush of warmth from the Spirit, and he threw his arms around his cousin and hugged him tightly. Carlos hesitated a moment, then put his arms around Whit and returned the brotherly embrace. He held tightly to Whit as if he didn't want to let go, and then he started to cry. Whit just held on to him and allowed him to express his grief, silently thanking God for this miracle. If losing the use of his legs could bring Carlos to a new and better life, then Whit considered that a price worth paying. He prayed that with time, Carlos would be able to see it the same way.

Chapter Eight

WHIT CAREFULLY CONSIDERED HOW TO go about seeing that Claudia's burial was taken care of. He had control this time, but that didn't mean Jose wouldn't cause trouble in one way or another. He talked it over with Mary and concluded that just doing a graveside service, as they had done for Sofia, was best. There were not many people that would attend, and avoiding any kind of formal service would help prevent more opportunity for family members to create problems. Once again Whit had to emphatically insist that Mary not attend. She understood, but it saddened her, especially when she had grown to care for his aunts more than most of their own children ever had. She was consoled by knowing that in their newfound sphere beyond the veil, these sweet women would surely be mindful of her and know of her love for them.

Whit had a careful conversation with Carlos about attending his mother's service. Initially Carlos insisted that he wouldn't go—that he didn't want anyone in the family to see him this way. Whit sensed there was more to it than that. He still knew next to nothing about what had happened the day Carlos had been shot, but he believed there were reasons why he didn't want to face his brother and cousins again due to whatever had happened and why. Whit hoped to be able to eventually help Carlos cross the bridge of coming to terms with that day, but that was somewhere in the future.

Together they devised a plan for Whit to take Carlos to the cemetery for the brief service. Carlos had become quite efficient at transferring in and out of a car; Whit's truck was a little more challenging because it was higher off the ground, but Whit had taken him out before and they had become pretty adept at getting him into and out of the truck. Whit knew how to unobtrusively give him the minimal help he needed. They would show up, keep to themselves, and leave. Whit would be giving a prayer to dedicate the grave, just as he'd done for Sofia. Other than that, the brief service was up to the priest of the church that Claudia had attended until she'd gone into the care center. Carlos admitted that he was nervous, but he also said with some anger that maybe it was good for his brother and cousins to see what their criminal involvements had done to him. He put some colorful words into the sentence that Whit tried to block out, but he couldn't deny that he felt the same way. He knew it wouldn't change anything, but he still thought that they should actually see with their own eyes the fact that Carlos was permanently crippled due to their bad choices.

The day of Claudia's burial came and went uneventfully. Mary had taken the initiative to buy Carlos a new button-up shirt and tie and slacks, and even shoes that he could wear. He declared that he really liked all her choices, and when Whit helped him put the tie on, they both agreed that Mary not only had good taste but maybe some foresight as well in helping him create a new look for himself.

Whit kept silent about the conversation he'd shared with Mary regarding their hope that Carlos might one day be able to use these clothes to attend church. Whit didn't know whether it would ever happen—and even if it did, it would likely be a long time in the future. But it was something worth working toward, and he prayed it would happen eventually.

Carlos maintained quiet dignity while he encountered family members who would hardly look at him, let alone speak to him. But there was a stark quiet among the family members gathered that hadn't been there when Sofia had been buried. Whit wondered if it was Carlos's presence that made the difference. As always, it was startling for Whit to see his cousins with their spouses and children; it was often easy to forget that they had families of their own—a new generation being raised in violence and dysfunction. Whit probably forgot because he had to force himself not to think about it.

The service ended quickly, and Whit came away with a fresh dislike for the hollow words spoken by the priest in charge—words that were devoid of any real hope on behalf of those who had passed on or for their loved ones who remained. The priest had clearly stated that the relationships the family had shared on earth had now come to an end, and in the afterlife it was strictly heaven or hell, judged by a harsh and unloving God—and they could only hope that Claudia had not gone to hell.

Driving away from the cemetery with Carlos, Whit broke the glum silence by declaring, "I just have to say that I don't agree with him . . . with what he said. I highly respect other people's right to worship any way they choose, and if people believe in this guy and the church he represents, that's their choice. But I want you to know that I don't agree with him. I know, Carlos, that your mother is in a better place, that God loves her and He loves you; He loves all of us. And I believe that . . . no, I *know* that we have the opportunity to be with our loved ones in the next life. What point is there to *this* life if we can't continue relationships with the people we love?"

"You really believe that?" Carlos asked after thinking about it for a minute.

"I really do," Whit said, then they settled back into silence and nothing more was said until they got back to the rehab center.

"Are you okay?" Whit asked him.

"Yeah," was all Carlos said, and he didn't seem to want to talk. Whit hung around for a while until Carlos came right out and said he just wanted to be alone, but Whit promised to come back the next day, and Carlos said he'd look forward to it. As Whit turned to leave the room, Carlos said, "Hey. Thanks, man. You been real good to me."

"We're family, Carlos," Whit said. Knowing better than to get too mushy, he just added, "I'll see you tomorrow." He stepped out the door, then on a hunch, he turned around and quickly added one more thing. "I pray for you, bro; just thought you should know." Carlos looked surprised, but Whit felt it was best not to expound. He had *always* prayed for Carlos, for all of his family members. But he'd never told any of them; none of them would have cared. Perhaps Carlos was now in a position to know that he was being prayed for; perhaps now it would matter to him.

With Claudia now resting in peace, Whit and Mary set to work to follow through on their plan to make some big changes in their lives. They continued visits to Carlos and Whit's mother, and Whit continued working his regular hours in the garden in order to honestly earn the money he'd been given as a salary. He knew Mr. Lostin wouldn't know the difference, but he also knew Mr. Lostin believed him to be a man of integrity, and he certainly wanted to be that. Above all else, God knew the hours he put in, and he would not leave this house and this job and the great blessing both had been to him without knowing he had done his very best—and perhaps better.

When things had settled down a little, Mary called Janel and had a long talk with her, catching her up on all that had happened and their plans to move. The two women talked on the phone at least once a week, and Whit also had conversations with Janel here and there. She still felt like family to them, and they knew they would always keep in touch. Janel was excited for the new beginning that was before them, and she was also happy to report that her own family members were doing well and that she had made the decision to stay permanently where she was. They all got along well, and she had a sense of belonging there. They all agreed that was good news, and once again expressed their mutual gratitude for modern technology and how it was possible to share letters, photos, and videos via the Internet.

Whit continued to feel haunted by the unsolved mystery of his father-in-law's death—and the very idea that he could have served a life sentence for it. He didn't mention his feelings to Mary because there was nothing new to say, and he didn't want to trouble her with any kind of worry or concern. He prayed that he would be guided by the Spirit either to find some new information that might shed understanding on what had happened that night, or if that were not possible, that he would be able to find peace over it and stop feeling this way. But peace eluded him, and he didn't want Mary to know how often he got up in the night to check the house and make certain his wife and children were safe. Or maybe she knew, and was simply choosing to avoid the topic as well. Either way, he just kept praying and moving forward, knowing there was nothing he could realistically do about the dilemma. Besides, there were other things that needed his immediate attention.

Mary continued to sort and pack, and they worked together to care for the children and keep up with their Church callings. Together they served in the nursery on Sundays, and they took their home teaching and visiting teaching assignments very seriously. Whenever it was feasible, they accepted Cinda's offer to babysit while they attended a session at the temple. The gospel was the strongest bond between them, and living it to the best of their ability was what they believed would keep their marriage and family strong. God had blessed them greatly and protected them from horrible things. They both felt they owed Him much and the very few hours they spent each week in service in the Church was a small price to pay, indeed. Mary also kept up with her humanitarian efforts, and she felt blessed to be able to manage it while handling everything else. She was also glad to know that she could continue her work no matter where she lived.

In the midst of all this, they were both actively engaged in searching for a place to live temporarily in the area, and they were also looking online for local job opportunities for Whit; in addition, they were sending his resumé out to several places around the country where a job opportunity might arise that could take them away. They talked to Carlos about how they were planning to take him with them when they left, and they were surprised with how thoroughly enchanted he was with the idea. While worried about being a burden to Whit and his family, he could humbly admit that he was grateful for their willingness to take him in. Whit couldn't help thinking more and more that Carlos ending up in a wheelchair was the best thing that had ever happened to him. And his hope was increasing that eventually Carlos would agree.

Whit carefully and prayerfully began to talk with Carlos about how he had turned his life around. They started with a conversation that took hours where Whit simply told Carlos his story—how the deaths of his father and brother had impacted him, how he'd given in to the gang mentality in a distorted effort to channel his anger. He told him about his time in prison and how the genuine caring of certain people had brought him back to the religion that his parents had always lived. Since his mother had married a Mormon, his was the only household in the family that had lived Mormonism, and the others had made it clear they had no interest in the faith.

But now Whit told Carlos in simple terms how it was the gospel and the Atonement of Jesus Christ that had saved him and turned him around. He told Carlos how he'd put his life in order, burned off the visible tattoo, and served a mission for his church. They talked frankly of how the gang Whit had belonged to had not reacted well to his declaration of independence from them. He'd been badly brutalized, resulting in some broken bones and a lot of stitches, but he'd considered it a price he had to pay, and he'd been glad to pay it if it earned him the right to separate himself from them. He told Carlos how he had stood his ground and how he had eventually come to an agreement with the others that they could all live and let live with a kind of grudging respect. Whit had promised to keep all their dirty secrets if they promised to leave him and his family in peace. Carlos had known some of that, but he'd never heard it from Whit's perspective, and his regret for being even minutely involved in any of that prompted many words of remorse. Even though Carlos had not been actively involved in the worst of it, Whit had to work hard to reassure him that it was in the past and he held no blame toward him.

"Truthfully," Whit said, "I don't blame any of them. I've come to see it as a kind of disease. It's like you grow up breathing bad air; it makes you sick and you just can't avoid becoming infected. I feel sorry for them, Carlos. I feel sorry for their kids especially. But I've come to accept that I can't change them; I can't fix it. If there was something I could do, I would do it, but I know in my heart that what I *can* do is protect my own family and make life different for them. If my kids grow up and live *good* lives, then I have made a difference. You can make a difference too, Carlos. You've already endured your punishment. They aren't going to come after you the way they did me, because they know they're to blame and they don't want to stir that pot. You're free now. You don't need them, and they don't want you. But who needs to be wanted by people like that? Think about it. You've lost the use of your legs, but you've gained the opportunity for a new life."

"That's what I want," Carlos said.

"Okay then," Whit said with triumph. "I am going to bring you some stuff to read and we'll keep talking."

Carlos liked that idea, and Whit brought a Book of Mormon on his next visit. He had marked certain scriptures and read them through with Carlos. He knew that his cousin had had *no* exposure to scriptures, and his reading skills were childlike since he'd dropped out of school way too early. But even young Primary children could read and understand much of the Book of Mormon, and Whit gave him specific reading assignments that were not lengthy but contained great truths, and on each subsequent visit they talked about it. Whit just wished he had more time to spend with Carlos, but he sensed some trepidation and hesitation in Carlos, and he wondered if he was moving too fast. Maybe his cousin needed to move more slowly; maybe he needed time to think and digest some of this. He was considering huge changes, and while his physical life had changed dramatically, changing his spirit could be more painful and overwhelming in some ways than what he'd already been through.

Staying busy and moving forward, Whit and Mary continued their quest each day. Finding a place to live seemed the most urgent issue. Whit needed a job, but they had a little money to get by on for a month or two. The house had to be vacated by the end of February, however, and they needed a place with certain minimum requirements. The most difficult requirement to fill was the handicap access Carlos would need. Any house or apartment they could find to rent that was in their price range just wouldn't work. Whit had asked some landlords if they would be all right with him building a wheelchair ramp and adding some amenities to a bathroom. He offered to pay for the additions himself and promised they would look attractive and add value to the property, but only one of them was mildly interested in that option. However, even in that particular case, the home was a long way from the care center where Ida was living, and it wouldn't be available until the middle of March.

Whit and Mary took to praying more fervently for guidance in finding the right place to live but as days passed February came, and no feasible options became available. They kept reminding each other to have faith and to remember that God would take care of them as long as they did their best. Mary pointed out that Mr. Lostin would probably be able to convince the board to let them stay just a couple of weeks longer if that became necessary in acquiring the one house that was a possibility.

"Or," Whit said, "we could stay in a motel for a couple of weeks if we have to. It's far from ideal and it wouldn't be easy or cheap, but we could manage. We were ready to do that when your father was going to kick us out before he . . . died." As soon as Whit said it, he wished that he hadn't. The fact that Mary's father had been angry over his daughter marrying an Hispanic man and was kicking them out of the house had been a heavily labored issue in the courtroom during the trial that had eventually proven that Whit had been innocent of the crime. But the memories were ugly, and the unanswered questions were haunting.

Whit could tell by Mary's eyes that her memories had gone to the same place but she hurried to say, "Yes, we can do that if we have to. Something will work out." Then she quickly distracted herself by getting back to work on her sorting and packing. S and P, she had come to call it. She'd even gone so far as to say that she was employed by the S and P Corporation. Whit thought it was funny, but Adrienne *really* thought it was funny, which was probably why Mary kept referring to it that way.

Adrienne seemed wholly unconcerned with the prospective move. The friends she went to school and church with didn't live that close anyway, and they always had to drive some distance to arrange playtime with any of them. Because they attended the Spanish-speaking branch, the branch boundaries covered a large area. They would prefer to stay within those boundaries, but they knew that might not happen, and since their eventual plan was to leave the city anyway, they didn't figure it would matter much. They could keep in touch with friends from the branch as much as they chose. The Church was true wherever they went, and friendships were forever if they really mattered and were nurtured.

Little Christian was thriving and doing well. He caught a little cold that brought on some sleepless nights and the typical challenges of a baby who couldn't breathe through his nose, but it cleared up without any complications. He was growing quickly and brought so much joy to their family that it was impossible to comprehend how life had been before he had arrived. Whit marveled every day at the blessings of his beautiful family, and he never began or ended a day without thanking God for having Mary and the children in his life. He considered them a gift that was a direct result of his choosing to turn his life around, serve a mission, and commit himself to living the gospel. If he'd not made that choice, he would not have had all that he had now. It was as simple as that. And he knew that God deserved all the credit for enabling him to make such dramatic changes and for blessing his life so abundantly as a result of those changes.

Just into the second week of February, on a particularly pleasant day, Whit was busy in the garden when his cell phone rang. He grabbed it and glanced at the caller ID, surprised to see that it was Alejandro Perez. This was not generally the time he might call to discuss home teaching appointments. Whit answered cheerfully and was surprised again when he asked if he could come by in a while and talk to Whit about something.

"Sure," Whit said. "Just call when you get here, and I'll unlock the gate."

"Great. I'll be there before three."

"See you then," Whit said and hung up. Logic dictated that this might have something to do with Carlos, but he couldn't imagine what. Was there some kind of problem? Oh, how he prayed that this good man's association with his family was not bringing some kind of trouble into Alejandro's life!

He found it difficult to concentrate while he waited for his visitor, frequently glancing at his watch. He had called Mary on her cell phone to let her know that Alejandro was coming then he forced himself to keep pulling weeds. He was startled to hear, "Hello there, brother," and he turned around to see Alejandro standing nearby. "The gate was open.

Mary said I would find you out here." He glanced around. "It's looking pretty good."

"It's getting there," Whit said as he took off his gloves. He motioned toward the patio and said, "Let's sit down."

In the minute it took them to traverse the lengthy stretch of garden back to the patio, they both reported that their families were doing well and agreed that the weather was nice. Once they were seated, Whit got straight to the point. "So, what's going on? It must be important for you to drive all the way out here."

"I wanted to have this conversation face-to-face."

"You're making me nervous," Whit said with a chuckle that exhibited the truth of his statement.

"No need for that." Alejandro chuckled as well. "I'll just get right to it. Suzy and I have talked about it and we want to have Carlos come and stay with us when he gets out of rehab, for as long as he needs . . . until he can figure out a new life."

Whit felt a little breathless. "Wow," he said and chuckled again. "I don't know what I expected you to say, but it wasn't that. Mary and I just figured we would take care of him; we're the only family he's got."

"I know. He told me you had invited him to live with you, and I'm sure you would manage; you always do. But . . . this house doesn't have wheelchair access, and you're moving soon. My house *does* have ramps and stuff because we had Suzy's dad with us before he died. When he moved in he gave us the money to have all that stuff remodeled for that reason. We like Carlos. And I think he likes us. Why don't you let him stay with us at least until you move and get settled, and then we'll see how it's going."

Whit still had trouble taking this in. He didn't know if it was the incredible generosity and charity of this man and his dear wife, or if he just felt disoriented over considering all of the facets of the situation. "Have you talked to Carlos?" he asked, buying himself a little more time to try to sort out his deeper thoughts.

"I mentioned it as a possibility and asked him what he thought."

"And?"

"What do you think he said?" Alejandro countered with a little laugh.

"He probably doesn't want to 'be no trouble to nobody,'" Whit said, doing a fairly accurate imitation of his cousin that made Alejandro laugh again.

"That's about it, but he admitted that he needs help and he has nowhere to go. He knows that you would do anything for him, but he also knows the situation with your needing to move, and he's worried about making it harder for you."

Whit remained thoughtfully silent for a long minute until Alejandro asked, "Is there a problem?"

"You know Carlos's background, right? I mean . . . you do know how he ended up in this condition, right?"

"Yeah, I know."

"And you're not worried that his associations might catch up with him? Cause problems for you and your family?"

"As far as I know, not one of them knows where to find him now. How would they find him when he leaves there? He doesn't want anything to do with them. No, I'm not worried. They don't know where *you* live, right?"

"I've had to take some careful precautions," Whit said. "What if you're out with Carlos and someone recognizes him and follows you home? You always have to be looking in your rearview mirror—literally and figuratively. I don't know what happened when Carlos got shot, but I know there's more to it than what he's told me." Whit leaned back, sighed deeply, and added, "You also have to remember that a murder occurred in my home, and I nearly went to prison for it. I don't know for sure whether any of them know where I live. I am still haunted by the fact that I have no idea what happened that night."

"Then maybe you should figure it out," Alejandro said, as if that were the most important point of the conversation. It only took a moment's thought for Whit to earnestly know that he had done everything he could possibly do without endangering himself or his family. The matter was in God's hands.

Whit ignored the issue and moved past it. "Logically I don't believe there's any reason to fear that anyone cares where Carlos is, or that they ever will again. He's become useless to them. I just want you to be sure that this is right, and—"

"Listen to me," Alejandro said and leaned forward, looking Whit squarely in the eye. "Suzy and I aren't so naive about this gang stuff. We'll just leave it at that. But more important, we've prayed about this, and fasted too. We didn't want to even bring it up unless we were sure it was right, and we are. If God wants us to take Carlos into our home, then we have to believe He will protect us. And we believe He will. I just need to know if you're okay with that. We just want to help him with this adjustment. Since we took care of Suzy's dad, we have some experience with the whole wheelchair thing, and with Suzy working where she does, she might be able to help him get a job eventually. Let's just do it until you move and get settled, and then see how things are."

Whit took all that in and couldn't come up with a single protest. What he felt most prominently was relief, because he honestly hadn't known how they would handle caring for Carlos with everything else that was going on. But he would have done it, and he knew that God would have helped him if there had been no other way. Well, obviously there *was* another way, and God was setting it before him as a merciful gift. Truthfully, he believed that Brother and Sister Perez had a lot better chance of influencing Carlos for good than he could. He and Carlos had too much history, and a lot of it was ugly. But these good people only knew the Carlos who had been humbled by this dramatic change in his life that had rendered him utterly helpless. Perhaps they had a chance to help him change.

"I think this is an answer to many prayers," Whit said. "If you're sure—and you obviously are—then I think that this is a great blessing for us, and especially for Carlos. All I can say is thank you." Alejandro smiled as if having the privilege of caring for Carlos truly made him happy. "And promise me that you'll be honest with me, and if problems arise, you'll talk to me so we can solve them together."

"I promise," Alejandro said and stood, holding out his hand to shake Whit's as he stood also, then they shared a brotherly embrace and Whit walked him out to his car.

Whit walked back into the house where Mary was waiting with her curiosity piqued. "I must know what that was all about. From the window your conversation looked pretty intense."

"Carlos is going to stay with Alejandro and Suzy . . . at least until we get settled."

"Really?" Mary asked and put a hand over her heart. "I've been so worried about how we would manage—more than I wanted to admit. And I didn't want Carlos to feel like he was falling through the cracks, so to speak, while we get settled. He's already struggling so much with feeling like a burden, and . . ." Her voice broke slightly.

"I know what you mean," he said. "But why didn't you say something?"

"Because I didn't want my concerns to make this more difficult for you. And you know that I would gladly take him in for the rest of his life if it's necessary."

"I know," he said and wrapped her in his arms, "which is one of a thousand reasons why I love you."

A few days later, Whit and Mary spent most of the day helping move Carlos from the rehab center to the Perez home. Alejandro and Suzy and their two teenaged children were eager and excited to have Carlos in their home, and they all behaved as if it were a holiday to have him move in. Alejandro and Whit helped Carlos figure out how to maneuver around the places in the house where he would need to go. He had come a long way and been well trained in caring for himself, and it was rare when he couldn't manage on his own; he'd also become very comfortable with both Alejandro and Suzy, and he seemed confident in his new surroundings. In fact, Whit could have sworn there were a couple of times when Carlos was trying very hard not to cry.

Whit wondered what the source of Carlos's emotion might be. He hoped it was gratitude, and perhaps he was even feeling a glimpse of the Spirit that was abundantly present in the Perez home. Whit had told Mary that there was no better way to convince someone of the truthfulness of the gospel than to have them live in an LDS home where the gospel was actively being lived. And Whit knew the full reality of the stark contrast between living in such a home and the kind of home in which Carlos had grown up. Claudia had tried her best; she'd had good intentions and had certainly loved her children, but other influences had been far too strong and they were all Carlos had ever really known.

After Carlos had settled in and gained some familiarity with his surroundings, they all barbecued hamburgers and shared a tasty meal that was accompanied by a great deal of fun and laughter that complemented the good food. Whit kept looking at Carlos and tried to imagine all of this through his eyes, then he tried to recount the circumstances that had combined to make all of this come together. God surely worked in mysterious ways.

The following Sunday, Whit and Mary walked into the chapel for sacrament meeting to see Carlos in his wheelchair, sitting at the end of the back row next to the Perez family.

"If I faint you'll have to catch me," Whit said to Mary while they both stood frozen and flabbergasted.

"I can't," she said, unable to move. "I'm holding the baby."

"I think a part of me never believed it would happen, and I certainly never thought it would happen so quickly."

Mary chuckled, regaining her composure. "Oh ye of little faith!" she said and hurried toward Carlos to greet him.

Carlos gave Mary a big smile before she hugged him, then he said proudly, "I wore the clothes you bought me." He smoothed his tie as he said it, and Whit suddenly felt deeply moved, almost to tears. He had *never* believed that he would ever see *any* member of his family inside a Mormon church. *Never!* At least not in this lifetime. But Mary had been right. Maybe he *did* need more faith. It was a miracle for sure. He hoped and prayed the miracle would come to full fruition, and that with time Carlos might embrace the gospel and fully accept all of its blessings into his life.

Whit shook Carlos's hand and smiled widely at him. Their handshake was the kind that two brothers of the gospel would share, not the kind that members of the same gang would exchange. That in itself felt deeply significant to Whit. "You clean up pretty good," he said to Carlos.

"Yeah," Carlos said, smoothing his tie again.

Since there was room on the bench with the Perez family, Whit and Mary sat there as well. While Mary was getting Adrienne and the baby settled for the meeting, Whit leaned over to Alejandro and whispered, "How did you manage this?"

"Oh, it was rough," Alejandro said with light sarcasm. "I asked, 'You want to go to church with us, bro?' and he said, 'Yeah, that'd be cool, bro.'"

"Seriously?"

"Seriously. What did you think I did? Threaten to not feed him if he didn't come?"

"Maybe," Whit said and chuckled. "Well, it's a miracle; that's for sure."

"I didn't do it," Alejandro said humbly.

"Oh, I know who deserves the credit, *bro*. But you are making a huge difference in his life—a difference I'm not sure I could make."

Alejandro just smiled slightly and said, "It's all just part of the good news . . . *bro.*"

Whit felt close to tears again as the meeting began. He kept discreetly looking down the bench to the end where Carlos was sitting. He appeared to be interested, and during the songs he was actually singing—or trying to—and sharing a hymnbook with Alejandro's son.

During the closing hymn, Alejandro whispered to Whit, "I need to see if he wants to go home. I don't know if he's up to the other meetings."

"Physically or spiritually?"

"Both maybe."

"If he needs to go home, I'll take him," Whit said, but when the meeting was over Carlos insisted that he wanted to stay, that he liked being there; the people were nice, and it was better than what was on TV.

After church, the two families chatted out in the parking lot and decided to combine what they'd both been planning to do for Sunday dinner and eat together. Whit and Mary went home to change their clothes and get their food and some things for the baby, then they went to the Perez home and spent the remainder of the day. The two families had quickly come to feel like one, with Carlos being the common bond. And the evidence of the miracles deepened as Carlos brought up a couple of questions in the midst of casual conversation that provoked a lengthy gospel discussion. The most remarkable moment was when Alejandro and Suzy's son bore a firm testimony to Carlos of the power of the Book of Mormon and the truthfulness of the gospel. No one spoke for a good couple of minutes after he finished. Carlos was apparently mesmerized, and everyone else was a little stunned by the power of the moment. The baby made a funny noise that broke the tension by provoking laughter, and a while later Whit found Carlos outside on the deck that was just off the kitchen. It was nice that he could go outside and get fresh air without help from anyone else.

"How you doing?" Whit asked.

"Good," Carlos said.

Whit didn't want to make too big of a deal of the changes taking place, mostly because he didn't want Carlos to feel awkward about it. But he did say, "It was great to see you at church. I want you to know it means a lot to me that you went, and I hope you can find some answers there."

"It was good," Carlos said, then he changed the subject. They talked a little about the sporting events he'd been following on TV, how good the Perez family had been to him, and he wondered if it was going to rain.

That night Whit held Mary close to him in bed and they recounted the miracles that were taking place in Carlos's life. Then they talked about how the month was moving along and how they had to be out of the house soon. They said an extra prayer together then went to sleep, mutually wrapped in the faith that everything would work out—somehow.

Chapter Nine

A WEEK LATER WHIT STILL didn't have a job, they still had nowhere to go, and Whit was beginning to feel helpless in regard to providing for his family and seeing that their basic needs were met. He reminded himself that they were far from homeless—they had money that would last a while yet, and he had faith that God would help them. But he was finding it a little more difficult every day to keep believing that it was all going to work out all right. In talking it through with Mary, he had to clarify that he believed everything *would* be all right, but he wondered what kind of refining experiences they might be required to go through before they got to *being* all right.

"Whatever that might be," Mary said with the firm conviction he needed from her, "we will get through this together. I think you're just tired."

"No more tired than you," he said, but she protested, reminding him of the long hours he'd been putting into his work in the garden. In fact, he had actually completed the hours he technically owed to the company that owned the house. But he was mindful of the generous bonus they'd been given, and he wanted the garden to be in as good a condition as possible before they left.

Mary encouraged him to leave it alone for a day or two and do something else. When he refused, she insisted; then she actually ordered him to leave the house. "Go visit your mother," she said. "Just . . . sit with her for a while and do some deep breathing."

Whit found her advice to be a bit strange, but he did it anyway, and he felt it reviving him. His mother mostly ignored his being in the room, but he observed her quietly, indulging in memories of when she had been herself and the closeness they had shared in the years following his mission.

He *did* breathe deeply as he merged his memories of her at her best self with the hope of her being that person again after she passed through the veil. He was then struck with a feeling that rushed into him with such unexpected force that he gasped—the feeling that she would be passing through the veil very soon. Had Mary felt prompted to urge him to spend this time here? Probably. But did she understand the reasons?

When his mother fell asleep, Whit went to find Mr. Silver, the director of the care center, to ask him how his mother was doing medically. It had been more than a week since he'd last checked, and he wondered if there had been any changes. He was told that Ida was sleeping more and more and had very little appetite, which was typical of patients who were approaching death.

"Although," he said, "she has occasionally had a sudden burst of energy and gotten up in the night and become very agitated, pacing and ranting about things that seem to frighten her. It's taken some effort to calm her down."

"She's experienced a lot of frightening things in her life," Whit said with sadness. Then he was struck by an idea that didn't make any sense to him, but he vocalized it before he had hardly thought it through. "Is there anyone in particular who has been with her when this has happened? Someone who might be able to tell us something specific about what might be agitating her?"

"I can do better than that," Mr. Silver said. "We always have cameras running in the patients' rooms that simultaneously record the video surveillance we use to keep them safe. Those recordings are still on the computer because we save them for a week, and it's not yet been a week. I would have to get our technician to locate the exact pieces, but I can do that."

"Would you?" Whit asked. "I don't know why, but I think I'd like to know. Thank you for your time."

Whit went back to his mother's room and watched her sleeping peacefully. He wondered what horrors of the life she'd lived were haunting her, and he wondered if there was any point in his discovering what they were. Was it just a fruitless endeavor that would only give him something else to be haunted by?

The following morning, Whit was doing well at suppressing his worries about his mother and other troubling issues. He was thrilled when Mary announced that they all needed a break. There were a few simple errands that needed to be done, but they weren't complicated and she declared that they should all go out together, complete the errands, have lunch out, and then do something fun. Since it was Saturday and Adrienne didn't have school, it seemed a perfect plan, and Whit was no less enthused about it than Adrienne. In fact, he kissed Mary and said, "You're a genius, Mrs. Eden."

"I have my moments," she said with a smile and kissed him back.

As soon as they'd had breakfast and cleaned things up around the kitchen, they were on their way out of the house. Mary watched Whit efficiently strap Christian into his baby seat in the back seat of the truck, thinking of how she loved such simple moments. She loved the way he talked to his son in silly voices, making an utter fool of himself. Then he made sure Adrienne's seatbelt was securely fastened and tickled her a little, making her giggle before he got into the driver's seat and drove away from the house. Mary took a deep breath, consciously leaving behind all of the craziness of getting ready to move that had been consuming them, as well as the stress of having no idea where they were going to live. She wished that it could be possible to just take Carlos and Whit's mother away from here and become a family of gypsies until they happened upon the right place to settle. It was a silly fantasy, but she'd been indulging in it more and more, and that's exactly where her mind was when she heard Whit say, "What the . . ."

Her heart quickened, knowing he only *almost* swore when something really startled or concerned him. She turned to see him looking in the rearview mirror and pulling over to the side of the road. She turned around to see the flashing lights of a police vehicle right behind them. Her heart began to pound, and her stomach tightened with a dread that was distinctly connected to Whit having been arrested and tried for murder. She didn't even have to ask if he was speeding because she knew he was meticulous about the smallest details in obeying the law. He'd been so dramatically on the other side of the law for so long in his youth that he had swung that pendulum completely in the other direction, and he wouldn't even tempt police attention with a parking violation.

"It's probably nothing," Whit said in a soothing voice, but his gut told him it *wasn't* nothing. He turned to Mary, took her hand tightly and said in a voice that Adrienne couldn't hear, "But if there's a problem I want you to stay calm and know that everything will be all right."

"What are you saying?" she demanded in a quiet panic but by then the officer was at the window, and Whit rolled it down.

"Is there a problem, Officer?" Whit asked with perfect respect.

"License and registration, please," was all he said. Whit handed them over, and the officer walked back to his vehicle with them.

"What's happening, Daddy?" Adrienne asked.

"I don't know, sweetheart. Just look at your book. Everything will be all right."

"What did you mean?" Mary demanded quietly, squeezing his hand as if she might lose him at any second.

"I don't know. I just . . . have a feeling that . . ."

"That what?" she said in barely suppressed panic, spoken in a whisper.

"I don't know, Mary. It's probably nothing. It wouldn't be the first time that I was simply taken in for questioning over something. That would be the worst-case scenario, so . . . just . . . stay calm."

"Easier said than done," she insisted, then they sat in silence until the officer returned.

"Are you Whitmer Eden?" he asked.

"I am," Whit said, his heart thudding. That should have been obvious from the license and registration.

"I need to ask you to get out of the vehicle."

Whit sighed, knowing his instincts were right on. One of his cousins had probably gotten into trouble, and he was guilty by being related until proven innocent.

"Stay calm," he said quietly to Mary as he opened the door, but he could see that she wasn't. "And if I have to leave with him, go home and stay there, and call Donald Vega."

Mary wanted to scream and had difficulty not giving in to hysteria. Donald Vega was the attorney who had represented Whit through all his legal difficulties in the past. He was also a member of their branch and a wonderful man. But why would Whit think that was necessary? She recalled him saying he might be taken in for questioning. Of course having an attorney with him was best. She reminded herself that he was innocent of *any* wrongdoing and tried to do as Whit had ordered and stay calm. She wished she could hear what was being said between Whit and the officer, but the truck door was closed and the window had been rolled up.

Whit stood to face the officer, making sure his persona evidenced complete humility and respect. He knew from experience that arrogance and/or defensiveness brought on nothing but trouble in dealing with the law. "Is there a problem?" Whit asked again, the innocence in his voice completely genuine.

"Are you aware that there is an APB out on this vehicle?"

All-Points Bulletin? Whit wanted to demand to know why, but he simply said, "I had no idea. Is there a reason for—"

"I also have a warrant for your arrest," the officer said.

"What?" Whit demanded, unable to hold back his shock. He wouldn't have been surprised to be taken in for questioning, even though it hadn't happened for years. But a warrant for his arrest? He wondered now if this officer had been waiting just outside of his neighborhood, waiting for him to leave.

"I don't know what it's for," the officer said respectfully, "but I have to take you in."

Whit took a deep breath and hurried to say, "Okay. I'll go with you, but . . . please don't put me in cuffs in front of my family. Just . . . let me speak to my wife a moment."

The officer motioned for him to open the truck door, but he stayed *very* close. Whit opened the door, forced a relaxed voice and expression as he said to Mary, "I need to go with the officer. Everything will be all right. Just . . . go home . . . and call Vega. I love you."

"What's going on, Daddy?" Adrienne asked, now more concerned.

"Everything's all right, sweetheart," he said, then felt the officer's hand on his arm.

Mary slid quickly into the driver's seat, praying frantically and trying to stay focused enough to drive in spite of her pounding heart and churning stomach. She glanced in the rearview mirror to see Whit and the officer just standing near the police vehicle, and she wondered what on earth could be going on. She drove away, feeling like she couldn't return to the sanctuary of her home quickly enough, nor would she be able to call Donald Vega with enough speed.

After Mary had driven away and turned the corner, the officer asked Whit to put his hands on top of the car. He then frisked him and put him into handcuffs. "Thank you for waiting," Whit said.

The officer just made some kind of indiscernible noise in return and guided Whit into the back seat of the vehicle. Once the car was in motion, a tangible sickness washed over Whit. He couldn't begin to imagine what this was about, and he felt horrified to think of Mary enduring the very things that would surely trigger every ugly memory she had concerning her father's death and Whit's subsequent arrest. He turned his mind to prayer, knowing that God was the only one who could really make all of this work out. He could comfort Mary through the Holy Spirit, and be with her while Whit couldn't be there.

* * *

Mary tried to remain calm for Adrienne's benefit while she took the children into the house; she assigned Adrienne to watch over her brother while he played with toys on the floor of the common room so that she could make a phone call. Mary spoke with Donald's receptionist and quickly explained the situation. Less than five minutes later Donald called her back and said he was on his way to the station to find out what was going on.

"Remember, Mary, that Whit knows better than to say anything until I get there, and they are legally required to inform us of the charges before any questioning can begin. He hasn't done anything wrong. We had miracles last time; and this time—whatever it is—is surely insignificant in comparison."

"I pray that you're right," Mary told him. "Thank you. I'm so grateful you're there."

"I will call you as soon as I know something."

Mary thanked him again then had to force herself to be strong for the children. Adrienne's concern was becoming evident. She had been clearly aware of all of the events surrounding Whit's previous arrest; in fact, she had testified on his behalf. She too could be having some difficult memories triggering fear for her now. So Mary distracted her by preparing a picnic they could eat in the garden, since they hadn't been able to go out to lunch. She assured her daughter that as soon as Daddy had a chance to talk with the police officers he would be home. She prayed that was the case and hoped that her emotions were just blowing this all out of proportion.

* * *

Since Whit had been arrested as opposed to just being picked up for questioning, he expected to go through the whole humiliating booking routine when they arrived at the police station. But for more than an hour he was left to wait in a squad room with a lot of desks, a lot of noise, and no one telling him what was going on. There he sat in handcuffs, his mind taken back to the horrors of multiple valid arrests in his past, of his time in prison, of being on trial. But there was a deeper heartache now. He had a family, and all of this was impacting them. He felt despair creeping into him and hurried to turn his thoughts to prayer in order to ward it off. He thought of Paul from the New Testament. He had turned his life around, changed his name, and committed himself to the service of Christ. He had still endured persecution and hardship, but he'd had perfect peace in knowing that he was right with God. He'd always been a hero for Whit, especially since reading his story had contributed hugely to Whit's determination to change his own life. In that moment he found comfort in thinking of Paul, and he called memorized scripture to mind. *For this thing I besought the Lord thrice, that it might depart from me. And he said unto me, My grace is sufficient for thee: for my strength is made perfect in weakness. Most gladly therefore will I rather glory in my infirmities, that the power of Christ may rest upon me. Therefore I take pleasure in infirmities, in reproaches, in necessities, in persecutions, in distresses for Christ's sake: for when I am weak, then am I strong.*

Whit repeated the words in his mind multiple times, mingling them with a prayer that whatever was happening might result in a positive outcome and that he could continue pursuing a respectable life, doing good things for his wife and children and whatever else the Lord might have in mind for him.

Whit became distracted by a noisy ruckus proceeding up the hallway and then into the squad room. In fact it was so noisy that *everyone* became distracted by it. His heart beat wildly and his mouth went dry when he realized that three of his cousins were being walked past him, all in handcuffs, each with two officers at each side as if they knew it would take that much manpower to prevent any problems. Whit had to blink and stare to believe what he was seeing. But there was Claudia's son, Jose, and Sofia's sons, Julio and Angel. Whit waited for them to notice him then felt sick when they did. He saw surprise in each of their faces, then they launched a verbal tirade at him as they moved past, telling him in essence that they knew he thought he was superior to them but he was never going to get away from his family and he would forever be punished for trying to leave. Julio snarled that if they were going down, Whit would go with them. Whit felt nauseous to realize that it was actually possible. He was amazed at how many cruel and taunting words the three of them could manage to throw at him in the short time it took them to be walked past him and down a long hallway. Jose actually spat at him. Thankfully it missed and hit the floor, but Whit was shaken to his very core.

After they could no longer hear the noise his cousins were making, everyone in the room went back to work, for which Whit was grateful. He wondered what all of these people must be thinking of him in regard to what they'd just learned in the last minute about his past and his criminal associates. It was difficult to hold back his tears, and since his hands were cuffed he had no possibility of discreetly wiping them away if they fell. He was startled by a woman's voice saying, "Sorry you had to endure that."

He turned to see a female uniformed officer squatting down to wipe up the spittle off the floor with a paper towel, then she sprayed some cleaner in that spot and wiped it up again with another paper towel. He wished he could clean away the effect of their words so easily. She tossed the dirty paper towels into a wastebasket, then she stood and put the spray bottle on a desk. Whit couldn't speak due to the knot in his throat, but the distraction had helped push back the threat of unwelcome tears.

"Are you hungry?" she asked. "Thirsty? I bet you'd like to get out of those cuffs."

Whit wanted to say *all of the above,* but his cynicism came through as he asked, "What's the catch?"

"No catch. Come with me," she said and took hold of his arm, urging him to his feet.

"Is my attorney here yet?" he asked, realizing she must know what was going on if she was actually taking him somewhere else.

"He is. He's been waiting."

"Waiting for what?"

"I'll take you to talk with him and get you something to eat."

"I'm not hungry," he lied, feeling too nauseous to eat. "Some water would be nice."

"Fair enough," the officer said, then she took Whit into a room where Donald Vega was sitting at a table on one of four chairs.

Vega immediately stood and asked, "Are you okay?"

"Relatively speaking," he said, and the officer unlocked his cuffs. Whit took a quick glance around the room to note there were no cameras and no mirror that would indicate an observation window.

"I'll get you some water," the officer said and left the room, closing the door behind her.

"Do you have *any* idea what is going on?" Whit asked as they both sat down across the table from each other.

"None. They just told me to be patient and we would get everything worked out. That's it. I called Mary and told her that much. She said to tell you she loves you and they're all having a picnic in the garden, and she said they made wishes for you. I assume you know what that means."

Whit was blessed with a clear image of his family picnicking in the beautiful garden and of his wife and daughter throwing coins into the angel fountain and making wishes and saying prayers on his behalf. He missed them, but the image made him feel a little better. Together they waited for another twenty minutes, neither of them having anything to say. The officer brought bottled water and sandwiches for both of them. "Just in case you decide you're hungry," she said. Donald encouraged Whit to eat and he did, glad that it actually helped settle his ongoing nausea a bit. He would have far preferred picnicking in the garden with his family. He thought of the outing they should have been having and felt angry one more time that this kind of thing had interfered with his life. He especially hated the way it impacted Mary and the children. Thankfully, Christian was too young to understand, and he prayed that he might grow up never being aware of such things in his father's life.

Whit was surprised but figured he shouldn't have been when Detective Wilson came into the room and closed the door behind him. "Sorry about all the waiting," he said, and something occurred to Whit. An apology wasn't likely to precede a criminal interrogation, and he was *not* in an interrogation room. And the female officer had apologized to him, as well. While he was trying to convince himself that this wasn't nearly as serious as it appeared, the detective added, "I apologize for all the drama, but now that we've gotten *past* the drama, I can tell you that your being brought here was mostly for show."

"What are you saying?" Donald asked before Whit could manage to speak.

Detective Wilson sat down and seemed fairly relaxed. "I have been involved with more than one case that has brought me close to the workings of this family, Mr. Eden," he said, looking directly at Whit, even though Donald had asked the question. "I knew that if your cousins were arrested, it would be better for them to know that you had been arrested too. We got a judge to agree with our methods, and the warrant for your arrest was official enough, but there are no charges and there was no booking . . . as you must have noticed. Still, you had to be arrested. That way your cousins will never wonder if it was *you* who turned them in."

"Turned them in for *what?*" Whit asked, both relieved and alarmed.

"I'm afraid that's all I can tell you for now. We need you to stay here for quite a while yet, I'm afraid . . . for the sake of appearances. Then we'll take you home." Wilson turned to Donald. "Thank you for coming, Mr. Vega. I don't believe Mr. Eden needs your services any longer, because nothing is going to be talked about. Feel free to call his wife and let her know that everything is all right, and that he'll be home before bedtime. Beyond that, we ask that you keep this confidential and ask her to do the same."

"I will, thank you," Donald said.

Shortly after Whit was left alone to ponder his relief and confusion, he was escorted to a men's room then back to the same room where he was left on his own with nothing to read, nothing to look at, and no one to talk to. His cell phone and everything else that had been on him had been confiscated when he'd been brought in. He was glad to know that he could talk to God. He wondered how many poor souls were left alone in such situations with no idea how to even pray.

Whit thanked his Heavenly Father for knowing he could be home for bedtime, and he expressed gratitude that this was turning out to be nothing of any great concern; as long as Detective Wilson's theory worked and his cousins—and their gang associates—all believed that he too had been arrested and questioned. It was the fact that his cousins *had* been arrested that baffled him. Generally their crimes were too crafty to leave enough proof for an arrest. They all covered for each other like a bunch of modern-day Gadiantons. For three of them to be arrested, he had to believe that something *big* had come into police hands that would justify such action. He knew that an actual arrest had to have evidence to back it up.

Given *that* thought, Whit spent a couple of hours fantasizing about what it would be like if the three stooges who had tormented and taunted him earlier today all went to prison to pay for even a portion of their crimes. He imagined in detail what it would be like for him to take his family and Carlos away from here and never come back. He imagined living in a quaint little house with a beautiful yard and garden, and going to work each day at a job he could be good at and love. He imagined going to church with people who would surround them with love and safety and protection. He imagined Carlos eventually embracing the gospel and being baptized, even going to the temple. He imagined being the one to baptize him, and then being his escort the first time he went to the temple.

They were certainly on the right path for that, and his confidence was growing that eventually it would happen.

Whit knew that the only thing keeping him here in this area was the need to be close to his mother. As bad off as she was, he couldn't help hoping and praying—as he had been for many months—that she would be released from her mortal misery and taken to a better place where she could be reunited with Whit's father and brother and find joy and rest from all her worldly sorrows. He knew that given her present condition, she could either hang on for quite a while or she could go very soon. He felt that he needed to continue looking for a place to live locally, which implied it would still be a while, but he looked forward to the day when his mother was released, which would subsequently release him and his family to leave here and never come back.

He had considered—and discussed with Mary—the possibility of having his mother moved to a different facility elsewhere. But the cost, the likelihood of finding good care, and the trauma such a move might cause for her made it illogical and impractical—and prayer had made it clear to both of them that they just needed to stay until she passed on. Whit would gladly wait for whatever amount of time was required. He loved and honored his mother deeply, even if she hadn't recognized him at all for a very long time. She still deserved his deepest homage, and he would remain close by until the end. When he knew she had peacefully moved on, he would start a new life. Until then, he needed to find a place for them to live in this area and continue to look for work. Funny, he thought, how those overwhelming challenges didn't feel so daunting now that he knew he would no longer be in police custody by the end of the day. His gratitude far outweighed his stress!

* * *

Mary was hugely relieved when she got Donald's call and knew that there was a logical explanation for what had happened. Whit would be home before she went to sleep that night, and just knowing he would be beside her in their bed throughout the night made everything all right. The idea of having the worst of his evil-doing family members behind bars also gave her deep comfort, and she hoped that whatever was going on resulted in their being put away for a long time. She knew nothing of the details of their crimes, but she knew what kind of people they were, and she loved the idea of three less such people being out on the streets.

Once she got off the phone, Mary eagerly relayed the good news to Adrienne; they knelt together to say a prayer of gratitude and to ask Heavenly Father to make sure that everything went all right and Whit would indeed get home as scheduled without any complications. After their prayer, they set about making some of Whit's favorite cookies, which kept them both distracted. Christian slept through part of the project; when he awoke, Mary fed him. Afterward, she sat him in his highchair with toys and Cheerios, where he played contentedly while his mother and sister baked cookies and prepared dinner.

Adrienne loved to help in the kitchen and Mary loved to include her in cooking and baking projects, even though that meant it usually took longer. But they sat together to share the nice meal they'd prepared, and Mary was glad to know she had something decent to feed Whit when he got home, depending on what time that might be and whether he was hungry. She kept wondering what exactly was going on and imagined the moment when she would be in his arms and know that everything was all right. She had memories of such moments and longed to experience it again. Filled with gratitude that this was nothing serious and that all would be well, she focused on the children, completely putting S and P on hold. The day hadn't turned out as they'd planned, but it could have been *so* much worse, and she was *so* grateful!

* * *

Early in the evening, Whit was given another escort to the men's room, then they returned him to his quarters and brought him a sandwich and some water along with a can of soda and a little bag of chips. No longer nervous or upset, Whit ate everything but still felt hungry. Perhaps he was just hungry to get out of here and get this over with. There were no windows in the room, but Whit knew from the clock on the wall that it was well past dark when two plain-clothes officers came to get him. They put him in cuffs while one of them whispered, "Just until we get in the car."

"Okay," Whit said and was escorted from the building and into an unmarked vehicle. They were about three minutes from the station when one of the officers leaned over the seat to unlock Whit's cuffs and take them. "Thank you," Whit said, then he realized they were heading in the opposite direction of his home. He felt mildly nervous but only said, "May I ask where we're going?"

"Wilson asked us to make one stop before we take you home. No worries. Everything's good."

"Okay," Whit said, but he didn't necessarily feel convinced.

After another fifteen minutes or so, the officers pulled the car into the driveway next to a house in an average neighborhood. The garage door went up and the car pulled inside, then the door went down behind them.

"Where are we?" Whit asked.

"A safe house," one of them said, as the car doors unlocked.

"A safe house?" Whit echoed, unable to disguise his alarm. He knew the term. It's where they kept people who were in danger from criminals.

"It's not you we're keeping safe," one of the men said, and they all got out of the car. "But we *are* keeping someone safe who wanted to see you."

Whit felt confused and concerned as he followed the officers through a door into a typical kitchen area, past a dining table and around a corner into a sparsely decorated living room. And there, watching sports on TV, sat Carlos in his wheelchair.

So much suddenly made perfect sense, but Whit felt a little unsteady as his understanding settled in. During the space of a couple of loud heartbeats he knew that Carlos had told the police enough to have his brother and two of their cousins arrested, and Whit had needed to be arrested to remove any apparent guilt from him. But if Carlos was in a safe house, that could mean only one thing. Even if those who had been arrested went to prison, they would be in contact with others who were still on the streets, and Carlos would be in danger.

Whit's heart tightened in his chest. Through the course of another few heartbeats while Carlos turned off the TV and turned to face him as the officers left the room, Whit recalled his own deal with the gang he'd left: he would keep their dirty secrets and they would leave him alone. At the time he'd made the decision, he had discussed it with his Church leaders and he had prayed and fasted about it extensively. Even though a part of him had believed that he should truthfully report all the criminal activity of which he'd been aware, he had known that in his case, he had needed to just keep it to himself and that God approved—that it was necessary in order for him to care for his mother and aunts and live in safety. He had expected that Carlos would do the same; they had even talked about it. But Carlos had had no interaction with any of the family since the shooting—at least not that Whit knew of. And maybe there was a lot more that Carlos hadn't told him.

As their eyes met, Whit saw his own poignant emotions mirrored in the countenance of his cousin. "Why?" was all Whit could say.

"I had to, bro," Carlos said, and Whit sat down so that he could be at eye level, and because he was feeling a little weak. "It was the only way I could make things right with God."

For all the changes that Carlos had been making in his life, Whit was surprised to hear God come so quickly into the conversation. "What do you mean?" he asked with earnest sincerity.

"I been thinkin' about doin' this for a long time, man," he said. "I didn't talk to you about it cuz I didn't want you in the middle, you know? It was my idea to do it. I told Perez what I wanted to do, and he helped me find that Detective Wilson's number. That's it. It's all on me."

"What did you do, exactly?" Whit asked.

"I testified," he said with a quick lift of his chin and firm determination in his eyes. Whit was startled by the way he thought how that same look might be on the face of a righteous Nephite warrior going into battle. "It's all done and over. They videotaped the whole thing."

Whit felt so proud of Carlos, but he also felt afraid on his behalf, and his fear trumped the pride he felt for his cousin. "Carlos, I don't have to tell you what they'll do. You have to know that—"

"I'm not sticking around long enough t' see what happens, man. I'm outta here."

"What do you mean?" Whit asked, his heart pounding as other pieces of evidence began to fall into place.

Carlos grinned, then he chuckled. "I'll be outta here before sunrise . . . on my way to a new life; new name and all that stuff, man."

Whit could hardly breathe. "Witness protection?" he muttered, trying to take in what that meant. Tears rushed down his face before he had a chance to realize they were coming. "Then we'll never see you again."

"Yeah, you will!" Carlos said with an enthusiasm that Whit didn't fully understand. "In heaven, bro. Eternal families and all that. You think I wasn't payin' attention in Sunday school?" He laughed in a way that seemed completely out of place for the situation.

"Were you?" Whit asked, trying to understand.

"Hey, bro," Carlos said, leaning more toward Whit. "This ain't no sad day. It's the best day o' my sorry life . . . so far anyway. The *only* sad thing for me today is leaving you, but it's worth it, man. Don't get me wrong; I'm gonna miss you and miss you bad, but . . ." Now Carlos had tears glistening in his dark eyes. "But . . . it's all gonna be behind me now . . . just the way it should be. I knew I had to do it. I just knew it! As soon as I knew that all the rest was true, I knew it was the only way I could make it right with God, you know? Now when I get baptized I'll know that I'm really clean, you know? I'll know that I made it good."

Something between a sob and a painful cough jumped out of Whit's throat. "What did you just say?"

"Do I gotta repeat it, man?" Carlos laughed, and his eyes sparkled, and Whit now understood the source of his happiness. But he could only shake his head as emotion overtook him so forcefully that he couldn't speak.

"It's all good, man," Carlos said. "I was readin' that book, and I just couldn't stop readin', you know? I didn't understand lots of it, but Perez helped me some, and he told me I just had to pray about it." He let out a scoffing chuckle. "I ain't never prayed before. I didn't think I could. But Perez, he taught me and he helped me at first. And I couldn't stop readin' and I didn't want to even sleep. It was like I been in the dark my whole rotten life, and then I was just sittin' there and I was in the light and I knew what I had to do, but I knew I couldn't do it till I came clean. Perez helped make arrangements. I guess the feds been talkin' to a stake president or some kind o' president and I get my new name and stuff after I get on the plane. Don't know where I'm goin' except that I'm gonna be stayin' with some Mormon family somewhere and I'm gonna be baptized real soon. And they're gonna help me get some education; a GED or something like that, and then I can get a real job, they said."

Whit shook his head and reached for Carlos's hand, squeezing it tightly. The connection seemed to transfer his emotion into Carlos and he too began to cry. "It's gonna be great, you know? So, it's a happy day. I don't exactly know how they'll work out gettin' me baptized and all with havin' a different name, but they assured me that once my name has been legally changed, it will all work out. And anyway, God knows who I am." He chuckled. "That stake president guy, he knows I'm gettin' a different name, so it's all good. And I'm gonna get t' the temple one o' these days, and that means that you and me'll see each other again someday when we get t' heaven, cuz we're family." Carlos sobbed. "And nothin's more important than family, right?"

"Right," Whit managed to say, then he scooted his chair closer and wrapped Carlos in his arms. They held to each other and both wept, sharing a bond so deep that it could never be put into words. Neither were there words to express the sorrow of their parting permanently as far this mortal world was concerned and their contrasting joy in the changes taking place in Carlos's life that would have eternal significance. There was nothing—*nothing*—Carlos could have told him that could have made him any happier than his having a testimony of the truthfulness of the gospel and his willingness to do anything to embrace it and bring it fully into his life. He understood now why he had to do what he'd done. Whit didn't know what Carlos said in his testimony to the police, but he knew that whatever it was, it would make a tremendous difference in the battle against crime in this city.

Chapter Ten

WHEN THEY HAD BOTH CALMED down a bit, Whit drew back from their embrace, chuckling as he wiped at his tears, grateful for the box of tissues nearby; he took advantage of them while sharing some with Carlos. "I don't know what to say, bro . . . except that . . . I'm so proud of you, and so . . . happy for you. It's going to be hard not to see you again, but knowing that you are living the gospel and living a good life will make me happy every time I think of you. Promise me that you'll never let it go! Promise that we *will* be together in heaven, because you are going to live up to everything God asks of you. Promise me!"

"I promise, brother!" Carlos said emphatically and shook Whit's hand firmly as if to seal the agreement. His use of the word *brother* as opposed to the typical abbreviation that was used so casually among his family was a testament to the changes and Carlos's deep conviction.

"Then everything will be all right," Whit said, smiling at his cousin. "God will protect us all, and He will comfort us and help us through whatever comes."

They both sat in complete silence for a couple of minutes before Whit noticed that Carlos seemed mildly nervous. Carlos looked down and cleared his throat tensely while Whit wondered what he might say. He lifted his face to look at Whit and said, as if it was something that had been memorized, "There's one more thing I got t' say before you go, and I know you gotta go soon, cuz it won't be long before they come t' get me."

"Okay, I'm listening," Whit said. "We can't leave anything unsaid."

"Yeah," Carlos said as if he were drawing courage from Whit's words. "The thing is . . . I just want you t' know that no one I know had nothin' t' do with Mary's dad gettin' whacked, and nothin' t' do with you gettin' blamed for it. Everyone was shocked by it, you know? Even Jose didn't know nothin'. I want you t' know that, so you don't have t' wonder. Even though Jose and me was glad the old man got what he deserved and . . ." Carlos hesitated, chuckled with an expression of self-recrimination and said, "I guess I gotta stop thinkin' like that. What would Jesus do and all that, you know?"

"Yeah," Whit smiled. "I know. You'll adjust. Go on."

"We was glad t' know he was gone, especially after what he did to our family, but we didn't have nothin' t' do with it. I wanted you t' know."

Whit straightened his back and felt his heart quicken. "*What* did he do to our family? Or do you mean *your* family? The whole family or just *your* family?"

"*My* family," Carlos said, looking stunned. "Except he knew your dad and he didn't like him at all. I thought you knew all along, man."

"I don't know anything except what you just said; my father worked for him for a while. And your mother used to work for him; more specifically, she worked for his wife, because he didn't like having Hispanics in his home." He thought as he said it that his own father had been white, so the bigotry wouldn't have been a problem. Or Whit had always assumed it hadn't been, or that there had been no connection to the more current issues. He told himself to just listen and focus. Time was short.

"You can sure say that again, man. That man treated Mama bad. He hurt her lots o' times."

"*Hurt* her?" Whit echoed, fuming at the very idea.

"Yeah, he hit her; she came home with bruises on her face, and Papa would get all worked up and threaten to kill him and Mama had to calm him down. Then one night she came home and it was bad, and Papa went over there. Mama was scared and followed him, but she found the two of 'em goin' at it, you know? That's when Papa died."

Whit gasped. "I thought he died of a heart attack."

"That's what the coroner said. But he'd fallen down when old man Cranford hit him, and his head hit somethin'. Mama said he'd been bleedin' real bad and went unconscious, and they called the ambulance but there was nothin' they could do. The way I always saw it was that if Papa was gonna die from a bad heart, it shoulda been at home in his bed, peaceful like, you know? Like my mama went. Funny how it was the same with Sofia. She shouldn't o' gone that way, you know? Anyways, me and Jose always figured it was Cranford's fault that Papa died when he did, whatever the coroner said. Mama tried to make herself believe he woulda gone anyway, but it was a bad time. Mama had to keep workin' for Cranford cuz she needed the job, even more cuz Papa was gone and couldn't make no money. Cranford never hit her again after that, but she sure learned to stay out of his way, you know? And I don't think there was no problem with your dad workin' for the old man; never heard of any. Only that your dad didn't like him. But nobody did, and your dad's been gone a long time. Then when Cranford got whacked, we was glad about it, but I know none of 'em had nothin' t' do with it, cuz they were all sayin' they wished they woulda done it. And you know if they'd done something they woulda been braggin' about it."

"Yeah, I know."

"That's what I wanted you to know," Carlos said.

Whit forced his mind away from what he'd just learned about Mary's father and Carlos's family. And thoughts of his own father were disheartening, even if it had nothing to do with the problem. It made him sick, but it wasn't surprising, and it didn't change anything. He *was* glad to know for certain that no one in his family or anyone in the gang they associated with had had anything to do with Walter's murder. In some ways it deepened the mystery of what had happened, making the crime seem even more unsolvable. He focused on the moment, knowing his time with Carlos was running out. Whit knew well enough that the safety of someone going into witness protection depended on living absolutely by the cardinal rule of never—ever—being in contact with anyone from their old life. It was simply a risk that couldn't be taken.

Whit told Carlos how grateful he was to know what he'd just been told, and he wished him every happiness. He felt prompted to use these final minutes to share his own testimony of the truthfulness of the gospel. He spoke firmly of his convictions in regard to the Book of Mormon, the First Vision of Joseph Smith, and especially of the divinity of Jesus Christ. They were both overcome with fresh tears as Whit spoke words that meant the most to him in his life, and Carlos clearly felt the Spirit in what he was hearing. Whit could see and feel his convictions, and he knew he didn't have to worry about his cousin following through with embracing the gospel and truly changing his life. He wished they could keep in touch so he could know all the details, but he would have to be content with imagining the life that Carlos was living. And that was okay, because they would be together in the afterlife, and then he would know everything. That was the essence of a perfect brightness of hope, he concluded. The hope of great eternal blessings. Anything he encountered in this life was endurable as long as he could have that perfect brightness of hope.

When they were told by an officer that they needed to wrap it up, Whit embraced his cousin again and once more told him how proud he was of him and how happy he was for the decisions he'd made, the courage he'd exhibited, and the sacrifices he'd made. His last words to his cousin were a tearful admission of how much he loved him and how he would miss him—and that he should never forget it. Carlos tearfully replied, "The same back at you, bro." Then Whit left the room and hurried out to the garage.

He found Detective Wilson there leaning against a second car in the garage. "You okay?" the detective asked.

"Yeah," Whit said. "It's hard to say good-bye, but I'm very happy for him."

Wilson nodded and they got into the car. Whit was glad to be able to sit in the front seat and not feel like a criminal anymore.

After they had driven in silence for a few minutes, Whit asked, "So, what's going to happen to my cousins—the ones in jail right now?"

"They'll be going away for a long time; probably life. Murder, rape, drug trafficking. And there were others arrested, as well; not just your cousins."

Whit squeezed his eyes closed. He was sickened by the magnitude of the crimes committed by these depraved men. He sighed and reveled in the reality that they would be taken off the streets and away from the public, probably for good.

"Carlos did a good thing, then," he said.

"He sure did."

"And he gets full immunity?"

"The DA was impressed. He figured Carlos had already been punished enough for his crimes, him being the victim of that shooting and getting the worst of it. So yeah, he gets immunity and a new life. But he's giving up everything to get those scumbags off the streets. I think he deserves a new life."

"I think he does too," Whit said and smiled to think of the aspects of Carlos's new life that Detective Wilson could never appreciate. But it warmed Whit's heart and eased his sorrow greatly. He felt jealous for a moment—jealous of Carlos being able to make a clean break and start over. Even though members of Whit's former gang had been removed from society, there were still people out there who knew his past—people he couldn't trust. He reminded himself that he and Mary were working toward the goal of leaving this area for good. He only wished it could happen sooner.

After several more minutes of silence, Whit decided to take advantage of his time with the detective. "Did Carlos talk about what happened? The shooting? He never told me anything."

"So you'd said." The detective smiled slightly but kept his eyes on the road. "He didn't remember exactly who shot him, but it was all about a grievance between his brother and some loser from one of their rival gangs. They were pretty gutsy going right into that neighborhood. We're pretty sure we already have the guy who pulled the trigger doing time for something else, but we don't know for sure."

Whit nodded. "Okay, thank you. You didn't have to tell me."

"I think you have a right to know."

"Does this imply that you no longer think I'm guilty of murder? You were very convinced."

"I *was* convinced," he said firmly. "The evidence is still pretty stacked against you—except that your daughter's testimony to the contrary couldn't have been faked. I know kids enough to know that. And now that some time has passed, and I've seen more of you and your family, I have to admit that I agree with the jury."

Whit sighed. He didn't know why that mattered, but it did. "Well, thank you, Detective. I'm glad to hear it. But I sincerely hope we never cross paths again."

"I could agree with that."

"Although . . ." Whit said and then wondered if he should even bring it up. He decided he was more likely to regret *not* bringing it up when he had the chance. "I must admit that we're still haunted by wondering what really happened to my father-in-law. I know the chances of solving the crime at this point are next to nothing, but if new evidence ever surfaces, will you let me know?"

"I will," he said.

"I assume nothing has come to light since we last talked about it?"

"I'm afraid not. You're right. The chances of solving it now are next to nothing. It's rare that a cold case gets resolved, but if it shows up again for some reason, I will let you know."

"Thank you," Whit said.

A few minutes later, Detective Wilson dropped Whit off in front of the gate of his home. He thanked the detective and watched him drive away. Since he now had his cell phone back in his possession, he dialed Mary's phone. She answered so quickly that he knew she must have been staring at the phone, waiting for it to ring.

"Oh, it's you!" she said when she heard his voice.

"Yeah, it's me," he said with a little laugh, so grateful to hear her voice, to be home, to consider the miracles that had taken place today. "I'm at the gate. Do you think you could open it?"

"Oh, right now!" she said and hung up on him. He chuckled and put the phone in his pocket. The gate opened and before it had swung far enough for him to walk through she was running out the door and across the driveway, hurtling herself into his arms. He laughed and picked her up and spun her around, then he set her on her feet and kissed her, and kissed her, and kissed her.

Once he'd gotten used to accepting that the drama of the day was over and that he was back home with his sweet Mary, he said, "I assume the children are asleep."

"Yes, but . . . I promised Adrienne you would be here when she wakes up in the morning."

"I'm very glad to say that is a promise we will both be able to keep." They both laughed, hugged each other tightly again, then walked into the house, their arms wrapped around each other.

"Are you going to tell me what happened?" she asked after they'd come through the front door and locked it.

He made sure the gate had closed from the remote that controlled it. "I didn't figure either of us could get any sleep until I told you everything."

"Was it horrible?" she asked, holding out a hand toward him.

He took her hand and said, "Some of it. But I also witnessed miracles today, Mary." He shook his head. "I still can't quite believe it."

"What?" she insisted. "Tell me."

He decided to just give her the bottom line and he could fill in the details later. "Well," he said, urging her to the couch where they could sit down to face each other, still holding hands, "I was arrested for the sake of appearances, so that my cousins would know that I had nothing to do with the fact that *they* were arrested. Once I was told that, Donald called you and I just had to wait until they could take me out after dark. I still didn't really know what had happened until they took me to a safe house to talk to Carlos."

"I don't understand."

"Mary," Whit took her other hand as well and tightened his gaze on her, "Carlos testified against them." She gasped. "His interview was video-taped and witnessed and he is on his way into witness protection. We will never see him again." He wasn't surprised when she began to cry, but he hurried to add, "He did it because he wants to be baptized, Mary, and he knew he had to come clean with God in order to truly make a fresh start." Mary gasped again, more loudly. Her tears increased, but there was a sparkle in her eyes that he understood. "He told me the feds had worked out an arrangement with the Church and he was being relocated with a Mormon family that would help him get an education, a job, and most importantly to get baptized." Whit fought for his composure, then finished, "He talked about going to the temple, about . . . us being together as a family in heaven."

"Oh!" Mary sputtered and threw her arms around him. They sat together on the couch until long past midnight while Whit filled in the details, including the disturbing information Carlos had given him about her father and Carlos's family. They speculated a bit on whether or not that could have had anything to do with the murder, but given the fact that Carlos knew that none of the family or gang members were responsible, it didn't seem likely. They both admitted that they hated the unsolved crime hanging over them and concluded once again that they would just have to learn to live with it.

When there seemed nothing more to say for the moment, they went upstairs where Whit gratefully watched each of his children sleeping peacefully. Then he crawled into bed next to his wife, and his gratitude deepened. He thought of Carlos and said in a sleepy voice, "Godspeed, Carlos."

"Amen," Mary muttered in a voice that was even more sleepy, and then they slept.

* * *

The following day Whit was sitting by Adrienne's bed when she came awake, and she jumped into his arms, giggling. Since it was Sunday, they went to church as usual, which is when it became starkly evident that Carlos was absent. People asked about him, and they all gave the same response—that he'd had a chance to make a fresh start elsewhere, so he'd taken it. Whit missed him but still felt in awe of the miracle and was so grateful. It had all happened so fast and was so strange that it seemed like a dream. After church they ate the leftovers of the food Mary and Adrienne had prepared the previous day, then they just enjoyed a peaceful day and speculated pleasantly on what Carlos might be doing.

On Monday, once Whit and Mary had completed all their errands, they picked Adrienne up at school so they could go bowling—which was something Adrienne loved—then they went out to dinner at one of Adrienne's favorite places. The next morning after Adrienne was off to school, Whit and Mary sat down together to examine the situation and talk about their options. Since they'd both been giving the matter a great deal of thought and prayer, they decided that Whit would call the gentleman with the house available the middle of March and tell him they would take it. The disadvantages were that they had two weeks in the interim with nowhere to live, and it was a longer drive to the care center where Ida lived. The rent was also a little more than they wanted to pay, but the landlord was willing to rent the house without a long-term lease, which would make it possible for them to leave when a job opened up elsewhere and Ida no longer needed them.

It felt strange to both of them to realize that they no longer needed to consider taking Carlos with them, which meant they didn't need handicap accommodations. That was one of the reasons they had originally wanted the house they were now talking about—the owner would allow Whit to make those changes. But the decision still felt right. They concluded that once Whit had spoken to the owner of the house, Mary would call Mr. Lostin and humbly ask if they could stay two extra weeks if they either paid rent or Whit compensated with more work on the gardens. Technically, he had already done that, but they didn't need to tell Mr. Lostin that was the case. They decided the worst he could do was say no, and then they would need to stay in a motel for a couple of weeks. They knew if it was just up to Mr. Lostin, he would gladly agree, but his orders came from a board of directors and it was their decision. Still, they could try.

Whit called the owner of the house they had decided to rent, then came to tell Mary, "Never mind. The house isn't available. The people who are in it have decided to stay until summer."

"Oh," Mary said with obvious disappointment. She then sighed, straightened her shoulders, and said, "Well, we just need to start looking again. Since we don't have to consider Carlos's special needs, it should be more simple." She was then overtaken by tears and muttered, "I miss Carlos."

Whit put his arms around her and said, "I know. So do I."

"He was always very sweet—at least he was to me."

"Yes, he could be very sweet. And he became so much more so these past several weeks. I've really grown attached to him."

"Me too," she said. "I'd really gotten used to the idea of him always being with us. Now it feels . . . wrong."

"I know what you mean," Whit said. "But all things considered, I feel so happy for him that . . . it makes up for it."

"Yeah," Mary said. "I'm happy for him too. I just . . . miss him."

Having said that, they went to the computer to start looking for available apartments and houses for rent. A few days later they still hadn't found anything suitable, and they were both getting very discouraged about the whole thing. But they kept reminding each other that God would look out for them, and surely He had a plan—even if he wasn't letting them in on it just yet.

Adrienne came home from school complaining of a sore throat, and by evening she had a fever. Mary focused on caring for Adrienne and keeping the germs contained so that they could hopefully prevent anyone else from getting sick. Since Christian was crawling and was accustomed to Adrienne being his playmate, keeping him contained in areas away from her was no small challenge. It was Adrienne's idea to stay mostly in her parents' bedroom during the day, where there was a television available. Mary liked that idea and told her it was a very good one. At the end of the day after Adrienne had gone to her own room, Mary could disinfect everything before she and Whit settled in for the night.

The family had all planned to go and visit Ida that evening, but Whit went on his own. Feeling an instinctive need to spend as much time with her as possible, he tried to go for a little while every day. He arrived at his mother's room in the care center to find her sleeping. But he liked to watch her sleep. She looked at peace, and there was none of the confusion and frustration that was often a part of her waking hours when she couldn't remember where she was, what was going on, or who she was with. Whit considered what a terribly difficult thing it had been to watch his mother slowly disappear within her own diseased mind. He longed for her to be released from her internal torment, and he couldn't deny his own selfishness in wanting to be able to stop seeing her suffer. He also wanted desperately to get out of this valley and never come back. But his mother could hang on for a long while yet, and he already knew they needed to find a place to live nearby and be content with staying for as long as it took. Since he didn't have a job *anywhere,* it was all in God's hands. If it weren't, Whit would really be depressed. Since he knew that God would get them where they needed to be—eventually—he knew he just had to faithfully endure day to day and do the best he could.

When his mother continued to sleep and Whit began to feel the need to be at home, especially since his daughter was ill, he carefully kissed her brow and left the room. At home he found Adrienne sleeping, her fever lessened by the medicine Mary had given her. Mary was just getting Christian ready for bed, and Whit took over in order to give her a break and to enjoy a few minutes with his son. Christian had become chubby and was more often than not a happy child. His curly hair had lightened from black to dark brown, but his eyes were still dark, and his features bore a strong resemblance to those of his father—at least that's what other people often said. Whit couldn't see it. He just saw Christian as being his own little person, and he was truly precious.

A few minutes after Mary sat down to nurse the baby so he would go to sleep, Whit's cell phone rang and he moved away from her so as not to disturb them. He was surprised to hear from the director of the care center, and his heart started to pound, wondering if this call was to inform him that his mother had passed away, but Mr. Silver simply said, "I was told you were here visiting your mother but I didn't get there quickly enough. I wanted to visit with you. I wonder if you might have some time to come in tomorrow and meet with me."

"Of course," Whit said. "Is there a problem with my mother?"

"No, not at all," Mr. Silver said. "It's about those video recordings you wanted to look at. I have them ready. I've reviewed them and I would like to discuss them with you. Perhaps there might be some clue here that could enable us to better help Ida if such a thing happens again."

"Of course," Whit said again. "I can come in any time. What works for you?"

"Would ten in the morning be okay?"

"Sure, I'll be there," he said, and they ended the call.

After they put the baby down for the night, Whit told Mary about the call and admitted that he wasn't sure he wanted to see the recordings. "I almost have the same feeling I had when that cop pulled me over."

"That was frightening for both of us," she said, "but it all turned out very well in the end."

"That's true. I guess I just need to face it and not fear what I don't even know."

Adrienne slept well and in the morning just had some sniffles and a low-grade fever. It didn't appear to be anything too serious, and she quickly contented herself in front of one of her favorite videos while enjoying some scrambled eggs, toast, and orange juice. It was raining outside when Whit kissed Mary and asked her to say an extra prayer for him. He couldn't shake a feeling of dread over this appointment. She assured him that everything would be all right and sent him off.

Whit arrived at the care center early enough to go and sit with his mother for a short while before his appointment with Mr. Silver. Ida exhibited little interest in eating her breakfast, and there was a vacant look in her eyes. Even when Whit spoke to her, she ignored him as if she were deaf, which he knew she was not. He tried to think of her in better times and was relieved when the time for the appointment arrived and he was able to leave her room. Mr. Silver greeted him kindly, but his tone was somber as he situated two chairs side by side so that he and Whit could sit and look at a computer monitor where the video would be played. It took Whit a few minutes to become accustomed to the angle of the camera in his mother's room, and to adjust his eyes to see her movement in the room when there was only minimal light there from a little night light. Mr. Silver did a great deal of fast-forwarding, but he had obviously studied this enough to know where to stop and listen to what Ida was saying as she frantically paced the room. At first Whit couldn't understand what she was saying, then he did and wished that he hadn't. He truly wished that he hadn't.

Mr. Silver played several different pieces of video where his mother in essence repeated the same thing, an event she was recalling in vivid detail. He explained that in some cases this kind of thing happened, where something traumatic could somehow break past the barrier of an otherwise nonfunctional memory. Whit felt sick in more ways than he could count. His mother could remember nothing positive about her life; not the people who loved her or the happy memories of good things she had done. But she could remember *this* with so much detail that she rehearsed it over and over. Mr. Silver told him it had happened more than a dozen times, with her summoning up every bit of energy she had to get up in the night and pace the floor with this kind of ranting until she would finally crawl back into bed and cry or, in a couple of instances, collapse from exhaustion. The staff was always aware of what was happening on camera, and they had kept an eye on her until she'd needed to be helped back into bed. They all knew that trying to intervene and convince the person that something was not what they believed was only likely to cause more problems; at least that had been the case with Ida.

"I just keep thinking," Mr. Silver said, "that this must be some kind of hallucination or something. Surely she can't mean what she's saying, but perhaps if we could figure out the source of it, we might be able to help her to stop having these episodes and—"

"It's not a hallucination," Whit said, barely able to eke out the words. More forcefully he said, "You can stop it now. I don't need to see any more."

A horrible silence fell over the room until Whit final became aware of it and turned to see Mr. Silver staring at him, his eyes wide with alarm, as if he didn't even know what question to ask. "I've been wondering, you know," Whit said. "I've been wondering what happened, because we were never ever able to figure it out."

"Are you saying that . . ." Mr. Silver couldn't say it and Whit knew he had to, because he had to accept it, and he had to deal with it.

"Yes, Mr. Silver, my sweet mother murdered my wife's father, and she didn't even remember she'd done it . . . until now."

"Oh, Mr. Eden," he said in a hushed drawl. "That just can't be possible. I know your mother. She's—"

"Obviously it's possible," Whit said, wanting to run or scream, but knowing neither was an option. This had to be addressed. He motioned toward the screen and said with overt anger, "She just reiterated every detail of the crime, and I had believed she was asleep in her bed. I nearly went to prison because my fingerprints were on the gun."

"I just can't believe it," Mr. Silver said, but he was more compassionate than astonished.

"I can't either," Whit muttered and sank deeper into his chair. It occurred to him that he and Mary had both been haunted by the unanswered questions. They had prayed for answers so that it could be put to rest. But this was not what he'd expected or wanted. This was a *nightmare*!

They both sat in silence again for a few minutes, and Whit was at least grateful that this man didn't make him feel uncomfortable, especially given such an incomprehensible revelation.

"I assume," Whit finally said, "that some kind of legal measures must be taken."

"Oh, I don't think that . . . well . . . what difference does it make now? She didn't know what she was doing then, and . . ."

"Yes, but that's not really the point, is it. I'm not worried about my mother having to stand trial or go to prison, but . . ." He pulled out his cell phone where he looked up a number, then dialed it.

"Who are you calling?" Mr. Silver asked.

Whit just said into the phone. "May I speak to Detective Wilson, please? It's important."

"Is this really necessary?" Mr. Silver asked.

Whit turned his back to him, knowing he had to do this, and he had to do it now before the shock wore off. He could feel himself trembling from the inside out. He had to face this and get it over with. He could fall apart later. He wondered for a moment how he would tell Mary. How could he ever tell Mary? He had to force the thought away and prayed the detective would be available. If he had to wait for him to call back, if he was busy with a case or something else, Whit would surely lose his nerve, and—

"This is Detective Wilson," he heard through the phone.

"This is Whit Eden," he said. "I know you hoped to never hear from me again, but . . . I have discovered some information that might help solve that cold case we both have an interest in. Are you busy?"

"Not particularly. Where are you?"

Whit told him the address and name of the care center, and Wilson said that he would be there in ten minutes. Whit used those minutes to give Mr. Silver a more detailed explanation of what had happened. It helped him feel more like this man was his ally in handling this correctly, and it also helped keep him distracted so that the inner trembling didn't overtake him before the detective got there and they were able to deal with this rationally.

When the detective arrived, Whit introduced him to Mr. Silver, then said, "I'm going to let him explain." The three of them sat down, and Mr. Silver explained everything pertinent for Wilson to understand why they had been watching the video recordings of Ida's nighttime ranting.

As Mr. Silver began to play the recording again, Whit's hands started to shake, and he realized that his inner trembling was making its escape to the outer regions of his body. After the full retelling of the crime had occurred twice, Wilson said, "I've seen enough, thank you."

Whit expected to be barraged with questions, but the detective turned to Mr. Silver and asked, "Tell me about Mrs. Eden's condition."

Mr. Silver explained very matter-of-factly how Ida's physical symptoms indicated she was in the final stages of the disease, and mentally she had not recognized anyone she knew for many months now. Wilson considered that information through a silence that grew uncomfortably long. Without looking at Whit he said, "You're obviously very upset over this."

"What makes you think so?" Whit asked with subtle sarcasm.

"Your hands are shaking, and your breathing is shallow."

"Is it?" Whit asked, unaware of his breathing but looking at his hands as if they had betrayed him.

Wilson turned and looked him in the eye. "Do you honestly think I am going to arrest a little old lady who hasn't even been able to think straight for years?"

"What *are* you going to do?" Whit asked. Now his *voice* was trembling.

"I'm going to show this recording to my superior officer and we're going to close this case, officially and forever. No one else has to even know. We're going to let your mother rest in peace, and I am going to officially apologize to you for ever believing you were guilty of murder." He held out a hand, and Whit shook it as firmly as he could with his own shaking hand. "You're one of the finest men I've ever known, and I've rarely seen such integrity."

Whit either felt too stunned or too upset to speak. He just nodded, wishing he could control his shaking until he got home. Mr. Silver handed the detective a DVD while he said to Whit, "It's the only recording. The original has been deleted."

"Thank you," Detective Wilson said, nodding briefly at both of them. He took two steps toward the door, then turned and looked at Whit. "Aren't you a Mormon?"

"Does that matter?" Whit asked.

"Maybe."

"Yes, I'm a Mormon," Whit said. The detective smiled, nodded again, and left.

Whit tried to gather his thoughts and keep his composure in check. "Thank you, Mr. Silver," he said, "for your understanding and discretion. I . . . uh . . . I need to go home. I'll . . . check back later." He didn't want to add that he wasn't sure he could see his mother right now. He knew she was innocent in the most important sense; he knew she was not to blame. But he and his family had suffered so much over this that at the moment all he could think about was getting home to Mary. He didn't know how he was going to tell her, but he needed her. Oh, how he needed her!

Chapter Eleven

WHIT MANAGED TO GET OUT to his truck but he could only sit there, his knuckles turning white from his grip on the steering wheel. He struggled as if he were drowning while flashes of hearing the gunshots went through his mind. Then there were flashbacks of finding Mary's father dead, of being arrested, of being in jail, of being on trial, of fearing that he would go to prison. He thought of all Mary had gone through—and little Adrienne. He couldn't believe it! He just could *not* believe it!

He finally forced himself to calm down enough to drive home, finding it a blessing that his need to be with Mary was stronger than his fear of telling her. He had to just tell her. He had to tell her quickly and get it over with. At least Adrienne would be at school and with any luck the baby would be napping. He couldn't think about what to say; he just had to say it.

Whit found Mary sitting on the couch, reading a book. He said nothing before he went to his knees and buried his face in her lap, breaking down in heaving sobs.

"What is it?" she demanded. "Is it your mother? Is she gone?"

"No, it's worse," he managed to say. "So much worse."

"What?" She lifted his face with her hands and forced him to look at her. "Tell me, Whit," she insisted, wondering how much more drama they could handle.

"Oh, Mary," he muttered, "my mother did it. She's the one who did it."

"Did what? I don't understand."

"She killed your father, Mary," he said, and she gasped, then held her breath, but she didn't let go of his face. "She confessed it over and over. It was all there on the recordings. She knew every detail of what happened.

She did it, Mary. She knew about things he'd done to hurt her sister, and how my father had been treated unkindly when he worked here. She believed your father was responsible for her brother-in-law's death, and she saw how he was hurting you and Adrienne, and she knew he was kicking us out of the house. She kept saying it over and over. 'I killed him. I killed him and he deserved it.'" He gasped for breath, and Mary did the same. "We thought she didn't know what was going on but she did, and then she just . . . lost it. She killed him, and then she didn't remember. She honestly didn't remember, but she's held it inside all this time, and now it's . . . all there. She took the gun that day when I was moving her here. I thought I'd left it at the house, and since I'd left the door unlocked, I thought it had been stolen. But she'd taken it; she'd put it in her purse and she used a handkerchief to hold it because she didn't like guns, so only my fingerprints were on it. But she kept it hidden, and she used it to kill him. She must have barely touched it enough with the handkerchief to pull the trigger, because my fingerprints were still there intact. She killed him, then she went back to bed and forgot about it."

When he had spilled the worst of it at Mary's feet, Whit buried his face in her lap again and just let all the pent-up emotion pour out of him. He was aware of Mary's acute distress, and he could feel her shock even without looking at her. But all he could do was hold her and believe that, just like so many times before, they could get through even this together.

Whit couldn't deny the nagging fear deep inside that this—more than anything else that had confronted them in the past—could come between them. His greatest fear when they'd first become involved was that his past and the life he'd lived would spill over and have a negative impact on *her* and create problems that would impact *her* life. And that had certainly happened! She had graciously taken on many challenges and endured much heartache that would not have been present in their lives if not for his dysfunctional family and the horrors attached to some of its members. But never in a million years could Whit have imagined something as horrific as this. How could he have ever fathomed that bringing his sweet elderly mother into Mary's home would also bring this unthinkable invasion of violence with so many terrible ramifications? He wondered what to say to her and couldn't think of a thing. He wished *she* would say something but she didn't. And he couldn't even bring himself to look at her.

Minutes ticked away while Whit wondered what to say, what to do, how to cope with this. When he came up with no answers he suddenly and without warning shot to his feet. Without even glancing at Mary he muttered, "I'm exhausted. I need to be alone."

He rushed up the stairs, taking them three at a time, and on impulse he went into the guest bedroom instead of the room he shared with Mary. His initial reasoning was that he wanted a place where he could really be alone, then he remembered that Adrienne *wasn't* at school. She was still sick and resting in his own bed. Glancing into the bedroom he shared with Mary, he was glad to know that Adrienne was resting, and that the house was big enough that she wouldn't have overheard what he'd been saying.

In the spare bedroom he kicked off his shoes and climbed into the bed, pulling the covers up around his shoulders and curling almost into the fetal position, as if hiding in some kind of primal mode might make this bearable. For a few minutes he wondered about Mary, worried about her on so many levels he simply couldn't bear it, and he had to force her out of his head. His mind then catapulted him back to that horrible night, and he played the events over and over in explicit detail. He'd done it a thousand times before, examining everything he'd seen and heard and done, certain that eventually his mind would pick up on some detail he'd missed and he would be able to get some little clue that might help solve the crime. Now he carefully dovetailed the version he knew by heart with the repeated detailed confession he'd heard from his mother's nighttime ranting. He was stunned with how perfectly the two versions meshed. Every minute detail made sense; every hole in his theories and speculations had now been filled in with perfect and logical explanations.

Overwhelmed with shock and disbelief and with no way to even consciously reconcile a myriad of emotions, all he could do was mechanically rewind it and play it again and again. He never would have thought that he could possibly sleep in such a state of mind, but he woke up, surprised to realize he'd been sleeping. He was even more surprised by the dusky light in the room that indicated the sun was going down. It was February, so the days were short. But the hours of *this* day had slipped past him in a strange, disoriented state.

His first thoughts went to Mary, and he felt distinctly guilty for having abandoned her like that after dropping such a huge emotional bomb on her. His guilt deepened with a quick review of all that he had brought into her life that had given her grief. But even now he dreaded facing her and couldn't imagine what to say or do to even attempt to make this right. He *couldn't* make it right. He just couldn't.

"Oh, Mary," he murmured and pressed a hand over his heart as a combination of his love for her and his heartache on her behalf created a tangible tightness there.

Whit gasped when he felt a gentle hand on his arm, and a moment later Mary's voice spoke softly behind his ear. "I'm right here, my love," she said, and she snuggled up close to his back and put her arm tightly around him.

"Mary?" was all he could think or bring himself to say. What he wanted to say was, *What are you doing here? Why are you being so kind? Don't you realize what I told you earlier?*

What he heard in response to his unspoken outburst was her gentle, reassuring voice close to his ear. "I can't even imagine how difficult this must be for you, but I promise you that everything is going to be all right. I promise, Whit. I love you more than life, more than anything that we could ever come up against in mortality."

Whit turned around abruptly to see her face, as if looking into her eyes might prove that she couldn't possibly mean it, because he found it impossible to comprehend that she did. What he saw proved the opposite; she *did* mean it. She meant it with all her heart and soul. He could see it, feel it encompassing him with all the love she had always had for him. How could he have so quickly and thoroughly doubted her when she had proven the power of her love for him over and over?

"Oh, Mary," was all he could say before he wrapped her in his arms and buried his face into her hair that hung over her neck. He held to her as tightly as he would a life preserver if he were drowning. And she returned his embrace with the same intensity, feeding her love into him, giving him the strength to believe that what she'd said was true, that everything *would* be all right.

After a few minutes of silently adjusting to the fact that Mary knew everything and nothing had changed between them, Whit noted the silence in the house and asked, "Where are the children?"

"I took them to Cinda's," she said. "Christian's gotten so he likes the bottle more than me, anyway. Adrienne's fever was gone, and Cinda is sure she caught her cold from Rachel anyway. They'll all be fine for a while. I told her we had a little crisis to deal with and needed some time. She was glad to help. She reminded me that we've helped her through a few crises of her own. I figured we could use some time alone; it was apparent that you needed me more than the children do right now."

Whit brushed Mary's hair back from her face. "How do you always manage to know exactly what to do . . . what to say? I have trouble comprehending how you can be so good to me when I have brought so many awful things into your life."

"Whit," she said in a tone she might have used with a child who was due for a scolding. She leaned up on one elbow and looked down at him. "When I married you I was well aware of your past, your family situation, your life—just as you were with mine. We had full disclosure, and we exchanged sacred vows knowing that life by its very nature brings challenges. My vows were not spoken with any exceptions. If the situation were reversed, I know very well that you would have stood by me without question. Why would you think any less of me?"

"But this is *so* horrible. I can't even imagine how you—"

She put her fingers over his lips to stop him. "It *is* horrible." He saw a subtle glisten of moisture in her eyes. "But I've had a little time to let it settle in, and so have you. And I am certain if we look at the situation more carefully, we will see evidence of many miracles."

"Miracles?" he countered as if she were speaking blasphemy.

She put her fingers over his lips again. "Be quiet and listen to me. I can understand that this has upset you greatly, and you have a right to be upset, and to take all the time you need to come to terms with it. But I've been praying very hard since you told me what you learned, and I've had some thoughts come to me that I believe are impressions from the Spirit. While I was just lying here beside you while you slept, it was as if I could see a condensed version of your mother's life go through my mind; it was as if I could see her the way that God sees her. And then I remembered so clearly the words of the blessing she received when we were struggling with all of this initially."

Whit thought frantically, trying to remember, but he couldn't. He would have said so but her fingers were still over his lips.

"You don't remember," she said, as if his eyes had given his thoughts away, "because you weren't there. You were in jail. Brother Vega came to give me the report of how bad it really was. He brought President Martinez with him, which seemed to me a bad sign; it was like he needed reinforcements. But as you know, they're both good men and I was grateful for them. Whatever I may have told you about their visit I wouldn't expect you to remember, but *I* remember, Whit. I remember certain things so clearly that I have no doubt that God wants me to remember. President

Martinez gave me a blessing, then your mother asked if she could have a blessing too. Brother Vega gave it to her."

Whit began to feel emotional at the thought, especially in light of all they now knew. Mary moved her fingers from over his lips and pressed a hand to his cheek. "This was after it had happened, Whit. And she was told very firmly and clearly that Heavenly Father knew her heart and that her sins were forgiven and she would be watched over with great care from both sides of the veil."

Whit took in a sharp breath as the implication settled into his mind. If he had any room for doubt, Mary erased it when she added with tearful conviction, "I know it's true, Whit. Even at that point, that very day, Heavenly Father knew your mother's heart; He knew she wasn't in her right mind, and she had been forgiven. Our learning the truth now will give us peace of mind and closure, and we can get on with our lives with no reservations. *That* is a miracle, Whit Eden. The way all of this came together right *now* . . . at a time when things are changing for us, with Carlos leaving, his testimony putting your cousins away, his telling you what he knew about my father's life and death. God's hand is in this, Whit, and I know you can make peace with it, because I have. I really have. I was driving back from Cinda's and crying and praying and I just felt this . . . warm peace settle over me, and I knew everything would be all right."

Mary smiled and added, "You and I both know that the power of the Atonement is real, Whit. It covers everything about this life where circumstances beyond our control cause so much damage, and it covers all the ways we fall short after the best that we can do. Your mother is going to be just fine; her test here is over. Consider all the violence she was exposed to—how she lost her husband and son violently, how she lived in fear every day. Add to that what we learned from Carlos about how my father had hurt Claudia and how her husband's death came about. With your mother's mind beginning to fail, all of the rest just makes sense. I think she was more afraid than angry, and I think she was instinctively trying to protect us. She did it to *protect us,* Whit. She loves us all so much, even if she can't consciously remember that at the moment. But she will soon. And she will be just fine. And we are going to be fine, as well."

Whit took in everything she said—took it all into his mind where he sorted and reasoned it out, and he took it into his heart where he could feel it and let his emotions flow out of him unchecked while Mary just held him and allowed him to grieve. And most importantly, he took it into his spirit, and that's when he felt the most profound of all miracles filter through his every nerve. He became almost instantly consumed with a warm peace and comfort, just as Mary had described that she had felt earlier.

Whit lay staring up into the darkness with Mary close by his side, marveling at the miracle. How could the piercing pain and agony he'd endured not so many hours ago be gone, swallowed up in the power of the Atonement, utterly disintegrated in the Savior's powerful and loving hands? He could admit that there was sorrow in him for the difficulties of his mother's life—and even his own, and Mary's as well. But he felt no pain. It had been entirely eradicated and replaced with peace; perfect, unadulterated peace.

Whit's stomach growled loudly to remind him of the hours he'd gone without eating. A minute later Mary's did the same, and they both chuckled. "Perhaps we should eat something and go rescue Cinda from our children."

"Perhaps we should," Whit said, struck again with the amazement of how fine he felt—not in denial, but fine. And earlier today he had felt as if he could never be fine again. Thanks to a wife who loved him unconditionally and with perfect charity, and a Savior whose love he had come to easily know and recognize, he couldn't deny that all was well. Even the reality of having no idea where they would live or how he would make a living didn't seem like a problem. If God could eradicate such horrible suffering, then finding them a place to live seemed rather insignificant.

While they were eating some leftovers that Mary heated up, she said, "I know you probably don't want to talk about it, but I have to know exactly what happened before we can put this fully to rest. I assume you know what happened."

"Oh, I do," he said, not wanting to think about it, but he completely understood why Mary needed to know. "I'll give you the simple version, then you can ask me questions if you need to." She nodded, and he took a deep breath and forged ahead. "From what she said—over and over—and what I remember, I believe it happened like this . . . She must have gotten up in the night and opened the patio door to go out. When the alarm on the security system went off, it frightened her so she just hurried and got back into bed. You know how we kept that baby gate at the bottom of the stairs locked so that she wouldn't wander upstairs and alert your father to her presence in the house."

"Yes, of course."

"Well, when I came downstairs to investigate the alarm, I unlocked the gate and left it open. I found the patio door open, then I checked on my mother and she appeared to be asleep. I remember thinking that she was surely a heavy sleeper, but now I know she was *pretending* to be asleep so she wouldn't be found out for setting off the alarm. And now I wonder if hearing the alarm triggered something in her mind—sirens, maybe. Who knows? Because I had reason to believe the house had been invaded and I knew that the police would come in response to the security system being breeched, I hurried upstairs to check on you and Adrienne, and I didn't lock the gate. I don't think I even gave it a thought. But why would I have ever believed it could be a problem in the middle of the night under such circumstances? You remember I was in the bedroom with you and Adrienne, with the door closed, when we heard the gunshot."

"Oh, I remember," she said with chagrin.

"I hesitated investigating, thinking I might be putting myself in danger, and I thought it might be best to stay with you. That obviously gave my mother time to open the sliding glass door, which was left unlocked, and throw the gun out the window, then go back downstairs and get into bed. When I checked on her I didn't know if she was asleep or just huddling there, afraid. But the police came and I just let her be. I honestly think she fell back to sleep once the noise settled down, and she probably woke up with no memory of what she'd done, or perhaps with a feeling of having had a bad dream. Now it seems to have crept out of her subconscious, and I believe she's trying to unburden herself. I wish I knew how to help her know that it's all right."

Mary reached her hand across the table and squeezed his. "You'll know what to do."

Whit nodded, hoping she was right. What he wanted now more than anything was for his mother to feel peace. He knew that she would be all right once she passed through the veil, but he didn't know how long that would be, and in the meantime he didn't want her living with this horrible burden.

Mary asked him some more questions, and he told her how kind Mr. Silver had been. He told her that he'd called Detective Wilson and how compassionate he had been in the way he'd handled the whole thing. As he repeated all of this to Mary, he could see more evidence of the miracles she had pointed out earlier.

"So," she said, needing some clarification, "tell me about the gun."

He sighed and leaned back, having finished eating all he could. "The pistol technically belonged to my mother because I was an ex-con and couldn't legally own a firearm, but I wanted her to have it for protection. Before her mind started going, she knew how to use it and handle it safely. The ammunition was always kept in a place separate from the gun, and it was well hidden to keep it from ever getting into the hands of our undesirable relatives. We were *very* careful with it. When I was preparing to move my mother here, I set the gun down, not wanting to leave it in the truck, which I had left unlocked while I packed it. We left the house in a hurry, and I realized later I'd forgotten to get the gun, and I'd also forgotten to lock the door. I was under a great deal of stress, but I was horrified by what I'd done. When I went back, the gun was gone. I thought it had been stolen and took my mother to the police station that day to make an official report."

"I remember that."

"Now I know that while I was taking stuff out to the truck, my mother had picked up the gun and put it in her purse. She picked it up with her handkerchief because, well . . . she said in her ranting that she needed to hide that awful gun so no one would use it to hurt her or her babies, but she didn't want to touch it because guns were so awful. I didn't think to pick up the gun because I didn't actually see it when I checked the house the last time; it wasn't there and I didn't think about it at the time or I would have looked in her purse. Apparently she kept it hidden here at the house, and it's impossible to know if what she did had some premeditation in it or if it was just an impulsive act. It did happen right after your father had found out you and I were married and he had told us we needed to leave. I thought my mother was oblivious to most of that, but I think she was taking in a lot more than we thought she was."

"Obviously she was," Mary said sadly. "Your poor, sweet mother." She sighed. "I pray she goes soon, Whit." Tears came to her eyes and her voice tightened. "She hasn't really been with us for such a long time; she's so confused and unhappy. I want her to be at peace; I want her to be with your father and brother again, and I know that she will be."

"I know it too," he said. "I believe that for all of Joseph's challenges when he was on earth, he's progressed a great deal. I've just felt it."

"I believe it too," she said and reached over the table to kiss him.

Surprised by how late it was, Mary called Cinda to tell her they were on their way. She said it was no problem. The children were asleep and she was watching a movie and was quite accustomed to staying up late anyway.

During the drive to Cinda's home, Whit took Mary's hand and told her earnestly how grateful he was for her perspective and insight and especially for her love.

"You're the best thing that ever happened to me," she said with conviction.

"What about the gospel?" he asked.

"You always ask me that, so I'll tell you again: I wouldn't have taken the gospel into my life without you, and I'm learning more and more that it's all part of the package. This kind of love we share, Whit, is at the very heart of God's plan of happiness. With you and I together, always striving to keep God a part of our lives, we are on a path that is the essence of God's eternal plan. Nothing could be better than that." She smiled and repeated, "You're the best thing that ever happened to me."

Back at the house with the children tucked safely into their beds and sleeping soundly, Whit and Mary knelt beside their bed, holding hands while Whit spoke a prayer on their behalf, expressing their deep gratitude for too many blessings to count. They asked for blessings to be upon their marriage and their family, and for special blessings to be with Carlos as he made these great changes in his life, and for Whit's mother that she could be comforted and at peace until the time came when she would be allowed to return to Him and find perfect rest from her sorrows.

They both fell asleep quickly, wrapped in a mutual comfort that could be summed up in the things Mary had said to Whit earlier during their brief drive. Their marriage and the gospel and the love and sacrifice of their Savior had created a neat, beautiful package that compensated for anything else that life could throw at them.

* * *

The next morning Whit went to visit his mother and found her sitting in the big, comfortable chair in her room, staring out the window. Her eyes had that typical lost look in them, and her countenance looked gaunt and worn.

"Hello," Whit said as he usually did. She barely tossed him a glance, as if he were no different than the staff members who came and went, none of whom she probably remembered from hour to hour. He scooted a chair close to hers and sat down. "How are you today?" he asked.

She didn't respond, and for long minutes Whit just observed her, thinking of everything that had been revealed yesterday and the enormous gamut of emotions he had experienced. He was so grateful for the peace he'd come to feel regarding the matter, and prayed that his mother could find that same kind of peace. He had come to expect nothing from their time together, but he did usually try to at least offer her some kind of company and conversation when she was awake.

"Did you have some breakfast?" he asked.

"I think so," she said without moving her gaze from the window.

Whit remained silent for more minutes, his thoughts most prominently focused on Mary's description of his mother's life, of how she'd been given a little vision of how much she'd been through and how all of that violence and fear had impacted her. He liked the way Mary had said it was as if she'd been able to see Ida the way God saw her. For a moment he caught a tiny glimpse of the same thing. What he saw was a good woman who had always loved the gospel and tried to live it, even in the midst of so many difficulties. She had lost her son and her husband to violent deaths. Her daughter had more or less abandoned her, and Whit had spent time in prison after years of being in the middle of the madness.

Ida had watched her sisters suffer much, most especially from all the grief their children's criminal activities had brought into their lives. In that moment Whit saw the Alzheimer's as some kind of relief from the painful memories of his mother's life. He wanted to wish that the horrible memory of that one impossible event hadn't crept through, but in the course of twenty-four hours he had come to see what a blessing it was to have it in the open and for him and Mary to have closure.

Whit became deeply engaged in his thoughts and was surprised to hear his mother say, "I was married once, you know." She said it in Spanish, which was a bit strange when she had spoken in English a few minutes earlier. He knew she went back and forth. Most of the staff only spoke English, but Spanish was her native language.

"I *did* know that," he said, wanting to add that he was a result of that marriage. He wanted to remind her that she had fallen in love with a handsome American who had gone to her home country of Mexico on an LDS mission. And the rest was history. But he just listened to see if she would say anything else.

"I've been missing him," she said, still in Spanish. "I had a dream about him last night. I think it was a dream."

She gave a little soft laugh. "Maybe I was hallucinating."

Whit couldn't help thinking that with the way her life was winding down that maybe her seeing him was more real than any hallucination or dream. Maybe. Maybe not.

"I think I should like to be where he is," she said, and Whit's heart quickened. Was her spirit being prepared to leave this world? Under the circumstances he could only hope and pray that was the case.

"I've heard it's a beautiful place . . . where he is; very peaceful."

"Yes," Ida sighed. Whit just listened and waited and she added, "His name is Christian. No finer name." She turned quickly toward him and said with a moment of enlightenment, "I have a grandson named Christian; named after my husband."

"That's wonderful!" Whit said, fighting back the threat of tears. "What a great tribute to your husband."

Ida relaxed again in her chair as if the effort to simply turn and look at him had been exhausting. He sensed her relaxing as if she might drift off to sleep, and he had a sudden impression that there was something he needed to say to her. He scooted a little closer and cautiously took her hand. She looked at him with mild alarm, as if she were wondering why a complete stranger would hold her hand. But as he returned her gaze he saw her countenance soften.

"I would like to tell you something, and even if it doesn't make sense to you, I want you to just listen. Is that all right?" She nodded slightly, and he went on. "I want you to know that your Heavenly Father loves you, Ida." He found it interesting that he felt impressed to use her name when he would have usually only referred to her as his mother. "He knows every detail of how difficult your life has been, and He knows all the good you have done. He's forgiven your sins, Ida, and He's waiting for you to come back to Him . . . when you're ready. There's nothing to worry about, nothing to be afraid of. And Christian is there with him . . . waiting."

Whit was reminded of how he felt when he gave a priesthood blessing, and the words just seemed to flow out of him without any thought or effort. He saw a glisten of tears in her eyes, and for a long moment he believed that the words had penetrated her spirit, even if her mind could not comprehend them. He wished that she would know who he was, but he'd given up on that a long time ago. Still, she smiled and patted his hand and said, "You're such a nice young man. Thank you for being so kind to me."

"Being kind to you was never difficult," he said.

She smiled again, then leaned back and closed her eyes, saying, "I'm just going to rest. Take out the trash when you leave."

Whit chuckled and squeezed his mother's hand before he let go. Perhaps she'd had some tiny awareness that it was him. She'd certainly told him to take out the trash a great many times during the life they'd shared. He stayed until she was sleeping soundly, then he kissed her brow and went home to check on his family. Finding that all was well at home, he got online to resume his search for a place to live. He found a couple of listings that hadn't been there the last time he'd looked, and he told Mary he was going to check them out. One of them was out of the question; the neighborhood and the condition of the apartment made it an impossible choice. The other was a possibility, but only in the barest and most minimal sense. Whit told the building manager he would get back to him, but he already knew it didn't feel right. He reminded himself on the way home that something would turn up; surely everything would work out. He wondered about Carlos but he smiled to think of his new life.

That evening, Whit went back to the care center and took the family, although Adrienne was required to keep her distance from her grandmother so as not to spread germs. Ida still looked very tired, but she perked up when they placed the baby on her lap. He was getting big, and he was very wiggly and wouldn't stay there long, but Whit helped hold him there, and Ida laughed a bit at how adorable he was. She seemed in good spirits when they left her, and Whit felt his peace deepening over the recently revealed issues with his mother.

The follow morning he got an unexpected call from Detective Wilson who told him that the case of his father-in-law's death had been put to rest, and he said that he appreciated Whit's integrity in bringing the matter to his attention. Whit thanked him for being so kind and understanding over the matter. He then just simply said, "And as for that other matter we discussed the other night . . . after your arrest."

"Yes?" Whit asked, knowing he meant Carlos.

"I just want you to know that I got word everything is good there."

"Thank you, Detective. I'm very glad to know."

Whit took a deep breath when he hung up the phone. If not for their need to leave the house, he would consider life to be remarkably good. He resumed his search, knowing he had to do his part, then he went again to look at a couple of places. Again he was disappointed. There were such obvious problems that he just knew it wasn't right to move his family to any of those places.

An hour after he'd returned home, Whit got a call from Mr. Silver, who told him with kind compassion that his mother had passed away just a while ago. She had eaten some lunch with the help of a nurse, then had gone to sleep. When a nurse checked on her an hour later, she was gone. Whit thanked Mr. Silver, then hung up the phone and cried, but there was far more relief than grief in his tears. He had grieved for the loss of his mother many times over already. His prayers had been answered. And given what had happened in just the last few days, he couldn't deny that it seemed as if she had finally unburdened herself of this horrible thing she had done, either in a fit of rage and recrimination or out of a perceived need to protect her family. Either way, she'd not remembered. And then, once her spirit knew that the truth had set the record straight, she was able to leave behind the mortal world and all the horrors she had endured there. And perhaps her spirit *had* absorbed some of what Whit had told her. He knew even more than ever that it was true. Her sins *had* been forgiven, and now she was at peace—and she was with her beloved Christian. Whit could hardly be happier than to think of his parents together again.

He wiped his tears and went to tell Mary. He was glad to have Adrienne back in school so that they could have some time together as husband and wife, and they would tell their daughter the news later. As they reviewed plans for Ida's funeral service that they had previously discussed, Mary put her hand on Whit's arm to stop him mid-sentence.

"Do you realize what this means?"

"What?" he asked, baffled.

She just looked at him hard as if she knew he would figure it out, and then he did. "Good heavens!" he muttered as it dawned on him, then it filled his spirit with a firm comfort that made it evident God had known all along that they would *not* need to find a place to live in this area, because all of their reasons for staying here were no longer relevant. Claudia and his mother were in a better place. It had all been planned out long ago in ways that no mortal could have controlled.

"So," he chuckled, "do you think I can find a job and a place to live somewhere else in the country in the next ten days?"

"With all the miracles we've had in our lives, would you even doubt that such a thing could be possible? You've already submitted your resumé to several places. You should start by following through with those and letting them know you're available and see if anything has opened up. It will work out."

"I'm sure it will," Whit said and hugged his wife tightly.

Chapter Twelve

ALL OF THE ARRANGEMENTS FOR Ida's funeral fell easily into place, especially with the help and support of branch members who were always willing to step in and make a difference. Unlike with Sofia and Claudia, Whit felt it was more appropriate for his mother to have a complete funeral service at the church building. Ida Eden had been an active part of this branch of the Church for many years, and she had many friends there who would want to pay their respects and honor her. Whit didn't bother to inform any of his extended family members in the area; the remaining few of them who weren't incarcerated hadn't had any contact with Ida for years, and they wouldn't really care. That's not all—he preferred to not have any of them around.

With all of that taken care of as much possible, Whit focused on searching for a job—anything he was capable of doing, anywhere in the country. They knew now that there was no more need to pay for Ida's care, and her life insurance would pay for all the funeral expenses and leave some extra that had been intended to cover any leftover debts or unforeseen expenses she might have incurred in her later years. As a result, Whit and Mary knew exactly how much money they had to work with, and they could certainly afford to rent a truck and get just about anywhere they needed to go. They wanted to get away from here just as quickly as possible and make a fresh start, certain God would guide them to the right place. Whit just hoped they might get a positive response from at least one of the many companies where he had placed resumés and made recent inquiries. He'd done all he could for the moment, so he left that in the Lord's hands and focused on getting through his mother's funeral.

When he knew he could no longer find any possible excuse for putting it off, Whit found a place in the house where he could be alone, and he dialed his sister's number. When a man answered, it took Whit off guard. Of course he knew his sister had been married for many years, but he'd never actually spoken to the man. The few times he had called, either Crystal had answered the phone or he'd left a message on an answering machine.

He hurried and said, "Is Crystal at home?"

"I'm afraid she's not," the man said. "May I take a message?"

"Um . . ." he debated a moment before he said, "this is her brother, Whit. I—"

"Oh, hello Whit," the voice said with enthusiasm. Whit didn't even know this man's name. "This is Tom, Crystal's husband."

"Hello, Tom," Whit said. "It's nice to finally meet you." They both chuckled, and Whit felt remarkably more relaxed with him than he had *ever* felt with his sister, even when she'd been living at home when he'd been very young.

"You too," he said. "How are things going? Oh," he added in a tone of afterthought, "you usually don't call unless it's something important. Is this about your mother?"

"It is," Whit said.

He preferred to tell Crystal himself and was relieved when Tom said, "I'll have her call you back as soon as she gets home; it should be less than an hour. Feel free to call again if you don't hear from her within two."

"I will, thank you," Whit said. "And again, it's nice to meet you."

"You too, Whit," Tom said. "Take care now."

Whit disconnected the call and felt dazed for a minute. His knowledge of his sister having a husband and children had always been kind of an abstract thing. Suddenly it felt real, and he felt a little disoriented to think that she had a family—that they were *his* family too. They were active in the Church and so much more like him and Mary than Crystal had ever given herself a chance to find out. He invested a tiny bit of hope that their mother's death and his leaving the area might bring about some change in Crystal's attitude, and maybe they could actually get to know each other again.

When Crystal hadn't called back in *three* hours, Whit called her number again, almost certain she would not actually call him but wait for him to make the effort. The way Tom had worded it, he wondered if her husband knew the same thing. Crystal answered, and he said, "I met Tom . . . in a manner of speaking."

"So I heard," she said as if she resented it, and he felt suddenly angry over this ridiculous tension between them. He understood the need she felt to keep herself separate from the world she'd left behind. But why did that have to include him in such a harsh and strained way? Before he could think how to respond to what he was feeling, she said, "I am assuming you called because Mother is gone."

"That's right," he said. "I know you won't come to the funeral, but you needed to know."

He could hear the background noise of dishes being washed, but she said nothing for a long minute, as if she had to think very hard about anything at all to say to him. "Did she go peacefully?"

"At the end it was very peaceful. Some things that led up to the end, not so much."

He wondered if she would ask what he meant; he wondered if he wanted to tell her. What he wanted was for her to care, to show some interest.

When she said nothing he said, "Can I ask you a question?"

"I suppose," she said hesitantly.

"What are you afraid of?"

"I have no idea what you're talking about," she said defensively.

"Do you think that sharing a civil phone call with your brother is somehow going to contaminate you with an incurable disease? Do you really think that the people you want to avoid are people that I would have anything to do with? All of that is behind us both. So, what are you afraid of? If you understand faith at all, then why don't you try to exert some and stop being so afraid of things that have absolutely no bearing in your present life?"

"I think you're out of line and—"

"I think you need to listen just a little bit longer," Whit said firmly. Now that he had some momentum, he felt strongly compelled to say all the things to his sister that he'd always wanted to say. This might be his last chance. And then if she never wanted to talk to him again, so be it. "Listen to me, Crystal. I'm your *brother.* I know I'm an ex-con and I have tattoos, but I have served a mission and I have been a worthy temple recommend holder ever since. I was married in the temple and I have a beautiful family. Now that mom and her sisters are gone, we are leaving LA and we are not ever coming back; there's no one here who needs us anymore. Do you think it's possible that we could actually have phone conversations and exchange emails and get to know each other? Do you think we could at least exchange pictures of our kids? Seriously! This is ridiculous! You have no idea about what's really gone on here during these years you've been gone. I will not ever complain about being the one left to care for our mother, because I considered it an honor and a privilege, but there were sacrifices made at this end that you will never be able to comprehend. I'm glad you were able to get away from here and find a good life; I am *so* glad for that. But is it possible that you could let me into it, just a little bit? I don't need to know your last name or your address or anything else you don't want me to know. I'm not trying to *find* you and somehow taint your life with my sordid past. I just want to get to know my sister a little bit. Do you not think our parents would want that? They're finally together again, Crystal. I am so grateful to know that. How do you think they might feel about the fact that we rarely even talk unless someone dies? And even then you are barely civil. Why does it have to be that way? What are you so afraid of?"

"I have to go," she insisted as soon as he had stopped long enough for her to get a word in.

"Of course you do," he said. "You can look up the obituary online."

"Thank you," she said and hung up without even a good-bye.

Whit let out a frustrated sigh. He felt sure he would never hear from her again, and if he ever dared call her, he felt sure she would recognize his number and not answer. He didn't regret anything he'd said to her, but he wondered if he should have said it during a call concerning their mother's death. But then, when else would he have talked to her?

He kept stewing about the call for the rest of the day and throughout a night of sporadic sleep. He talked to Mary about it the following morning, and she believed he'd done the right thing, but he knew she would probably say that regardless. He appreciated her support, but he still felt uneasy about how things stood between him and his sister. Beyond Mary and his children, she was the only family he had. And Mary had no family at all. Perhaps with his mother's death, as well as having lost his aunts and having Carlos leave, he was feeling a desire to connect with family, and therefore the situation was bothering him more than it ever had.

Whit reminded himself that Crystal had her agency, and he also kept in mind that Mary and the children were the best family he could ever ask for. And as soon as he found a job, they would be off on a grand adventure to begin a new life together. He liked to imagine how the move might go and the kind of place where they might end up. But beyond loading everything they owned into a moving truck, he couldn't even grasp how it might be.

The day of Ida's funeral was as perfect as such a day could be. Surrounded by people who shared their beliefs, Whit and Mary both felt as if this were more like a wedding than a funeral. There was celebration in knowing that Ida and her husband were together again and that Ida was free from the disease that had robbed her of her mind a long time ago. There was also joy in the abundance of love these people had for Whit and Mary and also for Ida. In the talks given at the service and in conversations shared before and after, the Ida who had been so vibrant and full of faith before disease ravaged her seemed to come back to life through the sharing of memories and stories. She was well loved and remembered fondly, and Whit couldn't recall ever feeling such peace at a funeral. In fact, when it was all over and they returned home, knowing Ida was laid to rest until the day of resurrection, Whit had to confess to his wife that he actually felt joy. He felt *settled,* which seemed completely absurd since they could very well be moving into a motel by the end of the week. They had discussed the option of calling Mr. Lostin and asking for more time, given the circumstance of Whit's mother having passed away. But Mr. Lostin called the day after the funeral to tell them a realtor would start showing the house the following week and it needed to be empty and cleaned. Mary promised him that it would be.

Whit and Mary began a fast by sharing a prayer, then they each went to separate computers and started searching for options, praying about where to go, what to do, how to start. Twenty-four hours later when they broke their fast by sharing another prayer, they still had no feasible options or answers.

"Okay, well," Whit said, trying to act like the protector and provider in this family, "maybe we should shift our search to getting a storage unit for most of our things and a reasonable motel with Internet access so we can keep looking."

"That might be the way to go. Perhaps the job opening that's meant for you just hasn't opened up yet."

"Perhaps," Whit said, trying not to sound as discouraged as he felt.

Late in the afternoon he was standing at the window, looking out at the garden that had been his source of employment since the day he'd met Mary. He had told Mary that he would create a new garden wherever they went, but he felt sad to leave this one behind, and he knew that Mary did too. He took a deep breath and forced himself not to think about that, then he went outside to start disconnecting the angel fountain from its water and power sources. He had purchased a different fountain to put there so there wouldn't be an empty hole, but he needed to face up to getting it done. It seemed that once their very own sentimental fountain was removed from the garden, it was no longer officially theirs.

He was just getting started when his phone rang, and he pulled off a glove to grab it, stunned to see on the caller ID that it was his sister. He answered and was surprised to hear her husband instead. "Is this Whit?" he asked.

"It is," Whit said. "How are you, Tom?"

"I've had better days; how about yourself?"

"The same."

"How was the funeral?"

"It was very nice, thank you. The service was recorded. It's possible to email the recording if you think Crystal would want to hear it. I think she might enjoy it."

"That might be a very good thing," Tom said. "Thank you. I'll get back to you on that."

"What can I help you with?" Whit asked. "I can't pretend I'm not surprised to have you call."

"No, I suspected you would be," Tom said. "First of all, let me say that Crystal knows I'm calling you. I had to talk her into letting me, but she finally gave in."

"I see," Whit said.

"The thing is . . . when the two of you spoke a few days ago, she had the phone on speaker, and she didn't know I was nearby until after she hung up. I heard everything you said."

"I see," Whit said again in a lower tone.

"I'm going to tell you what I told her," Tom said, and Whit feared that his sister's husband was going to chew him out for upsetting her or causing unwanted drama. But Tom said, "Much of what you said is exactly what I've told her many times. I love her dearly, but I have trouble understanding why she is so fearful about having any association with you. Many times I tried to convince her that we should come to LA to see her mother, but she wouldn't have it. I assured her that it would not put us in any danger, but she was adamant. I have suggested she get some counseling and she has always refused—until now. I think that when she heard you say things I have said many times, it struck a chord she didn't want to hear but one she couldn't deny. So, my biggest reason for calling is to thank you for having the courage to say what you did. I think you were inspired."

Whit took a deep breath, then blew it out again. "Well, thank you, Tom. That means more than I can tell you, and . . . I'm very glad to hear that she's getting some help. I'm sure we both want her to be happy."

"Yes, we certainly do. And most of the time she is. She's a good mother and a good wife. I know all about her childhood and the things that were so hard for her. When those things surface, she's unhappy and even afraid. As long as those things are ignored, she's great."

"I'm glad to hear it. She gets that from our mother. She was amazing."

"I wish I could have known her, but . . . the thing is, I also think you're right about needing to get to know each other. I told Crystal that even if she didn't want to get to know you better, I wanted to. So, I don't know if Crystal will join me, but the kids and I would like to come to LA and meet you and your family. The kids have been nagging about going to Disneyland anyway, so we could do that while we're in the area, and—"

"I have to stop you, Tom," Whit said with a delighted chuckle. "What you just said makes me happier than I could ever tell you. But we are moving. We're nearly all packed and have to be out of this house within a few days because it's being sold. Our plan is to leave the area and make a fresh start now that Mom no longer needs me here. I guess you could say I'm following my sister's example in that."

"That sounds very exciting," Tom said. "So, we'll take the kids to Disneyland another time. As soon as you're settled, would it be all right if we come and get acquainted? Where are you headed?"

Whit chuckled again, this time somewhat awkwardly. "Um . . . the thing is . . . we have no idea." He gave his brother-in-law a two-minute explanation of the situation, then admitted that they were just planning to find a place to store their things until a job opened up.

"So, what kind of work are you looking for, exactly?" he asked. "What is it you do?"

Whit was a little stunned that Crystal hadn't even told her husband anything about his profession, which was something he'd learned from his father. He simply said, "I do gardening, landscaping. I can do anything related to that. Sprinkler systems; stuff like that. Although, I prefer the more aesthetic stuff. But at this point I will take anything to get us by until something more permanent opens up. I also have some experience with construction."

"You really did just say you do gardening?" Tom said and laughed.

"I really did," Whit said, his heart quickening.

"I actually know of a job opening less than an hour from here, and—"

"Um . . . I don't know if that's a good idea, Tom. Under the circumstances, I wouldn't even want you to tell me anything else without knowing that Crystal is comfortable with that."

"Fair enough. I will talk to her and get back to you. Whatever happens, we're going to hook up as soon as we can manage it."

"I'll look forward to it," Whit said, and they ended the call.

Whit left his fountain project and went to tell Mary what had just happened. Throughout the remainder of the day as he forced himself to complete the fountain project, he tried to convince himself not to hope that he could get a job in the same area where his sister lived, and that they might actually be able to begin new relationships. It all seemed like such a remarkable prospect, but it would take a miracle—or maybe more than one—to make it happen. But then, he'd been witness to a great many miracles in his life. Maybe it *was* possible.

He was disappointed when he hadn't heard back from Tom by the end of the day, but before going to bed, he and Mary and Adrienne went outside to throw coins into the new fountain that would soon belong to someone else. They all went out to the garage where the angel fountain was sitting, looking a little forlorn, but they talked about what it would be like when it was hooked up in some unknown place in some yet-to-be-discovered garden. They all agreed that it was a great adventure. Then they had family prayer and went to bed.

The following morning while Mary was gone to take Adrienne to school, Whit's heart began to pound when his phone rang, indicating it was Tom calling. He answered and was surprised to hear his sister's voice.

"Well, hello," he said eagerly. "I didn't know if you'd ever speak to me again."

"I know Tom already told you that you said some things I didn't want to hear. I'll admit I'm still having trouble with it, but I know you're right . . . about Mom and Dad not wanting us to not be connected. I think now I was wrong to never come and see her, but . . ." she began to cry, "I can't change the past. And I think it's going to take some work for me to

change the future, but . . . I'm willing to try, Whit. So . . ." He could hear
her taking a deep breath, then she cleared her throat and her voice became
steady once more. "If you will give me your email address right now, I will
type it in and send this email that is all ready to go."

"Really?" he said.

"Really," she said. "Just tell me and we'll leave it that. It's a step."

"Okay," he said and gave her the information while he was on his way
to the computer, so eager to see whatever she might send that he felt like
a child on Christmas Eve.

"We'll be in touch," she said and ended the call.

Whit only waited half a minute before an email from his sister popped
up. He had to just stare at her name there for a long minute, although the
email address gave no indication of her surname. But that was fine. He
then realized there were photo attachments, and he almost whooped for
joy. He felt the manifestation of another miracle as he looked at pictures
of Crystal and her husband and their three teenaged children. He couldn't
believe it! He became so caught up in the pictures that he was startled to
realize there was a lengthy letter.

Crystal wrote to sincerely thank him for all he'd done for their mother,
and to tell him how proud she was of him for the choices he'd made after
he'd gotten out of prison. She apologized profusely for not being there for
him, for not being more involved with their mother's care, and for not
being more of a sister to him. She admitted that she knew she had some
unreasonable fears, but she was going to work on that, and she asked for
his patience in working toward renewing their relationship.

Whit had to wipe his eyes as he read, and he couldn't wait to share the
email with Mary when she returned. Then through his blurred vision, he
saw the P.S. typed below his sister's name. It simply said: *Here is the link
for the job opening Tom told you about. It's at a reception center, and the man
who owns this place is someone we've known a long time. He's LDS and a good
man. Tom called him this morning and told him to look for your resumé. Let
me know how it goes.*

Whit held his breath and clicked on the link. Within just a moment
he knew that his sister lived less than an hour from Pocatello, Idaho. But
more amazing than his knowing was that she had willingly given him the
information. Perhaps their parents were very busy in their ministering
angel duties on the other side of the veil, because Whit surely felt new
miracles unfolding.

The job was for a head gardener-slash-maintenance director at a reception center. The center had extensive gardens and the capacity to host two events at a time during the summer months. Photographs of the gardens in full bloom took Whit's breath away, and he could only think that this could be his dream job. The requirements for the position were first and foremost a knowledge and ability to keep the grounds and gardens in pristine condition through every season. In the winter there would be snow removal and other related tasks. The job also required some basic maintenance skills in order to do minor repairs at the center. Whit knew he could do all of that as well. He'd not hired a plumber or electrician or mechanic or carpenter to do anything since his mission. He'd just figured out what needed to be done and had learned how to do it.

It only took him five minutes to email his resumé, even after making some minor adjustments to specify his relevant skills, and he marveled at the blessings of modern technology. He said a prayer then tried not to think about it—then he said another prayer and wandered around on the Internet, habitually searching for jobs that he might be qualified for anywhere in the country.

He wondered where Mary might be then remembered that she'd had a visiting teaching appointment she was going to take care of after she dropped Adrienne off; that's why she'd taken the baby with her. He usually watched Christian when she made her visits but this particular appointment was with an elderly sister who really enjoyed the baby, so Mary always took him, and their visits were usually quite lengthy. He felt frustrated because he couldn't even call her.

His phone rang, and he hoped it was her. He gasped when the caller ID said *Stardust Reception Center,* the name of the business where he had sent his resumé fewer than twenty minutes ago.

"Is this Whit Eden?" a jolly-sounding man asked through the phone.

"It is, yes," Whit said, his heart thudding. He kept in mind that a phone call was just a step, and sometimes it took a series of interviews to actually *get* a job and this might come to nothing. But oh, how he hoped!

"This is Bud Stardust. I just got done reading all about you, and I've heard good things from your brother-in-law."

Whit chuckled softly, mostly to cover his nervousness. "I must warn you, Mr. Stardust," he said, wondering if that could really be his name, "my brother-in-law barely knows me."

"Oh, he explained all that," this man said as if he fully understood and it was not a problem but Whit felt he needed to offer more clarification than that.

"If this is a job interview—and I hope it is—then I want to be straightforward with you, Mr. Stardust. I am looking for employment anywhere away from where I have lived my life up to this point, because I've had some unfavorable associations here. I don't like secrets, so I'm not going to keep any. I once belonged to a pretty rough street gang here in LA, and I did some prison time."

"And then you went on a mission and you've been clean ever since. Did I not mention that your brother-in-law already told me all that?" He chuckled in a jolly way that eased Whit's nerves.

"I just wanted to be sure of exactly what he'd told you," Whit said. "And I'm also part Hispanic."

"I know your sister, young man. Such things make no difference to me." He let out a full laugh that was *especially* jolly. Whit chuckled from the contagion of it and felt like he was talking to Santa Claus. *Mr. Stardust.* "Now, who is conducting this interview?" he asked, followed by another jolly chuckle. Before Whit could tell him to go on, he did. "I've read over what you sent me, and it seems you've got the bases covered rather well." Another chuckle. "You've certainly got all of the qualifications I'm looking for; you might just be the answer to my prayers, young man."

Whit had to sit down and force himself to remain composed. How could *he* be the answer to this man's prayers, when Whit could feel miracles falling down around him like snowflakes from heaven? He remembered then that Crystal had told him this man was LDS. It was just feeling better and better.

"Because it's winter, we've been managing with just hiring out for snow removal and repairs and such, but once spring comes I need someone I can really rely on, and I'll be honest with you, I haven't had good luck with hiring people for this position."

"And you think I'll work out?" Whit asked, his heart pounding so hard he felt sure Mr. Stardust could hear it.

"I'm hoping so, and I've got a good feeling about this." Jolly chuckle. "I tend to trust those feelings, young man, and I never felt it with the others that have gone before you; it was always just a matter of making do with who was available." Whit had to cover the mouthpiece of the phone to breathe in and out deeply, as it was sounding more and more like he had a job. "If you have the skills you claim, then the only thing I really need from you is a good work ethic and integrity."

Whit squeezed his eyes closed, silently thanking God. If he knew anything, he knew he could honor an employer with his good work ethic and integrity. Oh, how he wanted this to be what it appeared to be! "I can give you that," he said firmly.

"Then let's give it a try," Mr. Stardust said. "When can you be here?"

"Really?" Whit said, making no effort to hide his enthusiasm.

"If you want the job, it's yours."

"Oh, thank you! This is . . . a miracle for us! Truly."

Mr. Stardust offered another jolly laugh, as if he were genuinely happy over having contributed to a miracle. "For me too, Mr. Eden," he said.

"Please call me Whit."

"Okay, Whit. When can you be here? I understand you're living out of state and I know it can take some effort to move a family, but I would be awfully glad to have you get started as soon as possible. Do you think you could start in a week?"

"I can," Whit said, certain the other details would work out. He didn't know yet where they would live, but getting a motel in a new place where he had a new job felt a whole lot better than getting one here. They would certainly manage. They were mostly packed, and driving to Idaho was not so terribly far.

"Very good!" Mr. Stardust chuckled, but quickly subdued his delight and said, "Oh, one more thing I need to clarify. It can take some time to work out details with taking on a new job. I want you to know that I need things done to certain specifications; that's what makes the business work. I will do my best to communicate my expectations clearly to you, and if you have questions or challenges, I expect you to do the same. If I have a problem with any of my employees, I tell them straight up and give them plenty of opportunity to correct it. If for some reason this arrangement doesn't work out, Whit, I will give you plenty of notice so that you aren't left high and dry. If you're all right with that, then we have a deal."

"More than all right," Whit said. "I will be there in a week. I think I have all the information I need from your website."

"Let me give you my cell number; that's not on the website. If you have any questions or problems getting here, please call anytime."

"Thank you," Whit said and wrote down the number. "Thank you so much, Mr. Stardust," he concluded.

"Please all me Bud," he said and chuckled. "Everybody does."

Whit felt comfortable enough with this man to say, "I have to ask . . . is that your real name?"

His jolly laugh rang through the phone. "Bud is much better than the name my parents bestowed upon me; I've been going by Bud since I was a kid, so it's real enough. When I was a bishop lots of folks even called me Bishop Bud." He laughed good-naturedly. "Of course, Bishop Stardust had a nice ring to it."

"So, that *is* your real name."

"It is, indeed. Convenient when God gives you a name that looks so good on the business you've always dreamed of owning." He chuckled. "Which reminds me . . . how does a man named Eden end up being a gardener?"

"Just what I came to this world to do, I guess. I got the name from my father, and he too was a gardener. I'm sure we could trace our genealogy back to the original Garden of Eden if they'd kept better records."

This made Bud laugh heartily, and Whit joined him with perfect delight. He felt so much relief and joy and gratitude—and he already felt a deep affinity with this good man.

After the call ended, Whit let out an enormous whoop of excitement that would have awakened the baby at the other end of the house if he had been there and sleeping. Thankfully he wasn't. Then Whit dropped to his knees right then and there and thanked God for having a plan in place all along—a plan filled with miracles and blessings, not the least of which was the healing taking place between him and his sister.

With his prayer concluded, he got online to answer his sister's letter. Knowing he couldn't call Mary yet, he enjoyed being able to tell Crystal that he had already spoken with Bud Stardust, he had the job, and they would be on their way to Pocatello within a couple of days. He expressed gratitude for her email, for all she'd said that had warmed his heart, and for the opportunity to get to know her and her family. He thanked her for trusting him enough to give him this privilege of coming into her community. Knowing her fears and trepidations, he knew that must have been a huge step for her. It was one thing for her family to come and visit him and then go back to their own environment; it was entirely different to actually invite Whit to come and live in the same area. And he attached some pictures of him and Mary and the children. At the end of his letter, he added a P.S. that simply said, *Do you have any recommendations for a half-decent, not-too-expensive motel in the area where we could stay while we look for a place to live?*

Whit had barely sent his response to Crystal when he heard the garage door opening and knew Mary was home. Anxious to tell her the miracles that had just unfolded, and not knowing where to begin, he hurried out to meet her. She stepped out of the truck and put a finger to her lips to indicate he should be quiet. *Quiet?* He wanted to shout for joy and declare the good news at the top of his lungs!

"Christian is sleeping," she said in a soft voice, motioning toward the baby in the back seat. Whit unbuckled the baby seat and carried it carefully into the house while Christian continued to breathe evenly in peaceful slumber. Once he'd set the baby seat down, Whit took Mary's purse and set it down before he picked her up in her arms and twirled her around, laughing with delight while managing to keep the volume reasonably soft.

"What on earth are you doing?" Mary asked, laughing with him. It was moments such as this that reminded her that he was ten years younger and *very* strong. She felt weightless as he whirled with her in his arms, then he gracefully set her down on the couch, for which she was grateful, considering the dizziness he'd evoked in her.

"What is going on?" she asked with a laugh as he plopped down beside her and took her hand. She couldn't miss the smile that consumed his face and lit his eyes.

"Oh, my dear Mary!" he said. "You cannot believe what has happened since you left! I never imagined that so many miracles could pour out of heaven in so short a time! When God says that the windows of heaven will open, and he will send so many blessings that there isn't room enough to receive them, He means it."

Whit saw tears in Mary's eyes and he wondered why for only a moment. He didn't even have to ask to know that she had just received a spiritual witness to the truth of what he'd just said, and he had felt it too. Not only was the principle true, but God was witnessing to them that the miracles that were occurring were indeed His doing, and they were in answer to that very promise. Mary didn't even need to know *what* the miracles were to know that they were indeed miracles with a divine signature.

He had so much to tell her, and they had so much to do, but for the moment he felt more inclined to just pull her into his arms and hold her close while he silently thanked God for blessing his life so richly, for allowing him to share every aspect of his life with this remarkable woman. He pulled back to look into her eyes. He laughed softly and she did the same, then he kissed her and enjoyed it so much that he almost forgot all the glorious news he had to share with her.

Chapter Thirteen

"NOW, TELL ME!" MARY INSISTED. "I can't bear it another minute!"

Whit didn't know where to start. He laughed and said, "I'm just going to give you the bottom line, and then I'll fill in the details."

"Okay," she said with enthusiasm.

"Here goes," he said and took a deep breath. "Crystal called me. She apologized. She wants to work on healing our relationship. More on that later." Mary gasped and got fresh tears in her eyes. She knew how much that meant to him. "She asked for my email address and she had a letter all ready to send. It was an incredible letter, Mary. You can read it later. And she sent pictures of her and Tom and the kids. It's so amazing!"

"Oh, it *is* a miracle!" Mary exclaimed with a burst of laughter. "It is!"

"I'm just getting started," Whit said, and Mary's eyes widened as if she couldn't even imagine what might possibly come next. He could barely imagine it himself, and it had actually *happened* to him. "At the end of her letter she had a link to the reception center where Tom had told me he knew of this job opening. She told me the man who owned it was LDS and Tom had called him and told him about me, and had told him that he could expect to hear from me."

Mary put a hand over her mouth as if she suspected what might be coming and she didn't want an outburst of emotion to interrupt his story.

"I added a couple of things to the resumé because he was looking for someone who could do *other* things that I know how to do. More on that later. I emailed the resumé, and . . ." He wished there could be some kind of drumroll. After all the time they'd spent fasting and praying and searching, he figured that trumpets should be blaring, or angels singing— or something. Perhaps they were, but with the veil in place it just couldn't be heard with human ears.

"He already called, Mary. His name is Bud Stardust. He was delightful to talk to." He chuckled. "He sounds like Santa Claus. He interviewed me on the phone; we talked things over, and . . ." Whit's voice broke slightly, ". . . he gave me the job, Mary. I start in a week." He heard her sob from beneath the hand still clamped over her mouth, and he saw huge tears form in her eyes, but he had to finish. "Mary," he said earnestly and took her shoulders into his hands. "I have a job in another state, working for a good man, doing everything I'm good at and enjoy doing, and it's in the same community where Crystal and her family live."

Mary shook her head as if she couldn't believe it, then she moved her hand away from her mouth so she could throw her arms around Whit's shoulders. She held on to him and wept with joy and relief. They sat together for a long while as he filled in all of the details he'd skipped over. Mary kept weeping and exclaiming in awe. At one point they paused in their conversation to hold hands and offer a formal prayer of gratitude, then they kept talking about how abundantly God had blessed them, how amazingly so many elements had come together, and how excited they both were to begin their new adventure.

Christian woke up in good spirits and added more delight to the festive mood of the house. While Whit and Mary shared a late lunch and took care of the baby, they made some lists of what needed to be done and fine-tuned their moving plans. They decided that Whit would pick up a moving truck in the morning, they would spend the next day loading it, and the following morning they would be on their way to Idaho before the sun came up. With a little research they had discovered that it was about 850 miles away, which would take about twelve hours to drive under ideal conditions; however, they were traveling with two vehicles, one of them being a loaded U-Haul truck. Mary would be driving the family vehicle with the baby, and Adrienne could go back and forth between riding with her mother and her father. They concluded that they would stop at a place that was about two-thirds of the distance to spend the night, and they made reservations at a good motel room in that city. They both agreed that it felt great to actually know *where* they were going and when they would arrive.

Since the following day would be filled with emptying the house and cleaning it, they decided to take care of some errands that afternoon so that they would be all set to go. One of the things they did was to get new cell phones with new numbers, and they put the account in Mary's name from her first marriage, which would never connect them to anyone in LA. Since she had all the right documentation, doing so was not a problem. They both considered it a precaution that was likely unnecessary, but it just felt like more of a clean break to not even have anyone from this area know their phone numbers. They would keep the old phone account for another couple of days, until they had notified Whit's sister and his new boss of the new number, and then they would turn off the old phones and get rid of them. They would keep in touch with friends and members of the branch via email only. If for no other reason, Whit wanted to be able to tell his sister that he had taken such precautions. No one from his old life, not even other Church members, had any idea where they would be moving, and they would maintain unlisted numbers—if only for the principle of the matter.

When Whit considered how Carlos had literally and legally given up his past in every way, this seemed like a lesser way of making equivalent changes. They had no need to go into witness protection—for which he was grateful. And he had no reason whatsoever to think that any of his cousins would ever even try to find him. They had lived separate enough lives for many years now. But knowing they *couldn't* find him just felt even better. And he knew that it would mean a lot to Crystal if he could give her such reassurances while she was working on conquering her fears and coming to terms with letting the past go.

That evening, Mary called Janel and updated her on all the good news. They'd talked after Ida had passed away, and since Janel had been working in the house when all the drama of the murder had taken place, it had seemed only right to tell her of the poignant resolution. Now their conversation was filled with joy over all the miracles taking place. Since they'd become accustomed to a long-distance relationship, this would not be any change for them. Janel was the only person from their past who would have their new phone numbers—but since she lived in Texas, it certainly wasn't a problem.

Branch members had known for weeks of the impending move of the Eden family and of the date they would need to be out of the house, so several people had tentatively set aside time to help with loading the truck and cleaning the house. Mary only had to make one phone call for a network of volunteers to be put in place, and the following morning several men and women arrived early with many helping hands, cleaning supplies, and plenty of food to keep everyone going through the day. Whit and Mary mostly supervised, both marveling at how quickly and efficiently everything came together. Almost everything had already been boxed up except for the things that were being used every day. Now, women helped Mary decide necessities that would be needed for the journey to their new mysterious destination, since they would need to stay in a motel along the way. Some things would be put into the family truck for easy access. Others would go into the moving truck last of all so that they could be readily available if necessary. All those who were helping were well aware of Whit's and Mary's reasons for keeping their destination a secret, and because they all knew that it wasn't a matter of any of them not being trustworthy, they simply understood without questions or resentment. Therefore, as they worked, it became a pleasant joke about how the Eden family was heading off on a secret adventure.

Comical speculations began flying around about where they were going, and since they'd been careful to not even mention how many days they planned to be traveling, no one had any idea about their destination. Whit and Mary had purposely not told Adrienne anything about their intended destination so that she couldn't accidentally give away any information. The branch members speculated that the family might be going to Florida or Wisconsin or even New Jersey. Someone said, "Do they *have* gardens in New Jersey?" which provoked laughter. Many ideas were bandied about, but not one person even suggested *Idaho,* as if the very thought of it was being blocked from their minds.

Adrienne didn't go to school that day but was engaged in helping pack her own things, and she was being very responsible about it. They had already discussed the upcoming move with her teacher. Although Adrienne felt some sadness about moving away, she had a healthy attitude about being with her family and knowing they would be together and secure no matter where they went. She had already said good-bye to her teacher and classmates, and her only real apparent sadness was over leaving her friend, Rachel.

Cinda brought Rachel over after school so that they could help with the project. Rachel brought Adrienne a gift that Adrienne was excited to open. There was a little angel statue of two girls sitting close together, representing best friends. And there were also a couple of activity books that would be good for a long journey. Adrienne was thrilled with the gifts and thanked her friend and her friend's mother for being so kind. The mothers then sat the girls down in front of the computer and engaged in a quick project that they had previously discussed. They set up email addresses for the girls and quickly taught them the basics of how to email back and forth. The girls were told the strict rules of emailing, and since the parents had the passwords, they could keep track of what was going back and forth. But the prospect of being able to communicate this way excited the girls and helped ease the pain of separation. Right then and there, Cinda took a picture of the girls, then plugged her camera into the computer and demonstrated how the picture could be emailed. The girls both giggled when they opened their new email accounts and saw the picture appear there. Mary then demonstrated Skype and showed the girls how they could talk to each other on the computer and even see each other. They loved that as well!

By suppertime, the moving truck was ready to go, the house was completely clean, and everyone enjoyed a dinner that had been brought in by the Relief Society. They used paper plates and plastic utensils, since everything else was packed. The family then shared their final good-byes with people who were dear and precious to them. While parting was difficult, they eagerly anticipated the prospect of making new friends and becoming a part of a new ward or branch in Idaho. Adrienne was less emotional than they had expected her to be, and they figured all the conversations they'd had to prepare them for this day had paid off; she seemed prepared and even excited for these changes.

After the children were down for the night, Whit and Mary walked hand in hand through the garden, reminiscing about how they'd fallen in love here and how they would always cherish fond memories of this place. They had taken many pictures in the house and garden during the time they'd lived there, and had taken even more once they'd realized they were moving. They could take the memories with them, and they both felt content and ready to move on when they went into the house to get some much-needed sleep. They slept on beds that would remain with the house, along with much of the furniture that also technically belonged with it. An alarm woke them very early, and they hurried to get on their way. The sleeping children were carried to the family vehicle, and they hardly stirred. Whit and Mary hurried to strip the beds and stuffed the sheets and blankets into large trash bags, which they put into the back of the moving truck. They both walked through the house once more to make certain everything was in order, then they drove away, with Mary following the moving truck that Whit drove.

They were many miles away from Los Angeles before the sun came up, illuminating the road before them that was leading them to a new life. Whit and Mary could communicate with each other on cell phones set on speed dial and hands-off speaker mode, and Mary could let Whit know when the children were awake and needed to be fed. They stopped at a service station that also sold fast food, including breakfast items. They took advantage of the available food, the restrooms, and the gas pump. They also purchased some snacks for the road. When they were ready to set off again, Whit noticed a text from his sister on his new cell phone. He had emailed his new number and his reasons for changing it, and all of the other information he wanted her to know about this move he was making with his family. The text he received now said: *I assume you're on the road by now. Travel safely. Will find a place for you to stay before you get here. Will send details when I have them. Looking forward to seeing you!*

Whit smiled and took a deep breath of gratitude. "Wow!" he said out loud and chuckled as he set his phone nearby and put the truck in gear, aware of Mary in his rearview mirror as he pulled out of the service station. The hours on the road seemed long, but everything went smoothly. They arrived at their planned destination before dark to spend the night. A thought occurred to both Whit and Mary as they got out of the vehicles and felt the temperature of the air. They had both always lived in southern California or Mexico, and they were moving to Idaho—at the end of February. They hurried into the hamburger place where they'd stopped to eat before finding their motel, and once they'd ordered, Whit texted his sister to ask: *Is there snow there?*

Five minutes later he received the reply: *Oh, yes!*

"Um . . ." he said to Mary, "I think we need to go shopping." She looked a little disoriented and he said, "Where we're going, there's snow."

"Snow?" Adrienne squealed with excitement. "There's snow! I've never seen snow before! Can we make a snowman? Can we? Can we?"

Her parents laughed and Whit said, "I've never made a snowman before, but we'll sure try to figure it out." He had only been exposed to snow a couple of times in his life during some minimal travels, and Mary admitted that she had only seen snow once.

"Well, this really *is* an adventure," he said, and as soon as they'd finished eating they found a Wal-Mart and purchased coats, hats, and gloves for everyone, as well as boots and snow pants for everyone but the baby. But they did get some heavier baby blankets and some warmer clothes for the baby and for Adrienne. Later that evening when the children were asleep in the motel room, Whit enjoyed his favorite time of the day—those minutes of perfect quiet when he held Mary close, after they'd prayed together and before they fell asleep. They talked in the darkness of all that had changed in their lives so quickly and speculated on what tomorrow would bring. They hoped that Crystal and Tom wouldn't have too much trouble finding them a place to stay, and they hoped it wouldn't be too cramped or difficult a place to live while they found something more permanent.

They all slept well in spite of Christian waking up a few times due to being in a strange bed. But he quickly went back to sleep each time and so did his parents. The next morning they were packed up and on their way without too much trouble but without the rush and early hour of the previous morning. At least it was daylight. They went to a local diner and ate a good breakfast then they were on their way again. Adrienne sometimes rode with Whit, keeping herself well occupied with her activity books and the bag of other things she'd brought along. Whit enjoyed having her with him but most of the time it was more practical to have her in the other truck with the baby, since Adrienne did a very good job of keeping him happy and occupied when he hated being strapped in his seat for such long hours.

Adrienne *was* in the truck with him when she first saw snow on the ground. She got so excited that they had to pull over and actually touch it and play in it for a few minutes. The cold air that they were so unaccustomed to quickly urged them back to the warm vehicles, and they all knew they would be making a big adjustment in that regard.

When they stopped for gas and to use service-station restrooms, the temperature of the air made them very grateful for the coats and other warm clothes they'd purchased the previous day. A couple of hours later they stopped for lunch, knowing they were just a few short hours from their new home.

Before they started driving again, Whit texted Crystal and told her where they were. He was hoping for the information she'd promised about where they should go. He couldn't help feeling a little unnerved by not having a *specific* destination other than Pocatello.

They were less than an hour from Pocatello when Whit heard his phone signal that he'd received a text. Mary would have called because she knew he couldn't text and drive. So it had to be Crystal. He signaled and carefully pulled over to the side of the road, noting in his rearview mirror that Mary was doing the same. He picked up the phone to read the text, gasping as he did, then he had to read it again to be certain he wasn't hallucinating. He had been hoping that Crystal would find them a half-decent motel, but her lengthy text was yet another miracle.

Here's the address of where you need to go. I hope you have a GPS. It's about ten minutes outside of Pocatello, in a semi-rural area with a few neighbors within walking distance, but a lot of open space. The house is a rent-to-own thing, so you could buy it eventually if you like it, but you don't have to sign a lease. The house has been empty a while so it might need some dusting, but the power and gas and water have been turned on, and the house should be warm by the time you get there. I paid the first and last month's rent, and a deposit on the utilities that will be paid through the landlord. So you owe me for that. Whenever you can pay me is fine. I'm not worried. Drive safely, and text me as soon as you get there. The key is under the flowerpot on the porch. Yes, it really is. Sis.

By the time he'd read the text twice, Mary was knocking at the truck window on his side. He opened the door and handed her his phone. "Read this," he said, "and then convince me that the Red Sea hasn't parted for us in the last not-so-many days."

Mary gasped, then laughed as she read. "A house? We can actually unpack our things into a *house?* I was hoping for a decent motel and a storage unit."

"Exactly," Whit said. "And even if the house is a dump and we decide not to stay, it's a *house.*"

"Yes, it is. But I really don't think Crystal would expect us to move into anything too awful."

"No, I don't either. I guess we'll see." He kissed her. "Okay, shall we drive the final stretch?"

"Let's go for it," she said and kissed him again, then she squealed like an excited child and hurried back to the other vehicle, obviously freezing.

Whit got back into the truck and put the address into his GPS. Once it had coordinated the directions, it told him that he would arrive in one hour and four minutes. He thought it might take a little longer given the vehicle he was driving, but they were almost home.

When he knew they were just a few miles from Pocatello, Whit hit speed dial for Mary's phone and turned it on speaker so he could drive and talk to her. She did the same, and they were able to talk as they traversed that final distance. He could hear Christian babbling in the background and Adrienne talking to the baby to help keep him happy.

"This feels very strange," Whit said as they drove into the city. "Knowing I'm going to work here, that we'll shop here and become a part of this place we've never seen before now . . . just feels weird."

"Yes, it does," Mary said. "It's like some kind of time warp or something."

They made some inconsequential comments to each other as they passed grocery stores and movie theaters and shopping areas, following the GPS directions through the city and then on a long highway leading out of the city in a different direction. Whit closely watched the GPS as it measured the remaining distance, and he kept Mary apprised. His heart quickened as they came within a mile of where they were going to live, and he looked out over a seemingly endless expanse of snow-covered fields. It was breathtakingly beautiful beneath a clear, blue sky. He'd never seen anything like it. He told Mary so, and she agreed, repeating that it was incredible. He could hear Adrienne commenting, and the baby was surprisingly quiet.

Whit became so enthralled with the scenery that he was surprised to hear the GPS tell him that he would arrive in half a mile. He could see a small cluster of a few not-so-closely-situated houses a short distance up the highway, and knew the home they would rent was one of them. The house they were looking for was on the right, and he slowed the truck down and pulled over, unable to stop staring. It was a quaint, two-story home that looked a bit on the old side—which only added to its quaintness—but it looked to be in excellent repair. It had a large porch with railings and a huge yard that was completely covered in snow. And there was actually a white picket fence. Unbelievable, he thought. A white picket fence. A sidewalk that led from the gate to the front porch had been shoveled and was free of snow; everything else was a perfect blanket of white. There was a long, snow-covered driveway, a garage that was separate from the house, and some kind of shed in the distance in what appeared to be a *very* large yard. Whit *loved* the yard, even as blanketed by snow as it was.

He stopped staring and got out to meet Mary halfway between the two vehicles. She was holding Adrienne's hand and had the baby in her arms. He took the baby and put his arm around Mary and they just stood there, staring at it as if they were in some kind of mutual dream.

"It's so . . . *proverbial*," Mary said as if the word were magical. "I mean . . . it's like out of a story book."

"Yeah," Whit said while they stood there freezing.

"It really does have a white picket fence . . . and a railed porch and—"

"Can we go in now?" Adrienne asked, impatient with all the philosophizing.

"We certainly can," Whit said and opened the gate, leading the way up the walk. On the porch they found a little flower pot with some kind of shriveled plant in it.

"You're going to have to do something about *that,*" Mary said, as if his skills and responsibilities as a gardener would be measured by having a dead plant on his porch.

"I'll get right on it," Whit said with sarcasm. He handed the baby to Mary and bent over to find the key beneath the pot. He turned it in the lock, opened the door, and warmth rushed out to greet them. They stepped inside to feel not only the warmth from the heat having been turned on in anticipation of their arrival but the warmth of a home that felt cozy even when it was completely empty. They stood on hardwood floors and could see a large living area in one direction, an apparent dining area in another, and a quaint little upward staircase in front of them.

"It's beautiful," Mary declared as they both noted that everything appeared to be in excellent condition. Adrienne took hold of Whit's hand and held it as they explored the kitchen, which had new counters, appliances, and fixtures as well as a lot of cupboard space. There was a study on the main floor as well as a bathroom, a little breakfast nook, a large dining room, and the kitchen and living area. Adrienne hurried up the stairs, feeling the excitement that they were actually going to live here. Upstairs they found two more bathrooms, three bedrooms, and spacious closets. Upon further exploration, they found a full basement with a finished family room, one more bedroom, and another bathroom. There was a laundry room but no washer and dryer, which made them realize they needed to buy those. And there were two different storage rooms with a great deal of space. Mary could imagine one of them filled with food storage, and the other would be perfect for holiday decorations and other things that needed to be accessed only at certain times of the year.

Now that they'd seen the whole house, Adrienne began running around with delight, not only excited but full of many wiggles from the long journey. Whit wrapped his arms around Mary and the baby and they held to each other tightly.

"Welcome home, Mrs. Eden."

"Amen!" she said earnestly and let out a deep sigh. They held each other for as long as the baby would allow without wiggling, then they set him down on the carpeted family room floor.

Whit looked around and said, "I guess we'll see if it works out permanently . . . if we might decide to buy it, but . . . it sure feels like home."

"It really does," Mary added, then laughed. "Incredible!"

Whit remembered that he was supposed to text his sister when they had arrived. He hurried and did that, then they bundled up to start unloading some of the necessities that had been packed for easy access while Adrienne watched over Christian on the carpeted floor in the basement. In half an hour they had brought a number of important items into the house, and they figured if they could get to the mattresses—which they knew they could—and go to a grocery store, they could manage until the next day. Whit followed Mary into the house and left the door partly open when his effort to kick it closed fell short. They both went up the stairs and took a minute to decide for certain which room would work best for each child; the master bedroom was obvious with its larger size and connected bathroom. Whit went back down the stairs and stopped abruptly when he saw a dark-haired woman standing just inside the door. *His sister.* He had to stop for a long moment and just absorb the reality.

"Hello, Whit," she said. "The door was open."

"Hello," he said and hurried to close the space between them, hugging her as tightly as he could without hurting her, as if it could make up for so many years of no hugs at all. She hugged him back just as tightly, and he realized she was crying.

"I'm so sorry," she muttered, then pulled back and wiped at her tears. "Can you ever forgive me? For . . . everything?"

"There's nothing to forgive, Crystal. And . . . the miracles you have brought into my life just in the last few days more than make up for anything that might have ever been a problem. We're starting over . . . right now."

She nodded and laughed, then hugged him again. He'd forgotten how beautiful she was; her pictures had not done her justice. Crystal then motioned absently toward outside while she took off her gloves. "Tom and the kids are coming. We brought separate vehicles, but they're excited to meet you, and . . ." Crystal's eyes shifted as Mary came down the stairs.

"This must be Mary," Crystal said. Speaking directly to Mary she said, "I recognize you from your pictures." She chuckled awkwardly. "But then . . . who else would be here?"

"I'm so glad to finally have this moment," Mary said and rushed forward, hugging Crystal as if they were long-lost sisters. And in a way, they were. Both of the women got a little teary, and Whit felt a bit choked up himself.

When greetings seemed complete for the moment, Crystal asked, "So is the house going to work?"

"Work?" Whit said. "It's perfect! How did you manage?"

"I don't know. I just got online to look and there it was. The owner said it had been empty for a little more than a month—that his efforts to rent it just hadn't worked out. Don't think *that* was a coincidence."

"Obviously not," Whit said, and he loved how she could so easily make spiritual implications. In that respect, they were very similar.

"So, you really like it?"

"We really do!" Mary said.

"I confess that I know what your salary will be because I looked online and it had the salary for the position listed. So, I believe the rent is easily doable, and you told Tom you had a little money to work with." She told him the amount of the rent, and he was surprised to find that it was lower than he'd expected.

"Yes, we can manage that just fine," he said. "I can't thank you enough."

"I'm so glad I could help," she said and looked around. "Now, where are my niece and nephew?"

They went downstairs together where Crystal made a big fuss over the children, and they both took to her readily. They heard a loud knock at the door and Crystal said, "Oh, that will be Tom and the kids."

They all went upstairs to meet the rest of the family. It *was* Tom and the kids, and they had come with enough dinner for everyone from a local chicken place; they had also brought large packages of paper plates, bowls, cups, and plastic utensils. "To get you by for a while," Crystal said.

After they'd all officially met, Tom offered a blessing on the food at Whit's request, in which he thanked God for bringing this family back together and for the safe travels of Whit and Mary and their children. They visited over the meal and got to know each other a little better. To Whit it still felt like a dream, and when he occasionally met Mary's expressive eyes, he knew she felt much the same way. As soon as they were finished eating, everyone bundled up and started unloading the truck. Adrienne was once again put in charge of watching the baby in the basement where there was carpet, away from the cold air coming in through the open door.

Whit and Mary were pleasantly surprised with the help Crystal and her family were offering. While Tom and his two strapping sons helped Whit unload the truck and put things in their proper rooms as much as possible, Mary and Crystal and her daughter started unloading boxes marked *bathroom* and *kitchen,* hoping to find all of the essentials necessary to manage through the coming days of unpacking and getting settled in.

While Mary was enjoying the opportunity to visit with Crystal and her daughter as they worked, they became aware of a bit of a ruckus. The women came out of the kitchen to see about a dozen people filing through the front door, their arms already laden with boxes and furniture, except for the women who carried covered bowls and casserole dishes straight to the kitchen, as if they knew exactly what they were doing. One woman had a gallon of milk, a loaf of bread, a jar of peanut butter, and a box of cereal. Gradually Mary and Whit met the bishop and one of his counselors, two Relief Society counselors and a couple of other sisters, and a few members of the elders quorum who were all from the ward where Whit and Mary would now be attending church. Tom had found the information for the bishop of this area, had called him to say that a new family was arriving, and the rest had been taken care of. Before these people left, the moving truck had been completely unloaded, the beds had been assembled, and the kitchen and bathrooms were functional. There were enough casseroles and salads in the fridge to last a few days while they settled in. They had been given a ward list with numbers they could call if they needed anything, along with the location of the local ward building and the time of their meetings on Sunday.

After the ward members left, Crystal looked around the bare front room and said, "You're going to need some new furniture."

"Yeah," Whit chuckled. "Most of the furniture we were using went with the house we left behind. We bought some beds before we left, but we need a washer and dryer and some couches."

"And a table and chairs," Mary pointed out.

Whit chuckled again. "We have a budget for that—especially now that I actually have a job."

"Is there anything else we can do to help you tonight?" Tom asked.

"I think we're set," Whit said. "We never imagined being so well settled so quickly. Thank you for everything."

"Well," Crystal said, putting on her coat, "I'm coming over tomorrow about . . . shall we say eleven? And I'm taking you shopping. I know where to find all the best bargains. We'll get groceries and furniture and all that stuff." She looked at Adrienne and added, "And I'm going to take you all out to lunch to celebrate."

Adrienne clapped her hands. "What are we celebrating?"

"A family reunion," Crystal said, looking at her brother. She then hugged Whit tightly and said close to his ear, "I'm so glad you're here. We're going to have such fun." She looked at him and smiled. "I just can't believe what a fool I was to wait this long."

"Perhaps the timing was right . . . and necessary. I couldn't have left LA before now."

"Perhaps," she said, "but now we can make up for lost time."

"I'm counting on it," Whit said and put his arm around Mary's shoulders.

They all shared parting hugs, and after Crystal and her family were gone, Whit and Mary looked at each other and both laughed with delight then hugged each other and knew they had been more blessed than they could possibly imagine. A short while later, the children were asleep in their new rooms. Whit and Mary snuggled closely in the bed in *their* new room and marveled at how far they had come in so short a time, then they slept contentedly.

The next morning, Whit was able to return the moving truck to the local branch of the company through which it had been rented. Mary picked him up, and they were back home long before Crystal was due to arrive. She was true to her word in giving them a marvelous shopping excursion. Whit gave her a check for the money he owed her the minute she showed up. She thanked him and kissed his cheek, but later she insisted on paying for lunch for all of them.

The following day they went to church in their new ward, and the feeling of being home settled in more deeply. After church they used the GPS to find Crystal's home, which was about a half hour's drive from where Whit and Mary now lived. It was a large, beautiful home, and it was evident that they were financially comfortable. Crystal and Tom had prepared a wonderful dinner, and they all agreed that it was amazing how quickly they had all come to feel comfortable with each other.

During a quiet moment alone as brother and sister, Crystal asked Whit some specific questions about their mother's situation prior to her death and how it had been. Whit told her how the Alzheimer's had affected Ida and a little bit about how difficult it had been. But he felt strongly that it was best to avoid the details of other things for now, and perhaps it would never be necessary to tell her. He would know if he needed to when the time came, and either way it would be okay. They were reunited now and had a promising future of sharing their lives and giving their children the gift of cousins they could love and respect and trust. That in itself was a miracle!

On Monday morning, Whit called his new boss to tell him he was now living nearby and settled in. He wondered if it might be possible to come and meet him and see where he would be working, and if he could bring his family with him so that they could see it as well. Bud was thrilled at the prospect of meeting them all, and they set a time for that afternoon.

The reception center was beautiful, and Bud Stardust was everything Whit had imagined over the phone. He was built like a big teddy bear, not at all overweight, but with a large chest, wide shoulders, and big, square hands. He was as jolly in person as he had been over the phone, and he was very sweet with Mary and the children. Mary liked the way he told her that he expected his employees to put in their hours and meet their obligations but he considered it even more important that their employment didn't interfere with their family time—and he would never expect so much of Whit that he couldn't be there for her and the children when he was needed.

Bud gave them a tour of the reception center, and they were all impressed with how beautiful it was. The place had a great deal of class! The gardens were completely snowed under, but Bud still took them outside, and they stood on a patio that had been cleared of snow while he pointed out the two little footbridges that covered a stream that ran during the warmer months. There was a gazebo and a beautiful stone fence that surrounded the property. Bud told Whit about the different areas of flower beds and rock formations, and it was easy to imagine what it would look like in the summer. Whit felt even more that this was his dream job, and he liked Bud so much that he couldn't imagine working for a better man.

When Whit officially started work, the family was settled in enough to manage without him for the day. The refrigerator and cupboards were stocked with food, and the new appliances and furniture had been delivered. Mary had a lot of unpacking to do, but she was steadily making progress in between caring for the children. The next day she made all of the arrangements for Adrienne to start school, and the day after that a big yellow school bus picked her up right on the other side of the picket fence. Adrienne was so excited to ride the bus that she had no apparent anxiety about school at all. She came home with sparkling eyes and reports of the children she'd played with and how much she liked her new teacher. They talked while they shared a snack, then Adrienne emailed Rachel to share all the news.

Mary felt as if her life had become a perfect dream. She knew that life by its very nature was prone to challenges. But they were content, and she found herself thinking about what a great day it had been when Whit Eden had shown up at her door, applying for a job as the gardener. The rest was history.

Epilogue

WITHIN JUST A FEW WEEKS, Whit had settled comfortably into his job, enjoying it every bit as much as he had anticipated. No job was perfect, but this was the perfect job for him, and there was very little about it he didn't enjoy. And he hadn't actually started caring for the grounds yet. He couldn't wait until the snow melted and spring came, so that he could see the gardens come to life under his care!

He felt the same way about the yard at home. He enjoyed playing with Adrienne in the snow, and sometimes Mary joined them. They had built more than one snowman and had become somewhat accustomed to the cold, although he wasn't sure that he and Mary would ever become *completely* acclimated to it. They'd spent too many decades in a warm climate. Still, it felt like home, and the snow outside only added to the coziness they felt inside their new house. With all the boxes unpacked and their every need met, they settled in comfortably and loved their surroundings as much as they loved the new start they had made.

Mary enjoyed catching Janel up on all the news, and she emailed pictures of their new home, inside and out, to her and to some friends back in LA. People would be able to see that there was snow, but she purposely offered no other identifying information about their new location. Even though she felt no fear about the past catching up with them, she loved the feeling of making such a clean break.

Mary settled quickly back into her humanitarian work via the Internet and found it amusing that no one she communicated with had any idea that she had changed locations. That was the beauty of the electronic age. She found the work even more gratifying as it was enhanced by the safety and security of their new life and the settled feeling that now filled her spirit.

Within a few weeks both Whit and Mary had Church callings and they had twice been invited to the homes of other ward members for dinner, which gave them an opportunity to get to know people and make new friends.

Spring revealed remarkable gardens at the reception center, which made Whit look forward to going to work. It also revealed that their own yard was in need of a great deal of tender loving care and improvement, which made Whit look forward to going home each evening—as if being with his family didn't. It had been an adjustment for all of them to not have him working right outside the house, but they quickly got used to it, and they all enjoyed their evenings and weekends together.

Summer made the gardens at the center come fully to life, and Whit enjoyed putting them in pristine condition each time an outdoor reception was scheduled. Even though he never actually saw the parties, he loved thinking of the wedding and anniversary and birthday celebrations that were taking place in this beautiful place that he had the privilege of nurturing.

The yard began to show some slow improvement, but it finally felt like it was their home when Whit was able to install the angel fountain in the backyard, near the patio and not far from the house. They made quite a ceremony out of the first time it was turned on as the lights inside of it glowed and water flowed pleasantly through it. Adrienne quickly got coins with which to make wishes, but Whit told Mary quietly that he couldn't think of a single thing to wish for. He had everything he'd ever wanted. She agreed emphatically and kissed him.

* * *

Nearly a year after they had first arrived in Idaho, Whit and Mary officially owned the home that Crystal had found for them. Living in it and attending their new ward had made them absolutely certain it was where they wanted to stay forever. The house was adequate in size, but there was enough yard space that they could comfortably build onto the house should they ever decide they might want to. Whit loved his job, and Mary had gained a new enthusiasm for the humanitarian work she loved so much. She was also discovering the joy of doing genealogy. Adrienne and Christian were thriving, and their family felt complete.

Whit and Crystal had become incredibly close, and their spouses shared in that closeness. They socialized a great deal and became very much involved in each other's lives. Crystal loved to come and watch the children now and then, and the four adults went to the temple together once a month. Crystal's daughter was an excellent babysitter and always handled everything well in their absence.

Once a year's time had passed since the deaths of Sofia and Claudia, they were able to do the temple work for these dear and amazing women, with Crystal and Mary standing as proxy for them. And a day came when Whit and Mary both felt strongly prompted to follow through on having Adrienne and Isabelle sealed to them. For quite some time they had been working through the legalities of Whit officially adopting Adrienne and her deceased twin sister, Isabelle. Given the intervening challenges of relocating and the complicated nature of all the legalities, their progress toward this goal had been slow but now they felt they needed to put forth some extra effort to make it happen. It turned out that all of the proper approvals came through near the time that they were able to do the temple work for Claudia and Sofia. Crystal knelt at the sealing room altar with Whit and Mary, acting as proxy for Isabelle. The Spirit in the room was so strong that they all felt certain many angels were in attendance—those for whom the work was being done and also many other family members, perhaps for generations back.

Whit and Mary both had individual witnesses that Isabelle was now truly a part of their marriage and their family, and there was a strange, inexplicable shift in their family dynamic as it became evident that Adrienne had officially become Whit's daughter—for all eternity. For all the contentment they had felt with putting so much hardship behind them and finding a new life, it was this finalizing of their eternal family that gave them a feeling of being completely settled. Together they were determined to now use all they had been blessed with to help build the kingdom by serving others and striving to live the gospel. They knew that was what the gospel was all about, and nothing meant more to them than that—except perhaps each other, but then it was all part of the same plan. They did indeed have their perfect brightness of hope.

About the Author

Anita Stansfield began writing at the age of sixteen, and her first novel was published sixteen years later. Her novels range from historical to contemporary and cover a wide gamut of social and emotional issues that explore the human experience through memorable characters and unpredictable plots. She has received many awards, including a special award for pioneering new ground in LDS fiction, and the Lifetime Achievement Award from the Whitney Academy for LDS Literature. Anita is the mother of five and has two adorable grandsons. Her husband, Vince, is her greatest hero.

To receive regular updates from Anita, go to anitastansfield.com and subscribe.